CW01267003

TRE AMORI

Simon Wigg

First published by Lulu Books May 2024

Copyright © Simon Wigg 2024

ISBN 978-1-304-36146-2

Imprint: Lulu.com

First edition May 2024

Cover illustration and map: Francesca Pelizzoli

This is a work of fiction. Names, characters, places and incidents are either the product of the author's imagination, or are used fictitiously. Any resemblance to actual persons, living or dead, events or locations, is coincidental.

For Francesca, Sophia and Sebastian

N
W
E
S
Florence
San Sepolcro
A P P E N N I N E S
Tiber
Montone
Gubbio
Umbertide
M. Acuto
Borgo &
Torre di S. Giuliana
Lake Trasimeno
M. Tezio
Assisi
Perugia
M. Subasio
Spello
Montefalco
UMBRIA
Tiber
Orvieto
Spoleto
Narni
Rome

Contents

Prologue 1
PART I
Chapter 1. The Gothic Line 7
Chapter 2. The Flower Festival 25
Chapter 3. Meeting Hannibal 49
Chapter 4. Ornella 65
Chapter 5. Lucrezia 79
Chapter 6. Cafaro's Revenge 95
Chapter 7. *Buona Sera Signorina* 117
Chapter 8. The Sagrantino Harvest 127
Chapter 9. *La Madonna Azzurra* 141
Chapter 10. The Bronze Figurine 161
Chapter 11. *La Peste Nera* 177
PART II
Chapter 12. Wild Asparagus 191
Chapter 13. The Goddess of Dawn 203
Chapter 14. The Bureaucrat 225
Chapter 15. *Santa Chiara* 237
Chapter 16. The Boar Hunt 257
Chapter 17. A Late Renaissance 273
Chapter 18. *Stella di Natale* 293
Epilogue 313

Prologue

They came to live next to *la torre di Santa Giuliana*, in a room above a stable filled with sheep at night. Three child refugees, two boys and a girl. They arrived and left at about the same time as the swallows that swooped above in summer skies. A single season etched firmly in Father Giuseppe's memory.

Massimo and Giovanni were first. Father Giuseppe remembered the date: 25th April, 1944. The day American fighter bombers flew past heading north towards the town of Umbertide. The day he allowed himself a glimmer of hope. When his parishioners saw him smile for the first time since the German occupation began the previous September.

Massimo's parents had decided to send their only child to live with his aunt in the countryside. They were fearful of the terrible civilian death toll, of the awful collateral damage inflicted by Allied troops as they fought their way through Sicily and then up southern Italy. His aunt lived as a widow in Father Giuseppe's parish. She too had sought a place to hide, ten years earlier with her late husband, a lanky academic stoically opposed to Mussolini's regime. Unfortunately, his whereabouts was reported by one of the many hunters that stalked the valley and within a week he was killed by a gang of *squadristi*. That was in the days well before the outbreak of world war.

As stubborn in character as he was scrawny in looks, Massimo refused to stay with his aunt unless joined by his best friend Giovanni.

'*Dai, ti prego, ti prego mamma!*' both boys begged relentlessly of their respective mothers, until they acquiesced.

The two boys travelled together with other refugees in the dark of night. First in a dilapidated Fiat truck, whose driver spent more time fiddling under the bonnet with a greasy spanner than at the wheel. Then after separating from the rest of the group, on foot, relaxing only when they saw the tall stone tower as it gleamed above the oak trees in the light of a waning moon.

Luckily, there was little danger of being intercepted by Germans. The majority were still massed south of Rome, holding out against repeated attacks by the Allies at Monte Cassino. However, by the time Father Giuseppe's niece Livia arrived, Umbria was overrun with retreating enemy troops that were regrouping along new defensive lines. One a few kilometres to the south that bisected Lake Trasimeno just outside the provincial capital Perugia; another along the Apennines to the north. Worse still, were the rumours that the Nazi commander in Italy had set up his base nearby at Polgeto, a castle on the slopes of the conical Monte Acuto.

It had been Father Giuseppe's idea to invite his niece. He knew that his sister Donatella some 50 kilometres away in Spello could not afford to leave their shop, just as the two boys' parents had remained tied to their home-town Umbertide. But he also knew Donatella would want her child to be safe.

He wrote her a second letter to warn of the new dangers, but it was too late. By the time it arrived Livia was already bumping along on a wooden cart, sitting on a thin bed of straw clutching her belongings. She was alone in the back, nestled among barrels she was told were full of last season's olive oil and wine. She sat listening to the unshod hooves of the two emaciated horses ahead as they clinked on the small stones on the surface of the road; and she watched the fields idling by with their rows of self-seeded red poppies. Livia loved flowers.

'Supplies for Polgeto,' repeated the cart driver, a family friend in his late 50s.

It seemed to work every time. At each roadblock, during which her heart beat so strongly she thought it would burst. Livia lost count of how many times they were stopped. Of the number of noisy trucks that roared past, each filled with stern-looking young German soldiers, that engulfed them in black diesel fumes and clouds of dust.

Livia's cheeks, once moistened with tears as she left, were now caked in hardened brown crusts.

'And the girl? What is she doing with you?'

'She is my sister,' said the driver's companion, another family friend and much younger. 'Never wants to be left out.'

'You should have stayed at home, little *signorina*,' the sentries would typically say in heavily-accented Italian, followed by the formality. 'Papers *bitte*.'

Livia had understood her parents could not leave their shop and fields in the valley below that helped keep its shelves stocked. Many townspeople in Spello were dependent on it for their basic provisions and occasional luxury, such as sheep's cheese. But that did not stop her resenting them for sending her to be with an uncle she hardly knew.

'Uncle Giuseppe says there are many children from other towns to make friends with,' Donatella had said, trying to lift her daughter's spirits.

'Now remember,' her father had advised. 'If the Germans interrogate you, say you are joining family in the North.'

'Fellow fascists,' Donatella had suggested.

'That would only draw attention. Don't listen to your mother.'

It was all a bit bewildering. Luckily, Livia was never interrogated.

Livia's uncle hugged her tightly on her arrival at *Santa Giuliana* and presented her with a bouquet of sweetly-scented yellow *ginestra* and delicate dog roses.

'*Grazie zio, sono bellissimi! Mi ricordano di casa,*' the little girl said with a tentative smile.

He knew they were among her favourite spring flowers, ones that would remind her of Spello. A town already famous before the war, for its religious flower festivals. Within a few days this slightly withdrawn girl began to blossom herself as the memories of her fraught journey receded.

Livia had an immediate effect on 13 year-old Massimo, who at first sight promptly forgot all about Maria Celeste, a young teacher of whom he had clearly been in awe and who was the first to uncover a hesitant musical talent. He was the slightly shorter of the two boys and had a darker complexion. As with all boys after so many years of war, except perhaps the sons of the fascists and some other Nazi collaborators, there was not an ounce of fat anywhere on his thin frame. At least his aunt had been able to put some meat back in his diet -there were still some wild boar, hare and deer in the wooded hills that surrounded them. An occasional wistful glance betrayed a sensitivity and creative nature. He was fascinated by the two frescos in Father Giuseppe's church, particularly the altar piece by an unknown artist of dubious talent. He was once caught trying to restore the feet of *Santa Giuliana* lost in an earth tremor with a burnt umber paint he had found, before being admonished by his aunt.

'Shame on you Massimo,' his aunt said, although they both knew she was impressed and would have him restore others parts if she had any say.

Luckily, Giovanni's interests at that point had not yet focused on girls, or the boys' strong bonds of friendship might have been put to the test. He was an intense and highly inquisitive boy, able to absorb reams of facts and figures like a sponge and better at maths than his teachers back in Umbertide, although he was not remotely boastful about it or his academic ability generally.

Father Giuseppe took a shining to the newcomers and they reciprocated his warmth by listening to his sermons and engaging in his religious instruction, although they were fascinated much more by the history he told of the region and of the tower in particular.

He had not always been warm or even remotely compassionate. After all, he had lived under fascism for most of his life. He had entered the priesthood armed with a strong intellect, sharp elbows and a steely determination to work his way up the ecclesiastical ladder. All the way to the Vatican if possible. This first posting since he was ordained was supposed to be temporary, according to his superior the abbot of the *Badia di Monte Corona*. But then the Second World War intervened. As the hardships faced by his rural parishioners multiplied and the burdens of their daily existence grew, Father Giuseppe softened.

So it was that the trio snatched as much of Father Giuseppe's time as they could, hearing snippets of the tower's 1,000 year history. Of how it used to taunt marauding invaders such as Ghibelline soldiers armed with crossbows and swords. How it dared them to breach its impenetrable walls of white chiselled stone and harm those sheltering within. About the fires the garrisons would light on its flat roof, one in a line of towers that warned Perugia of enemies approaching from the north. They ventured back even further, to Roman and Etruscan eras before the tower was built.

Until one night just after mid-summer. When everyone froze during a fierce exchange of gun-fire that echoed through the hills for many hours; when bursts of tracer bullets cracked the air, puncturing the sky like burning arrows.

PART I

'Meanwhile the darkening clouds o'er the Apennine
range
Gather like wreathing smoke; grand and austere
and green,
From th' encircling hills in graded tiers descending,
Umbria watches.
Green Umbria, all hail! And thou Clitumnus,
hail
Presiding God! My ancient country stirs my heart,
And on my burning brow, of old Italic gods
I feel wings brushing.

GIOSUÈ CARDUCCI
Le fonti del Clitumno, 1876 A.D.
(translated by Emily A. Tribe)

Chapter 1. The Gothic Line
1944 A.D.

The red flags with their menacing black swastikas had gone. So had the raised salutes, the metal-tipped boots that sparked on ancient stones as storm-troopers marched. Today it was the screeches of swifts that echoed off the renaissance buildings in the main *piazza*.

Maria Celeste was late. Her heart was beating loudly, but not from the exertion of the brisk walk from her home in the outskirts of Umbertide. Nor from the fear which had stalked her on the simplest of daily errands for so long. It was pure elation and excitement.

On the way to the *piazza* she was serenaded with birdsong. By the calls of collared doves courting among branches of Mediterranean pine. The busy chatter of sparrows in the gardens. Even people who days earlier would hardly even have acknowledged her, waved and greeted her warmly as she walked by.

'Buongiorno.' 'Salve.' 'Che bella giornata.' 'È bellissima Maria Celeste!' 'Ciao amore.' 'Sposami.' They shouted, as she beamed back at them. All that is, but the young man she passed asking for her hand in marriage.

It was not hard to spot Julian, looking immaculate in his khaki uniform with pressed shirt and tie. He was sitting outdoors surrounded by empty tables, his smiling face angled towards the summer sun.

'I haven't kept you long, have I?' Maria Celeste said apologetically in English, as he rose to greet her.

'No, not long at all. I was enjoying a rare moment of relaxation. As well as my first good cup of coffee since the Sicily campaign,' said Julian. 'Or maybe it was Rome,' he added, correcting himself. 'Anyway, what can I offer you?'

He drew back a metal chair for Maria Celeste to sit opposite him.

'I'll join you with an *espresso*,' she answered. 'I am sorry, I got carried away preparing for the new school term. I completely lost track of time.'

The owner of the bar appeared and welcomed Maria Celeste enthusiastically, taking her order directly from her. Julian heard her congratulate him on the re-opening, while he apparently lamented the lack of customers. '*Pazienza. Torneranno.*' He had heard her say.

'You beat me to it, asking for your coffee. I was going to show off my Italian,' Julian said, jokingly, once they were alone again. Maria Celeste smiled. Julian caught her glancing at a brown leather attaché case, which rested next to his captain's hat on the metal table. He had felt compelled to fill an awkward silence.

'Our next orders. To free San Sepolcro to the north. Leaving tomorrow.'

She is even more striking than I remember her, he thought to himself. She was tall, elegant. She had deep blue eyes, like the heavens in her name. She reminded him of a fellow student at Oxford he had admired from a distance.

'So soon?' Maria Celeste could not conceal her disappointment. They had only just met. A few evenings earlier, as the whole of Umbertide burst into spontaneous celebration with their liberators.

'Too soon.'

Julian's cheeks turned slightly crimson in the dusty air, as workers cleared rubble from the adjacent *piazza*, a whole neighbourhood destroyed. Obliterated in an allied air-raid that missed its targets, a railway and a road bridge across the Tiber. Seventy lives lost in an instant. Including the parents of one of

Maria Celeste's pupils, Massimo. The tragic irony was that the bridges were anyway later destroyed by the retreating Germans, to impede the Allies' advance.

'You'll see the Piero della Francesca paintings before me then,' she said. 'You will protect them won't you?'

'Ah yes, his best-known work, the…' he said, trying to remember that famous fresco he had read about once. 'The Resurrection?'

'That's the one,' she said. 'I'm impressed! It's the most vulnerable, part of a wall in the medieval councillors' hall.'

'I guessed right! I'll try my best. But the instructions will be to do all it takes to retake the town,' he said in a regretful tone. 'Softening-up the target, as we say in the artillery.'

Maria Celeste's lips parted and her eyes widened with delight. They shared a connection.

'Tell me about Rome.' She looked him playfully in the eye, while taking off her white gloves as the café's owner brought her coffee.

'I will, but first tell me more about you.'

'Alright. But then it's your turn'. She refrained from reaching across to squeeze his left hand. It would be most unlike her. Even in war, when she had witnessed so many seize the moment.

Maria Celeste began her story. 'You are my first contact with England in four years, do you realise?'

A look of anguish crept across her face. Julian lent forward, inadvertently.

'I was travelling with two history of art friends from Cambridge.'

'You went to Cambridge?' Julian interrupted, even more captivated with the woman sitting in front of him.

'Well, not quite,' she said. 'My friends did. They went to Jesus. I was at Girton College, up the road.'

'Ah, the famous Ladies' College. Trying to be formally recognised as part of the university, if I remember.'

'Struggling for equality, yes. But just like the women's vote, we'll get there in the end.'

'Most surely. Quite right, too. It's hard to believe those old-fashioned notions still survive.'

She blushed slightly, as his words resonated inside her. He may be a bit rigid and awkward, but he seemed to have embraced the modern way of thinking. She decided he was a bit shy. In the company of women, anyway. Not so with the men he led into battle. There she imagined a man quietly imparting confidence and self-assurance to his troops.

'You know,' she said. 'My parents had very different ambitions for me. To put me on display in the debutante's circuit. I rebelled. Twice in fact.'

'Only twice?' he ventured, with a twinge of mischief.

'Oh, you mean my Italian odyssey? Maybe,' she said, shifting slightly in her chair and fidgeting with the tea-spoon next to her coffee cup. 'Anyway, when they finally acknowledged I was not cut out to be a debutante, they wanted me to read modern languages. Italian, specifically, for family reasons. I chose history of art instead. Two of my favourite hobbies rolled into one.'

'Very astute of you', Julian said, feeling increasingly at ease. 'Tell me, what were your favourite memories of Cambridge?'

'Hmm. Probably, as you might expect, punting on the Cam with summer picnics. Cycling into town to choir practice. I loved the sense of freedom my bicycle gave me. And you? Something about you tells me you were an Oxford Blue.'

'How flattering of you,' he said, sensing his cheeks redden for a second time. 'No, my father was the Blue, not me. Football. But at least I got into his Oxford college. He became an army chaplain in the first world war, you know. Refused a gallantry award for rescuing men behind enemy lines.'

'You must be very proud. The church? Not for you?'

'No. With war brewing, I went on to Sandhurst. But look, we have digressed from your story. Why are you here, sitting in front of me looking every inch a countess from the Renaissance'?

'Are my clothes so dated?' she replied, smiling.

'They are timeless,' he said. He wondered for a moment whether Maria Celeste might be with the SOE. He knew they had been parachuting operatives into France. Perhaps Italy too? She would be a perfect undercover agent.

'Well, where was I before you interrupted so rudely,' Maria Celeste said playfully. She wanted to speak of her dream to bring to life all that she had studied. To stand in the oval of sunlight cast on the floor of the Pantheon, feel the pain of those who lost their lives in the Colosseum, admire those vivid Caravaggios.

'We were in Florence when Mussolini declared war against England,' she said. 'That was in 1940. The consulate helped smuggle them out, through Genoa. But I was determined to reach our destination, Rome.'

'How were you going to manage on your own?' Julian was visibly nervous for her.

'I could speak Italian. I have relatives in the north in Bergamo. I thought the war would be over quickly. Many reasons,' she said, looking not at him but at the hat on the table. 'I know,' she added hurriedly, to pre-empt him. 'You are going to ask why we came in the first place. Why our families let us travel when Europe seemed to be on the brink of war.'

'So many people ignored the threat. I can understand.'

'We were so young and naïve. Some Italian contacts in London, who helped with the visas, assured us we'd be safe. It wasn't until we arrived in Florence that we realised Mussolini had been running a nasty fascist state in Italy for many years. That he'd been in power much longer than Hitler.'

'*Il Duce* ran a very slick propaganda machine, I know,' said Julian. 'Even Churchill bought into it in the early days. Looking after the welfare of the nation. Keeping the communists at bay. All lies, as it turned out. Anyway, I want to hear about you, not fascism.'

'Well, it became difficult to travel on public transport,' she continued. 'I found myself living here in Umbria. In this small town, frozen in time on the banks of the upper Tiber. A cousin in Bergamo helped get me a job as a teacher on Via Garibaldi. Filling-in where they needed help. Art, music, mathematics.'

'Maths?'

'Yes, very basic mind you. Are you surprised?' she remarked, finally looking up to meet his gaze.

'No. Just intrigued. Teaching English would hardly be appropriate, I can see.'

'Exactly. Anyway, I slipped into my new life like a night-gown. They made me feel so welcome.'

'Go on.' Julian was hooked.

'But I had to be cautious. I had to keep my thoughts to myself, even in those early days. Luckily, I managed to avoid the attention of the fascist thugs, the *squadristi*. My daily life only really began to get difficult when Mussolini was overthrown and the Nazis took over mainland Italy.'

Furrows appeared in her brow, as she moved into a darker chapter.

'Now everyone was scared. Afraid of informers. I had to change my identity. A whole family was murdered just north of here, as a reprisal for the success of our local resistance fighters. Several people disappeared, arrested by the SS while they slept.'

'Look, that's enough about me,' she said, her discomfort growing with every word. 'I want to hear about you. Tell me about Rome. Better still, tell me about England. I miss everyone so much.'

'I bet you do. So do I. I've been on the road for much of the war. First North Africa. Then the Sicily landings.'

'North Africa as well?' she interrupted suddenly. 'Then you are not with 1st Punjab? No wonder I didn't recognise the badge,' she said, looking once more at his hat. All of Umbertide had come to know something of the battalion of polite men in turbans and khaki shorts that had led the infantry assault into the town. But those soldiers had not fought in those earlier campaigns.

'No, you're right. That's the Crusaders' Cross of Montgomery's 8th Army. I am here on a different mission. Top secret,' Julian added inadvertently. What was it about this woman he hardly knew, that made his knees wobble and tongue waggle? First, he let slip the battle plans. Now this. Maybe it was the alcohol? Could she notice it on his breath?

'I can keep a secret,' she replied, with a glimmer in her eye.

'I know,' he acknowledged, thinking of her life under the Gestapo. 'I've been assigned as escort to King George VI's visit to the frontline troops. A morale booster. There is to be a parade here, right past your school building I believe.'

'Our King, coming here? When?' she said astonished, before remembering. 'I thought you said you were leaving for San Sepolcro?'

'Now that I can't disclose. And yes I did, I'll be rejoining my artillery unit when his Royal Highness leaves.'

At that moment Maria Celeste saw a woman in a blue and white dress walking purposefully towards them. She recognised her immediately. Normally when walking about town, she wore plain, quite boyish-looking clothes in drab sandy shades to avoid attracting attention. But this morning she seemed to be making a statement. 'Here, look at me,' her dress announced. And several men in the *piazza* were doing exactly that.

'Julian, this is my friend Sandra,' she said, standing up to present her neighbour.

'*Piacere di conoscerti*,' said Julian.

'*Piacere mio,*' Sandra replied. '*Parla italiano anche lei?*'

'*Un po*. I am awfully sorry,' he continued in English, while glancing at his watch. 'But I am late for a briefing. Must go now, I'm afraid.'

The spell had been broken.

'Wait for me, I'll take you to Rome,' he whispered in Maria Celeste's ear as he said goodbye.

'*XX Settembre,*' she replied, as he turned to walk away.

'It's in the dairy,' Julian beamed back at her.

'That's my home address! Number 4.'

'And a date'. He paid for the coffees and walked off to join his regiment. They were billeted outside the remains of the town's medieval walls, alongside some tobacco fields by the Tiber.

****

Sandra accompanied Maria Celeste home after meeting the captain. They walked side-by-side much of the way. The feeling of freedom should have been intoxicating, but Maria Celeste's heart weighed heavily in her chest. As did the burden of her secret.

'*Che bell'uomo,*' Sandra exclaimed, trying to lighten the mood. '*Ma, è molto inglese.*'

'Very English, I know. Polite, but a bit formal and stiff.'

'*Esatto,*' Sandra agreed. But she could tell from the tone of her friend's voice, that she was clearly annoyed that the meeting with Julian had ended so abruptly. That it was no time to jest.

'I am sorry to have interrupted you so rudely.'

'No matter. He was about to leave anyway.'

As they left the main *piazza* they passed the *Rocca di Umbertide*, a fortress with crenellated walls and an imposing medieval tower, the pride of Umbertide.

'Your very own *Braccio da Montone,*' Sandra teased. 'The modern-day hero of Umbria.'

The *Rocca* had been Braccio's temporary home. Both as a captive there and following his release for a large ransom, after he laid siege to the fortress with fellow knights from the nearby village of Montone.

'My Julian is a saint in comparison. Never. *Braccio* was duplicitous and greedy. Julian is principled and refined.'

'*Il tuo* Julian?' said Sandra provocatively, diverting attention away from another history lesson.

There was an attribute of Braccio's Maria Celeste did wish for Julian. His remarkable ability to survive, against all the odds.

Sandra steered their conversation onto a happier plane. 'My *papà* has found some help to move the piano. *Questo pomeriggio.*'

'This afternoon? How wonderful.' Maria Celeste tried to contain her excitement. The piano had been hidden in a garden shed since the German occupation. They knew the Nazis had been systematically stealing pianos and other musical instruments of value across Europe, especially from Jewish families abducted to ghettos and work camps.

'What's more, as no one in our family can play, he wants to have it installed in your house.'

'Never! I could never accept such a gift.'

'What about the loan of a piano? With regular invitations to recitals in lieu of interest payments?'

'No. Not even that.'

'What will you play for me?'

'It is going to be horribly out of tune. *Vedremo.*'

'I take that as a yes.'

They reached the large white neo-classical building where she taught, opposite the railway station and very near their homes. Maria Celeste could see her classroom from her bedroom window, it was so close.

'We have a teachers' meeting tomorrow. I can't wait to drop the fascist curriculum.'

'What a relief that will be,' agreed Sandra. 'No more indoctrination. Those awful patriotic songs I was forced to sing as a child. The infernal books praising the Romans.'

Remembering Maria Celeste still had a rather romantic image of ancient Rome, Sandra quickly changed the subject. 'I wonder how many of your class will be returning.'

'I wonder. It keeps me awake every night. What if I am asked to break the news to Massimo?'

Her excitement over the piano was short-lived.

****

Giovanni was struggling with his homework. It was most unlike him. He went across the hall to Massimo's bedroom.

It was the only good thing, living across the hallway from one another, that had happened since returning to Umbertide. When they discovered Massimo's parents had been killed in that air raid, and Giovanni's parents became his guardians.

'Mas, *facciamo un patto*. I'll help you with your maths if you help me with the war story. There is too much to write about. Can I see what you have done?'

Massimo did not reply, he was so engrossed in his writing. Looking over his shoulder, Giovanni began reading the opening paragraphs.

'*I was sent to seek refuge from the war with my aunt in a hidden valley full of sheep. A place we called la torre di Santa Giuliana. It had a tall watch-tower centuries old built of white stone and next to it Father Giuseppe's church.*

Everyone said we would be much safer there as the big battle would be fought in Umbertide. But Father Giuseppe was not so sure. He said the Germans would fight hard to defend the high ground. Places like the monastery on top of the hill behind.

Luckily, I made sure my best friend Giovanni came with me. He once lived across from my house in Umbertide. But during the war they moved to a different neighbourhood nearer our school.

We made friends at Santa Giuliana with a niece of Father Giuseppe's called Livia. She arrived on a horse-drawn cart from Spello, with all her clothes packed in a case made of cardboard. Livia was our age and very pretty, with short straight brown hair and green eyes. She wore glasses with silver rims. The glasses broke soon after she arrived but she was brave about it.'

'Mas you can't write about Livia like that- how embarrassing!'

That caught Massimo's attention. '*Certo che posso*. She has gone back to Spello and will never know.'

'What else did you say about her? Your first kiss while we were catching fireflies? Holding her hand while we hid from the Germans in the pigsty?' Giovanni was enjoying being mischievous.

'Stop it. What are you going to talk about? How you were always hungry? Stole vegetables from neighbours' gardens, bread from their kitchen tables?'

'Which you ate as well! And what about the time you hid from the SS under Miss Mary's long dress?'

It was not Massimo's proudest moment. The verbal volleys between the two best friends continued for a while, until Giovanni abruptly left the room and returned to his desk. He thought about Miss Mary and how they all had to call her Maria Celeste after the Germans took over. How she told them Galileo's daughter had adopted that name on becoming a nun. How she saved him and Massimo from joining the work gangs building fortifications to keep the American and English troops out.

His mind turned to *Santa Giuliana* and he began to write down random recollections of his time there. Learning about Hannibal from Father Giuseppe. About the action he saw and heard, both real and imagined. The panzer tanks advancing up the Nese valley. The sounds of shells exploding, machine guns, tracer bullets flying at night. About his hunger and his favourite food, *pecorino di fossa*, a sheep's cheese wrapped in straw and hidden from the Germans in holes underground.

A while later Massimo joined Giovanni in his room.

'Finished yet?' he asked.

'Almost,' came the muffled reply of someone deep in concentration, his pen struggling to keep pace with the narrative racing in his head.

Massimo walked to the window which framed the town's mystical guardian, Monte Acuto.

At least, he thought it mystical. Giovanni, by contrast, was less romantic. 'It's an isosceles triangle,' he once observed, commenting on its perfect conical peak and equal sides. 'Can't you see?'

He didn't really, not at the time.

'Nice view,' said Massimo, as he stood pressing his nose on the pane of glass. 'Much better than in your old house. We had to lean out of our windows to see Acuto in those days, remember?'

There was no response. Just the sound of a silver nib scratching curved lines of thought across the surface of Giovanni's notebook. The occasional dip into an ink well. Followed by the tapping of metal on glass to shake off any surplus that would otherwise scar the page with black splotches. Giovanni was very orderly and did not like making a mess. '*Sono meticoloso*,' he liked to say.

Some teachers reacted fiercely to homework covered with marks and smudges, although not Miss Mary. She even held an art class where they all had to flick paint onto white pages with abandon. But then the head teacher intervened and, shocked by the anarchic mess and waste, Miss Mary was restricted thereafter to teaching maths. And music. She taught Massimo the piano, for one hour on a Thursday afternoon. It was his favourite time of the week, by far.

Massimo's rambling thoughts returned to his old home. It was in a poor, crowded and very noisy neighbourhood, that probably had changed little since the Middle Ages. His home was across a narrow alley from Giovanni's, their bedrooms just a few metres apart.

'Remember the clothes line and pulleys you stole and rigged between our rooms?'

Still no answer.

'I'd send you some left-over bread and what would I receive in return? Yet another book, with pages missing.'

Giovanni used to decorate his walls with the illustrations torn from second-hand books his mother Antonietta would supply to keep his mind off his perpetual hunger. She had little notion of the literature she fed him, with the result that rather risqué pictures of young women began to adorn obscure corners of the room while battle scenes from Homer's Iliad and gods and goddesses from the Odyssey held centre stage as a parental distraction.

Massimo slipped into a reverie as the mountain ahead began to speak to him in silent whispers. The sound of the summer breeze whistling through tall grasses and thistles that turned yellow with the march of time. The groans of beech trees nestled in ravines bowing before the winter gales. The chants from the spirits of his ancestors, imparting their collective knowledge that helped fill the baskets of mushroom and truffle gatherers, that guided the hunters towards the wild boar and other quarry. He was not the only one to believe this. Many of his friends said the mountain was a sacred place of worship in the olden days. But not Giovanni. He said it was all nonsense and that they ought all to place their faith in modern science.

Some of Massimo's favourite memories were of the many walks with his *mamma e papà* on that mountain. He tried not to think of his parents as it made him cry. But at night they entered his dreams and spoke to him and told him that they too had joined the mountain spirits and that he needn't worry, that they were keeping a watchful eye on their only son in the valley below and that they loved him.

These memories provoked tears that filled his eyes as he stood with his hands in his pockets, shoulders rolled forward. A part of him wanted Giovanni to his forlorn state, but Giovanni remained hunched over his desk.

'I miss Livia,' he said. He couldn't bring himself to say he missed his parents as well. The nerve it touched was too raw to disturb.

'*Anch'io.*'

Finally, a response.

'You too? Gio, can we ask your *mamma* and *papà* to take us to see her when it's safe?'

****

Maria Celeste was not good at resisting temptation. The black and white ivories were feet away, the upright piano beckoning attention.

Luckily, the lid was locked.

'Please take away that key', she had implored Sandra. 'I have a lot of homework to mark.'

'Only if you play me my favourites. The Clair de Lune?'

'*Va bene, va bene.* I will, I promise. Now leave me in peace.'

As Sandra closed the front door, Maria Celeste picked the first piece of homework. She was a little nervous with her task she had set, asking her class to write about the war. But it had the senior teachers' approval. The class should be old enough and it could be therapeutic for them.

There was another knock on the front door. It was Sandra again.

'Mari, *un' altra cosa*. I forgot to mention that earlier today I heard that a British officer disobeyed orders to bombard San Sepolcro! *Il tuo* Julian, perhaps?' She closed the door a second time, leaving Maria Celeste alone to absorb the news.

It was a while before Maria Celeste regained her composure. She had never forgiven herself for missing the King's parade. A chance to see Julian, if only a glimpse. She had been giving a piano lesson to Massimo and it was all over so quickly.

Finally, after pacing around the sitting room several times, Maria Celeste began to read the first essay. It was by Giovanni.

It would be a few months before she heard who the saviour of The Resurrection in San Sepolcro actually was. It was a lieutenant in the Royal Horse Artillery. Julian at the time was on temporary leave, unfit for service. His drinking problem had worsened after leaving Umbertide. But Maria Celeste was never to know this.

****

Cesare arrived at his sister Vincenzia's home late at night.

'*Meno male*. You made it. What a state you are in. You look exhausted,' Vincenzia said, greeting him with a cursory hug. His clothes were those of a farm labourer, ragged and worn. A disguise for his journey back from meeting fellow Nazi sympathisers near Pierantonio.

'I am starving. Is there any dinner left?' he grunted, scanning the kitchen for signs of sustenance.

'*Si, ho fatto una minestra di pastina e fagioli. Siediti e mangia!*'

Vincenzia had kept the pasta and bean soup warm on the woodstove and laid a place on the kitchen table. Although firm with him, she could not resist fussing over her brother. Especially since they had lost their parents.

The large, burly young man washed his hands in a bowl of water, took off his coat, sat down and began eating noisily.

'*E il pane...Dov'è?*'

'*Ei furbo!* Don't push your luck. The bread's packed for the journey.'

'*Capito.* Now, are we ready? What supplies could you find?' he asked.

'Oh, some pecorino. Left-over wild boar salami. Flat bread. You'll see. Enough for four to five days. How far to safety?'

'Should get us past the latest German defensive line. You know what they are calling it? The Gothic Line. Don't know what it's got to do with the Goths. Anyway, it's going to be tough, getting into the Apennine mountains unnoticed,' Cesare said, before wiping his mouth with the back of his hand. 'Any *grappa*?'

'I am saving it for our escape.'

'Oh, come on. What about a toast to Benito?'

She relented and reached for a small flask in a worn canvas bag in which she stored the few provisions for their trip.

'A toast to *il Duce*. To the *nuova Repubblica Sociale Italiana*!' he pronounced loudly a few moments later, before sipping the precious distilled wine.

'*O tu, raggio di sole nascente!*' chanted Vincenzia, quoting an ode written in the 1920s. Although in truth, she no longer believed Mussolini to be a ray of sunshine.

'And to our friends the Nazis who installed him in Salò!' Cesare added, emptying his glass. He was referring to the German commandos that rescued Mussolini from his mountain prison after he was deposed, before installing him as puppet figurehead of the new German regime.

'To them too. Thank God. I've packed a few clothes for you Cesare. Including your black shirt from your time as a *squadrista*.'

'Oh Vini. You think of everything. What memories. Those days of mugging communists. What about my precious fez?'

'Now you're being silly. Your Balilla uniform was given away, remember. To that boy from San Sepolcro. Cafaro.'

'Cafaro. Ah yes. The pretty boy. Always being beaten up for his looks.'

'Made him a good fascist, just as you predicted. Now, turning to important matters, is anyone else coming with us?'

'No. The others are making their way separately. So as not to draw attention.'

'Good. We won't have to share our precious provisions,' she said, eliciting a wry smile from her brother in between mouthfuls of soup.

'You know, we got a special mention at the meeting,' he announced, pushing his now empty bowl to one side.

'What, you mean they finally recognised our good work?'

'Yes. They confirmed our total. Ten.'

Ten acquaintances from the neighbourhood they had reported for suspected collaboration with the partisans. Stolen from their beds by the SS in the dark of night.

'Could have been more,' she replied venomously. 'You know my hunch about that teacher with the presumptuous name, Maria Celeste? I heard her talking in English to a British officer the other day. I knew she was a spy. That *stronza*, and her friend Sandra. She was in the resistance too.'

'Don't you worry Vini. We'll get them. When Mussolini is back in charge.'

Chapter 2. The Flower Festival
1969 A.D.

Livia was very frustrated. Trying to get in touch with her boyfriend was nigh on impossible. Even the radio irritated her this morning, which was unusual as it was Beatles' hour and this band was her favourite. Best foreign group anyway. Her number one singer, as everyone knew, was Mina.

She switched the radio off, drawing a feigned protest from her mother upstairs who listened to the band, despite having no understanding of the lyrics, in a vain attempt to keep up with her daughter's generation. Her favourite singer was Mina too.

The telephone line crackled back into life and the international operator repeated the number.

'*Esatto, e questo numero,*' Livia said, her voice sounding unusually shrill.

The operator tried again, followed by another lengthy pause. Finally, someone answered in English. 'Good morning. The Royal Academy of Music.'

Then another break followed, again in English by 'Mr. Massimo? I am sorry he is not here at the moment. I believe he is giving a recital outside London.'

'*Chiamante, ha sentito?*' the operator asked Livia, making sure she had heard the reply.

'*Si, grazie.* I will try again later,' Livia replied despondently.

The line disconnected but Livia stood for a few moments, holding the receiver to her ear. As if Massimo's voice might just materialise across the airwaves. She had been trying to reach him for what seemed like the whole morning, but it was only about an hour.

Giovanni would comfort her. As he always did. She dialled a local Umbrian number and to her surprise, got through immediately.

'*Pronto?*' It was Giovanni's mother.

'Antonietta, s*ono io*, Livia. Sorry to trouble you, but is Giovanni back by any chance?'

'Livia, how nice to hear from you. You sound anxious, p*overa*.'

'It's nothing really.'

'I hope not. Giovanni should be on the train from Milan. I am collecting him at midday. I know he is looking forward to helping with the petal laying.'

This was the final stage of over ten months of preparations for Spello's annual flower festival, the *Infiorate del Corpus Domini*. Tomorrow, Saturday, was the *Notte dei Fiori*. From six in the evening through to dawn on Sunday the floral teams would be laying flower petals, filling compositions on the alleys along the processional route.

'Thank you so much. Please tell him I can't wait to see him. I hope to see you there too.'

'We wouldn't miss it for anything in the world. *Ciao tesoro*.'

'Oh, and how did his medical finals go?'

'I think they went well. You know him. He will say very little until the results come through. At least to his parents. You may have better luck when you see him.'

'I doubt it. He rarely speaks about himself, even to Massimo and me,' Livia answered. 'Anyway, I really look forward to catching-up on Sunday.'

'*È vero*. Good luck on Saturday. Hope the weather holds.'

'Me too! Goodbye Antonietta.'

Livia hung up. She picked up the car keys from the hallway and walked into the kitchen to prepare her lunch.

'*Mamma*, can I borrow the *Cinquecento*?' Livia asked in a raised voice. She was back in the hallway and looking up the stairs.

'Of course, darling,' her mother Donatella answered from her bedroom on the first floor. She had been unwell for a while and always had a slow start to the morning. 'But where are you going all of a sudden?' she asked, as shuffled across to the top of the staircase.

'I'm going for a short trip up Subasio.'

'Monte Subasio, by yourself? You'll miss your *infioratori* team meeting.'

'I just need a short change of scene. Clear my head,' said Livia.

'Are you sure? You won't be late, will you?' her mother said, trying to muster the energy to dissuade her daughter. 'You can't let them down.'

'I won't, I promise,' Livia said, before adding with disarming innocence, 'Tell *papà* I prepared a *parmigiana* for dinner tonight.'

'Wonderful. He'll love that,' her mother replied in the flat tone that acknowledged Livia was, once again, getting her own way.

Livia walked into their small garage, passing Massimo's Vespa that they stored for him, before entering the narrow alley on which their yellow Fiat *Cinquecento* was parked.

****

When Livia's team had asked her to design a floral pattern for the competition she yelped in surprise, drawing both hands to her cheeks. She then jumped up and down on the spot, burst into tears and hugged each team member in sequence.

'What, me? How?' she exclaimed.

'Donatella showed us a sketchbook you keep in your room. You've got a hidden talent,' said a team member called Laura.

'My sketches? Oh, they are mere scribbles. How can you possibly think me worthy of this honour?'

'I had a dream that you and I were visited by Santa Chiara,' said the most elderly of the team. 'Santa Chiara told us her biggest regret was to let you go. But that you would reward her one day with a floral composition that would tell her story to thousands.'

'Santa Chiara has appointed you, Livia. You won't let us down, will you?' said another, who also happened to be called Laura.

Superstition was clearly rife among the team, only one of whom (apart from Livia) had completed secondary school. They all held the local saints, St. Francis and Santa Chiara in higher esteem than the Pope, regarding them almost with as high a degree of reverence as the Virgin Mary herself.

'Yes. Of course I accept,' Livia announced with glee. 'And together we are going to tell that special story.'

'And win!' pronounced the first Laura.

Now it was the turn of the team to surround Livia and leap with joy- although the eldest could barely rise from her stooped posture and simply managed a toothless grin.

They disbanded and went their own ways after having agreed when to hold their first meeting. Livia skipped home to tell her parents and try to call Massimo, who could not be reached as usual but Giovanni did happen to be at home at the time.

'Gio, *ciao. Sono* Livia,' she blurted with excitement. 'Tell me you are free tomorrow to drive to San Damiano?'

'San Damiano? Santa Chiara's convent? What on earth for? What's going on?'

'I need inspiration. 9am sharp, at your house. I'll explain when we meet. You'll love it, I promise.'

So it was that Giovanni accompanied Livia on their first visit to Saint Clare's convent, just outside Assisi.

A successful visit it was too. Although the monastery was in need of funds for restoration. Nevertheless, both Livia and Giovanni were infused with a serene sense of calm which San Damiano imparted on most visitors and Livia came away with ideas for four compositions to present to her team.

One was a scene in which the young Clare first received her vows from Francis; a second showed an older Francis talking to birds while convalescing at San Damiano; the third depicted a Papal visit to the convent; while the fourth showed the famous scene in which Abbess Clare stood down a Saracen army trying to invade Assisi by invoking a huge storm, which drove the invaders away. It was the second time she had saved Assisi from the Saracens, both through power of prayer. After much deliberation, the team unanimously chose the storm scene.

****

'*Arrivo, un attimo,*' said Livia's mother, somewhat breathless, as she answered a barely discernible but persistent knock on the front door.

An imposing figure with thick fair hair and brown eyes stood before her. 'Ah, it's you Alessandro, *che piacere!*'

'*Buongiorno* Donatella. I've dropped by to ask if Livia needed any help.'

He had been dropping by quite a lot recently, thought her mother. Not the only one to be doing so either, since Livia's boyfriend went to music college in England and the long distance began to take its toll. 'Like bees to a honeypot,' she would say of the young men hovering about in her neighbourhood. But Donatella liked this one the most. Polite as they all were and charming but without any affectation. Strong in physique, she imagined a character as sturdy as a rock. Just the sort of man her flighty daughter needed. After all, with this strange illness sapping her strength that she was too afraid to do anything about, Donatella could also do with some stability in her household.

Her husband disagreed. So far as he was concerned, there was no man eligible for his daughter's hand in marriage in the whole of Umbria. Not even Massimo. But then, how could he not be protective of his beautiful, joyful and precious only daughter?

'You have just missed her. She'll be back late afternoon.'

'Forgive me for asking, but is she alright? I bumped into Livia's team just now. They were collecting fresh flowers from gardens in the neighbourhood for the contest. I was surprised Livia was not with them.'

'Thank you for your concern, Alessandro. She is fine. I'll tell her you came by,' Donatella replied, keen not to disclose any frailties of character, such as Livia's occasional bouts of selfishness.

'*Grazie*. I look forward to seeing you on Sunday.'

'*A domenica*!' she said, as he turned for home.

He knew there was a lot of pressure on her as creative leader of her floral team for the first time. What was supposed to be a religious festival had turned into a bit of a competition ever since the two parishes that hosted *l'Infiorata* decided to hold a prize-giving on the Sunday evening. Simple geometric designs of the past were increasingly replaced by progressively more elaborate and colourful story-telling compositions around religious themes.

Alessandro would be sure to wait for the procession at Livia's floral composition, in front of her family's shop on Via Cavour.

Better still, he thought, he would drop by on the Saturday evening to see if he could be of any help.

Livia's mother meanwhile prepared to join her husband at their shop. This was going to be a busy weekend. Thousands of visitors were expected, some finding their way into their shop looking for a light lunch, or a local delicacy to remind them of their visit. Shelves were stocked with local *Sagrantino* and *Grechetto* wines and extra virgin olive oils. The shop window enticed customers with a choice of Umbrian delicacies such as wild boar salamis, cheeses with truffle and many types of dried pulses, chick peas and beans.

Since her mother's illness took hold, Livia's help had been invaluable. But both she and her husband felt guilty they were holding her back, despite her insistence she work in the family business.

****

Snaking her way through a maze of alleys down to the valley floor in her yellow car, Livia was overcome by a delicious feeling of freedom. A few hours to herself with no responsibility other than to relive memories of those surreptitious trips up the mountain with Massimo. She had promised herself this short pilgrimage for a long time.

She began singing one of her favourite Mina songs, *Parole Parole*, while swaying rhythmically with such enthusiasm her little car became her dance partner and bounced from side to side in unison.

Turning onto a narrow road that led back up towards Monte Subasio, she had a nagging feeling she was missing something. The fresh flower collection! Oh well, her *infioratori* would manage without her. They knew which colours were needed. Her mind wandered back to those wonderful evenings of *la capatura* earlier that spring. How she and her team and various neighbours sat around drinking wine, sharing stories and laughter while plucking petals off dried flowers and placing them in numbered boxes.

'Santa Chiara told us her biggest regret was to let you go.' What was that all about? Her free-spirited nature? Time and time again these words played in Livia's head, as they did as she drove through clouds of dust a few minutes later. She could just make out the town walls and roof tops of Spello in her rear-view mirror. She had driven through the silvery-green olive groves and now spindly *ginestra* bushes bordered either side of the *strada bianca* as the unpaved road wound up the mountain. The yellow broom was in full flower and a sweet, sticky fragrance filled the car.

Glancing over her shoulder, she caught sight of quilts of corn blue in the fields beneath Spello. Here, chicory plants proliferated, as did waves of red poppies that undulated in the breeze.

Her mind wandered back to *la raccolta* -the many hours spent harvesting those flowers from local fields and the lower slopes of Subasio, then laying them out to dry in the sun before cataloguing them.

She suddenly thought she should have borrowed the Vespa. It was Massimo's Vespa which used to whisk the two of them away from the prying eyes in town. With a flutter of excitement, she remembered how she pressed against his back and wrapped her arms tightly around him as he drove up this very road. She would rest her chin on his shoulder and felt their fates closely entwined as they parted the cool mountain air together. She could not put a finger on why it had felt so special to her. It was just, well, right. The only kind of right she had known, since she was quite young. Barely a teenager.

As she climbed, the broom and oak increasingly gave way to pine trees. Livia was not so fond of pine, particularly these non-indigenous trees as it made her think of the cold. She was however looking forward to her picnic among the short beech trees that thrived in the cooler air near the mountain top. These trees nestled in protected ravines and hollows, while grasses and blue spiny thistles ruled the exposed high plateau of Subasio's summit.

Livia reached their favourite spot and stopped the car by the roadside. She took her key and locked the doors. It was an unnecessary precaution; she had seen no one in the last half-hour. But she did not want to take any risks.

The summer's first wave of heat had arrived early this year. A thick dusty blanket lay heavily above a fuzzy landscape. For a moment she thought she had left her glasses behind. Through the haze she detected some tall white clouds rising high above the distant horizon to the west.

Livia took a small bundle containing her book, her light lunch and bottle of water and strolled over the long grasses, heading for a small clearing with views down the mountain towards Le Marche and beyond, the Adriatic. She longed for Massimo to take her to the sea. To pick sea urchins off underwater rocks, scoop out and share their raw and salty flesh.

These fantasies were interrupted by a column of flies buzzing overhead. She smiled, knowing that she would shortly be in good company. Within a few seconds two large white *Maremmano* sheepdogs were walking towards her, tails wagging in recognition. Livia was so happy to see them again. Even though she knew that after their greeting, they would return to guard their flock.

Livia then followed a ritual she and Massimo had established, laying out a rug and tucking into a simple lunch of *pecorino*, a small loaf of bread, some chopped fennel in olive oil and salt, followed by cherries.

Normally they might read at this point, with Livia resting her head on Massimo's stomach as they lay at right angles to each other. Livia enjoyed telling silly jokes and her reward was a bouncy headrest as Massimo laughed out loud. She loved making him laugh.

She looked at her watch. A twenty-first birthday present from her parents.

'Mustn't be late,' reminding herself of the last of the meetings with her floral team. She wrapped up her belongings and began walking back to the car, following a path hewn by animals along a contour of Subasio. Spotting a horse silhouetted against the blue sky, her mind soon wandered away from the festival commitments. She thought it magical that farmers in the valley below left their horses, sheep and *Chianina* cows to roam freely on the mountain in the late spring, where they could feed on lush pasture in the cooler temperatures. She would allow herself one last indulgence. A small diversion. It would only take a few minutes. As Livia approached the deep hollow in the mountain her heart began pounding with the memory. Would it be there? Surely not. It had been a while.

As she approached the rim of the sinkhole, there it was. Spelt out in large white limestone rocks, a long way beneath her. LIVIA.

While she had rested in the shade of a small beech tree, he had disappeared to declare his love for her in stone.

By the time Livia made it back to the car, the thunderclouds looked very tall, dark and menacing. She hardly noticed them. Her thoughts had drifted back to that silhouette of the horse. Livia promised herself not to miss a photograph again, not to miss a vocation that became clear to her in this mountain-top vision. She would become a photographer; she would research photography schools; she would help her parents find her replacement at their family business.

****

'You shouldn't have waited for me,' Livia said, still panting after running home from her family store where the team meeting was held.

'We didn't,' answered her father Mauro nonchalantly. 'It was good, by the way. Not your finest, though. Lacked salt. But we Umbrians are used to salt shortages, aren't we?'

'Yes, we can blame the Pope for that,' she said, smiling. Her dad was always harping on about the times the Vatican tried to strangle the supply of salt, to starve Umbria into submission.

'What about the aubergines and tomatoes from Sicily?' she asked, hoping for a more enthusiastic response.

'You mean the ones I ordered for the shop? They were delicious.'

'*Dai*, Mauro *basta*,' Donatella said, protectively. '*Amore*, look at you. Still dripping wet from that storm. Go upstairs and change while I heat up the remainder.'

'*Grazie mamma*. What a day!' Livia exclaimed. 'I'll tell you all about it.'

'Did you make the meeting in time?'

'Of course I did,' she replied as she sprinted to her room.

Some ten minutes later, Livia sat blowing on her plate of *parmigiana* to cool it down.

'Sorry, I got distracted,' she said, noticing raised eyebrows across the table. Oh my, inquisition time.

'And?' prompted a disgruntled Mauro.

'And, I have finally made up my mind!'

'About what? Massimo?' he said provocatively.

'No *papà*, about college. I want to go to college. To study photography,' she announced.

'Whatever for? There is no money in photography. Just hours and hours in dark rooms being poisoned by chemicals.'

'Yes, for the best results. But you can also send your cartridges of Kodak or Agfa film to be developed. It's a booming field, I promise. *Papà* you love flicking through the colour magazines, I know. When you are not reading your comic books.'

'Well, who's going to pay for all of this?' he frowned.

That brought an abrupt end to the conversation. It was Donatella who eventually broke the silence.

'Alessandro dropped by today.'

'Did he?' Livia blushed.

'He was wondering why you were not collecting fresh flowers with your team. He offered to help tomorrow night.'

'With this tricky weather, you are going to need all the help you can get,' Mauro said. 'Unless the festival is cancelled.'

'Don't say that, Mauro. Just you wait, *la Madonna salverà L'Infiorata*. She always does. Anyway, I am tired. Time for bed.'

She stepped across to hug her daughter and kiss her goodnight.

'*Buona notte, amore.* We are so proud of you.'

Mauro stood up and helped his wife ascend the stairs into their bedroom.

'You will lock-up and turn out the lights?'

'Of course, *papà*.'

Half-an-hour later, noticing the lights were still on, Mauro walked back down to the kitchen in his pyjamas.

'Livia, I thought you were going to get a good night's rest?'

'I am worried about *mamma*. She seems to be weakening by the day.'

Livia sat at the table with an empty glass cupped in her hands and a plate still filled with her dinner.

'She is so stubborn, that mother of yours. Worries about everyone except for herself. Refuses to go to the doctor for tests.'

'I think she is too scared. Those oozing lumps she showed me in her left breast. They are frightening.'

'Help me get her to hospital when the festival is over, won't you?'

****

It was the next day and most of Livia's petal-layer team were gathered in the stockroom behind her shop, where all their numbered boxes of flowers were temporarily stored. They stood among cartons filled with red poppies, boxes of yellow *ginestra*, as well as cornflowers for the sky. Other boxes contained wild flowers such as elderflowers, anemones, roses and dog roses, ribwort, the pink thistle flower of the cardoon and yellow fennel. They also had boxes of petals from oxeye daisies and magnolias and from the local gardens, they packed boxes of freshly-cut carnations, marigolds and chrysanthemums. The judges seemed to favour the more vivid colours of the fresh petals.

Some of the women played cards indoors. Others waited nervously outside, knowing that other teams were already at work, while keeping an eye on the darkening sky.

Earlier, they had agreed as a team to postpone the petal-laying until the storm threat passed.

'At most, we are talking about a couple of hours' delay. Thunderclouds usually disappear by early evening,' Giovanni had advised them.

While everyone was fearful of a repeat of the previous day's storm, there was growing restlessness among them. They knew how long it took to lay twenty-four square metres of floral carpet. That the early morning deadline was fixed. Officials needed to judge, the public deserved to see the creations and the church required the procession to start on time. The Feast of Corpus Domini, held each year on the ninth Sunday after Easter, would not wait.

'I told you we should have chosen another composition,' said a frumpy team member. She was in her 50s, the second oldest of the team.

'*Perché?*' asked Giovanni.

'Are we not tempting fate? Here we are portraying Santa Chiara and her sisters praying for a mighty storm to frighten away the invading Saracens.'

'That is a bit ironic,' he admitted. 'But I understand everyone agreed to it.'

'We did,' agreed a sinuous young woman. She was the second Laura. 'At least Giovanni arranged for the large tarpaulin to work under, to keep us dry this year,' she added.

Laura quite fancied him. Even if he was a bit aloof and rather quirky, as she imagined all very clever people to be. He returned her compliment with an unexpected smile, while she blushed.

'If the wind blows as it did yesterday, the tent will be useless,' said the team's sage with the toothless grin. Despite being the oldest team member by some margin, her fingers remained so dextrous she was still among the fastest petal-layers in Spello. This lady had been involved in this festival since the beginning, so she claimed. She knew the woman who first placed petals outside her door to honour the procession in the 1930s.

'These storms can happen when Easter is late. Like this year. Pushes *l'Infiorata* into early summer,' she muttered, for the benefit of younger team members.

'Enough of all this negative chatter,' announced Livia suddenly, feeling increasingly anxious. 'I am not waiting any longer. I am going to start my drawing on the paving stones now. If it rains and I need to re-do them, so be it.'

'I agree. In the meantime,' said Giovanni. 'I'll be on weather watch.'

He set off to a look-out terrace above the town, where he would have a good view of any approaching storms from the west. Sometimes the thunder clouds bypassed Spello, unleashing rain in black curtains on the valley below instead.

Within half an hour Giovanni was running back to warn the team, accompanied by a ferocious wind. One that ripped fresh young leaves from trees and filled the air with precious petals. Minutes later the town was hit by cold horizontal rain, which gathered in streams that flowed down Spello's steep alleys.

****

Maria Celeste had never seen this side of her friend. It was a revelation to her. But on further reflection, she seldom saw her relaxed in a group as this evening.

For the day had been one of jubilation. Sandra had invited her to join her team of archaeology students as they celebrated their big discovery. One month into the big excavation on the summit of Monte Acuto. The mountain that watched daily lives unfold in the town of Umbertide. Where they once both lived, before moving to Perugia.

It was a very spontaneous gathering, which began at a bar in the afternoon and then rolled into the evening. Outside a dark sky threatened a storm of biblical ferocity and in the distance, lightning danced randomly above Monte Subasio.

Maria Celeste arrived just before the deluge, to find Sandra still wearing her dig kit. A blue boiler suit, walking shoes and a red bandana tied around her forehead. She even had her toolbox by her side, with its picks and trowels and brushes. The group was laughing and joking and Sandra was in its midst, enjoying the limelight and revelling in the attention having been crowned dig champion. A student band began playing and most of Sandra's friends took to the dance floor. Including Maria Celeste, who first drink was left untouched as Sandra pulled her away from their table.

'Have you ever danced with a woman before?' Sandra asked. She was smiling and quite giddy.

'Like this, never,' Maria Celeste replied.

They had just finished dancing to 'Rock Around the Clock' and the band began to play a slow number. The change in tempo was much welcomed.

Sandra led, one hand holding hers and the other resting gently on Maria Celeste's left shoulder.

'Relax, Mari. Pretend I am Julian,' Sandra said, feeling her friend rigid and detached.

'There, that's better. It's not so bad, is it?'

'On the contrary, it is quite pleasant,' Maria Celeste answered, almost nonchalantly.

'Still no word from him?' Sandra asked.

'None.'

'*Non preoccuparti*, you'll get to see Rome one day.'

Sandra pressed against her friend as she guided her gently across the dance floor. Giulia looked on with a tinge of envy. Not only had Sandra found the most ancient bronze figurines (she had found three), but here she was clearly enraptured by this tall woman from England.

****

Standing just outside the church of Santa Maria Maggiore, six clergymen dressed in white and gold held a large silk canopy high above the bishop. The sun shone and the air was so still it seemed repentant, exhausted perhaps from its frenzied exertions the previous evening.

The bells stopped ringing, giving the signal for the procession to begin. Soon the prelates were walking gingerly over the first floral carpet. It showed a white angel carrying a bouquet of flowers flying over a stylised, multi-coloured town of Bethlehem. The team behind this creation had at first waited for the storm to pass, but grew impatient and began laying petals just before it struck. Fortunately, they were able to borrow flowers from other groups that had to retire. Many compositions had been saved in this way.

A little later the procession walked on Livia's homage to *Santa Chiara*.

'All that work being trampled underfoot,' said the older Laura. 'Why can't they walk around it?'

'Tradition,' sighed the team sage.

'I agree with Laura,' lamented the younger Laura. 'All that hard work for nothing.'

'At least we'll be in Santa Chiara's good books. And we've a prize to collect this evening,' said the first, still convinced they would win. 'Don't we Livia?'

'Possibly, you never know. But don't raise your hopes too high,' Livia said, trying to manage expectations.

'Ah look, there is Alessandro,' the elder Laura said, spotting him among the jostling entourage behind the priests. 'Our hero, isn't he?' she added, nudging Livia gently in the ribs.

'Rather fancies our Livia, doesn't he?' said the sage. 'He's tumbled head over heels for you my dear.'

'Nonsense,' Livia replied, succumbing to a warm glow inside. One that did not feel quite right. Not yet at least. 'And anyway, it was Giovanni who saved the night.'

'I'm with Livia. None of this would have happened without Giovanni,' said the younger Laura, who had become quite infatuated with the doctor to be.

As Alessandro walked past, Livia found herself edging towards him.

'*Grazie*, Alessandro. You saved us last night,' she said.

She had never paid him much attention before. Now here she was, being quite forward.

'That was the least I could do. I was happy to be able to help you.'

He really had been a saviour. Rescuing together with Giovanni, the tarpaulin that had been ripped from its anchor lines, drying the site, organised the floral replacements and most importantly of all, restoring a sense of calm and self-belief among the team.

'Will you join us for the party after the prize-giving?'

'I would love to Livia. Thank you.'

Alessandro kissed her on both cheeks and turned to follow the procession along the Via Cavour. Down towards the triumphal Roman arch, *the Porta Consolare*, near the entrance to the town.

As he walked home, he was overtaken by a sense of euphoria. There was a lightness in his step. The thought of his upcoming military service was suddenly much less daunting. To mark his own personal triumph, he thought of stepping over the cordon that protected the monument for the first time. But he changed his mind, and followed the procession instead. His application to law school in Perugia could wait.

****

Prize-giving had ended and a clamorous throng heaved about in Spello's main *piazza*. The crowds swelled forward in waves between the food and merchandise stands. From the brightly-lit van selling furry soft toys and iridescent sweets in frightening shapes; to the pizza parlour offering re-heated squares with sparse toppings; and to the ubiquitous *porchetta* van, where customers in disorderly queues waited to be served pork buns by characters straight out of a Disney cartoon.

Spello's brass band had played intermittently through the afternoon. As the evening approached, there was a palpable relief for some to see dented trumpets and trombones being packed away by local musicians of all ages. To be fair, there was a smattering of talent sitting amongst them. Most of the band however, consisted of youngsters unable to match the enthusiasm of their parents. As well as the elderly, whose lungs and fingers were beginning to betray them but who steadfastly remained in the band for the companionship it offered. A band of rock musicians stood by impatiently, awaiting their turn, drawing heavily on cigarettes while holding bottles of Peroni. Their vocalist, clad all in white, from the cowboy boots to the gold-sequined trousers and jean jacket, nervously ran his fingers through swept-back dark hair thick with gel. Spello's very own Elvis.

The town's mayor, along with the town hall officials that preceded him had droned on for over an hour, in what was a thinly-disguised campaign speech. The local elections were to be held in a few weeks. To drum-up enthusiasm, they handed out Italian flags and arranged for a group of young men to wear red-shirts to reenact the centenary commemorations of the unification of Italy, as they had done every year since 1961. Nothing could stir the soul of a crowd so much as the sound of Italy's national anthem being played as Garibaldi's red shirts strolled proudly in its midst.

Livia's floral mosaic had not won. It did not even make the top three, despite the fact that around half a dozen teams had to withdraw and the procession walked over large empty spaces with no artwork along the way.

Rumours abounded, driven by superstition, that the people of Spello had fallen out favour, that Santa Chiara indeed had invoked the wrath of the heavens the previous evening as a sign of her displeasure. The pious had attended mass that day in large numbers to repent and some even planned a pilgrimage to the Basilica di Santa Chiara in Assisi, built after her death, to beg forgiveness for misusing her image. The fact that all this happened in the twentieth century did astound the clergy, but they welcomed the spike in church attendance and the full collection boxes.

Most of Livia's team believed that Santa Chiara was not offended in any way. She had suggested the subject in a dream after all. It was the mistakes they made on the night that cost them the prize. In the scramble to replace lost flowers, the patterns lost clarity and colours jarred. In any event, the floral canvas seemed to bear only a passing resemblance to the painting from which they worked.

Livia however, knew that she was at fault. Her creation was too busy, too cluttered. There were too many figurative, child-like figures representing Saracen soldiers. Santa Chiara had too many of her nuns confronting them in prayer. It did not flow or convey the story in the way she wanted.

'*Non importa*,' said Giovanni while holding his arm tightly around her shoulder, trying to console her. 'You can't expect a masterpiece at the first attempt.'

'I am not upset at all. I loved the whole experience. Wouldn't have missed it for anything,' she enthused. 'Mind you, I could have done without all this controversy and silly superstition.'

'Oh, but that only adds charm and poignancy to the whole festival. Don't you think? It is through occasions like this that we connect with the past.'

'Gio, you are sounding more and more like Massimo! Where has that scientist disappeared to?'

'On leave, until I get my results! Who knows, if I don't pass, I might head for the church. Like your uncle. Father Giuseppe. Anyway, I am on holiday. Talking of Massimo, how are you and he getting on?'

'Never thought it would be so tough. This separation. I feel that walk I did on Friday..'

'Without even telling us,' he interrupted. 'Left us to collect all those valuable garden flowers without you. That walk?'

'Yes, that one,' she said, turning a little red with embarrassment. 'Afterwards, it felt as if I was leaving him. A pilgrimage to say goodbye.'

There was a brief silence.

'He still loves you, I know.'

'Does he? If so, he doesn't show it. He didn't even write to wish me luck this weekend, let alone call.'

'Yes, he told me so recently, over the phone. Like you, he is finding the distance hard to cope with.'

'It's all that mysterious donor's fault. If there had been no sponsor, he would have been nearby. Studying music in Perugia, not thousands of kilometres away in a stupid foreign country,' she said, showing her frustration once more. Giovanni's parents swore it was not them and Massimo had received no inheritance. So, the origin of Massimo's benefactor remained a mystery.

'What if I broke-up with him?' Livia asked.

'I think Massimo would be deeply hurt,' Giovanni answered, taken by surprise.

'But eventually, he would come round, wouldn't he? He'd realise that childhood sweet-hearts don't always make it through to adulthood. You told me that, remember?

Giovanni did not recall saying that. He was too loyal to his friend to have said as much, surely?

They spotted the master of ceremonies as he strode towards the wooden platform to take the microphone and introduce the aspiring rock stars.

'What do you think has happened to Alessandro?' Liva asked.

'I don't know,' Giovanni replied, suddenly realising why Livia had been testing him. 'He told me he had to work on his law school applications. I'm sure he'll be joining the party. The whole of Spello is out tonight.'

The band took to the stage and began tuning their instruments, drowning Giovanni's reply in a barrage of drum beats, clashing symbols and over-amplified electric guitars.

The younger Laura, who had stood nearby with other members of the team and their families, immediately seized her opportunity. She had seen Giovanni catch her eye at least once, as he stood talking to Livia.

'Giovanni, will you dance with me?'

'*Mi piacerebbe*,' he replied.

As Livia watched the couple ease their way through the crowd to the dance floor, she fell into a sombre mood and thought about her mother. She realised for the first time that her knees were sore and her lower back ached from the hours bent over her floral creation. She was about to turn for home, when she felt a tap on her shoulder.

'Alessandro, where have you been? You're late!' she shouted in surprise.

Following Laura's example, she took him firmly by the hand and before he could find the words to reply to her, led him towards the band. All her worries and pains evaporated in an instant.

Later that night, as Alessandro headed home after leaving Livia at her doorstep, he noticed the metal chain under a Roman arch had been removed. This time he would march beneath it, and into the new life he had yearned for. With Livia. He could not believe his good fortune. Nor that first kiss, as she sat on his lap.

****

It was no coincidence that at the very same moment that Alessandro was passing under the Roman arch in Spello, Massimo was walking alone past an excavated section of a Roman wall in the City of London.

He and a group of fellow students from the Royal Academy had been to a classical concert at the Barbican. For a change, they had not been performing. He should have been relaxed, inspired by the rendition of Beethoven which featured various alumni from the college, including the first violin and piano soloist.

Only, he was far from at ease with himself.

He had been so wrapped-up in his student life in a foreign city, he had totally forgotten to speak to Livia before *l'infiorata*. He had made no attempt to call, or to write a letter. It had not even occurred to him to send a last-minute telegram to wish her and her team good luck. He knew she would be terribly upset.

Shadows lurked behind the broken outline of the wall, taunting him.

'You have turned yourself into a distant memory,' one whispered.

'She's drifted away from you, Maximus,' said another.

Why the name Maximus, he wondered?

Then a third voice intervened. He was never sure whether it was that of a man or a woman. Even the accent was unclear. It was a voice he heard often. He was convinced it was that of his benefactor.

The voice normally only spoke of his life in music. It encouraged him and inspired him and tried to elevate his self-esteem. Which he needed badly. Confidence had always eluded him, especially after losing both his parents when he was barely a teenager. It was constantly eroded by his mediocrity. Or rather, what he believed was his very average talent, when compared to that of his peer group at the college.

But the voice was steadfast in its support.

Tonight however, it spoke to him for the first time about a totally unrelated topic. The big party in Spello. It joined in the taunts reminding him how Livia would be the centre of attention. That a large group of admirers would be taking turns asking her to dance.

It made him feel quite ill.

He resolved to spend the following morning trying to call her.

Chapter 3. Meeting Hannibal
217 B.C.

Julian stood alone above the garrison town of *Arrezo*. He was looking for the tell-tale sign of a large army on the move, a dirty plume over the horizon.

His head throbbed. He had been drinking in secret again, to take his mind off the wretched war that kept him away from his new love that he had met only recently, as his legion rested on its march up from Sicily.

He removed his helmet to feel the soft breeze that brushed through the pine trees around him. To hear the rustling green needles. Although this morning, the soothing sound was drowned by the high-pitch serenade of the cicadas.

Suddenly, the insects fell silent. Julian instinctively turned around.

'Julius?' asked a tall legionary approaching him.

Julian could see from the transverse crest on his helmet that he too, was a centurion. The uniform also proclaimed he was a *triarii*, one of the heavy infantry units that formed the core of Rome's army. Like himself, he would be in command of two maniples of *triarii*, some 120 men in total. He looked young for his position, but then many men had risen quickly through the ranks to replace the fallen.

'Yes,' Julian replied sternly. He did not recognise him and was most annoyed that he had been caught off-guard.

'*Mihi nomen est* Alexander. It is an honour to meet a hero of the battle of Trebia. Consul Gaius Flaminius would like you to join him at a meeting with his closest military advisers.'

Alessandro had been waiting for this opportunity. To meet one of the most highly-regarded centurions in the Roman army. He wanted to befriend him, to learn from him. To hear how the heavy infantry units managed to survive largely intact and return to Piacenza, when half the force of lighter troops had perished at the hands of the Carthaginians that day.

'Good to meet you, Alexander,' said Julian, in a perfunctory manner. 'Flaminius would like to see me, would he? The question is, will that amateur heed my advice?' Julian continued, before adding, 'There are no heroes on the defeated side, only the vanquished.'

'I am sure he will,' said Alessandro, a little surprised by Julian's indiscretion. The sarcasm of veterans unafraid to speak their minds, he supposed. Mixed with a touch of exasperation. The growing feeling he noticed among the men, that there was no Roman commander in the field that could come close to the brilliance of Hannibal. Alessandro took a different view. So long as Flaminius was untested, he would give him the benefit of the doubt.

'Alright, I'll be more than happy to meet Flaminius,' said Julian. 'I need to tell him that Hannibal has already slipped past us in the night, heading south to Trasimeno. While we slept comfortably in this garrison town, he marched by so that he could pick the site for the next battle. One that suits him. Just as he did at Ticinus and Trebia, defeating us twice already since crossing the Alps. I bet you he will be waiting for us at that lake.'

'You think Hannibal's army now stands between us and Rome?'

'Yes, I do. What's more, he is trying to lure us into battle. Why else would he be committing atrocities among the local people? When he first arrived, he went on a huge recruitment drive among the Gauls that live in the Po valley. Now the Gauls and other tribes ambivalent towards Rome are joining him in droves. He doesn't need any force or bribes to boost his ranks.

Flush with troops and success, he wants to engage us, defeat Flaminius and walk unchallenged into Rome.'

'What's Flaminius ever achieved,' Julian continued, 'except to put his name to a new *via Romana*? He has no military experience whatsoever. *Roma* desperately needs to professionalise its army.'

Alessandro could have Julian arrested for these treasonable words. But he wouldn't. Rome needed every seasoned soldier it could find to defeat Hannibal. Moreover, Alessandro could learn a lot from him.

'I met Maria Caelestis on the Via Flaminia, you know. At a small settlement on the Tiber. We were marching up from Sicily to reinforce the army in the north. Our legion was one of four led by Consul Tiberius Sembronius. He at least had experience, as the naval commander who recaptured Malta from the Carthaginians.'

Julian was rambling now. He started talking about marriage and becoming a lictor in Rome on retirement. In spite of this strange outpouring of his inner self to a complete stranger, something about him struck a chord with Alessandro. He too had left a girl he loved behind.

Alessandro realised at this point that Julius was drunk. He could smell wine on his breath. He was in no fit state to meet Flaminius. He had to do something, quickly, to protect Julian from himself. Looking around to check no one was in sight, Alessandro clenched his fist and knocked an unsuspecting Julian out cold with a single blow to the jaw.

He arranged for Julian to be taken back to his tent to recover and went to join Flaminius and his advisers. Alessandro felt he successfully diverted attention away from Julian's absence, with valuable intelligence on Hannibal's movements.

****

Massimo wanted to flee. So many men had done so, gone into hiding in the mountains, taking young families with them as well as the fitter, elderly parents if they could. Some just fled on their own, unencumbered, petrified of rumours that the advancing Carthaginian troops were under orders from Hannibal to behead all local men of fighting age.

'I am scared too. We all are,' said Giovanni. 'But I am not leaving without my parents, you know that.'

Livia's mother was too ill to move and her father refused to leave her bedside. In a show of solidarity, Giovanni's parents said they would remain with them. As for Livia, she still believed Alessandro's legion would defeat Hannibal. That they would be saved.

'But Livia, the Romans are still far away to the north. The enemy have arrived at our lake already, unopposed,' Massimo had tried to argue.

It was hopeless trying to reason with her and anyway, there was no chance Livia would join him. Her relationship with Massimo was over. He had been too unreliable, taking off hunting for weeks on end. She was with Alessandro now.

The two young men stood side-by-side outside their hamlet on an escarpment overlooking Lake Trasimeno's north shore. Giovanni was almost a head taller than his friend. He had long limbs that moved gracefully through the forests, like the deer he stalked with his shorter companion, whose defining features were his broad-shoulders, chiselled jaw and fine hands with thin and dextrous fingers with which he crafted arrowheads and other hunting weapons.

'Please, join our village meeting first. Then decide.'

'Of course I will. Your parents have become mine too. We are in this together.'

Half-an-hour later they joined a crowded wooden community hall, surprised at how many people were still around. Reluctant maybe, to leave their precious land to the enemy. The fertile plain beneath them farmed by generations of their ancestors; the lake in front filled with fish; forests teeming with wild boar, deer and porcupine.

'Quiet everyone. Quiet.' It was the village chief.

The room fell silent instantly, as eyes filled with fear turned to him. Although he was quite ill and had a pronounced limp, he still held most of the community's respect.

'Look, I'm afraid I don't have any good news to give you. Hannibal's army were seen yesterday approaching the shores of our lake to the west. They have sent scouts ahead to look for a site to fight the Roman army, which is expected to march down from *Arretium* soon. Etruscans fleeing ahead of the Carthaginians tell us they are killing all men of fighting age they find.'

'What about those grey monsters?' interrupted one man.

'We are told all the elephants have died or been killed.'

'So there is some good news then.'

'I suppose so. We have little time, so let me get straight to the point. The Roman army will not arrive in time to save us. Nor frankly, are they really interested in our fate- they just want to preserve Rome.'

This provocative statement would normally have sparked a lively debate from the younger generation, that was more fully integrated with Rome than their Etruscan and Umbrian forefathers. But not today.

'The elders and I therefore encourage anyone who wants to leave, to do so now, before it is too late,' he continued. 'But not all of us can or want to go. So, for the sake of those who stay, I offer to reach out to Hannibal, to make a generous offer of grain and other food stores to his army in a show of our support. Who will accompany me?'

'What's the point? Those savages will steal our food and rape our women, even if we side with them,' shouted one man, breaking the silence that followed.

'No-one? What about you?' the chief said pointing at Cesare, a flagrant opportunist who spent a lot of time trying to cultivate relationships among the elders.

'Frankly Chief,' Cesare replied, 'I believe the only way we can get an audience with Hannibal, is to convince his scouts that we can help him win.'

This was a step too far for many, especially Livia.

'We'll help Hannibal choose a battle site,' Cesare continued. 'We'll tell him where he can hide his troops in ambush.'

Giovanni seized the moment for reconciliation. Livia was now red with anger.

'Look, let's alert the Romans at the same time,' he said. 'They can then adjust their tactics to turn the surprise on Hannibal.'

Everyone seemed to like that idea.

'I would be happy to warn the Roman army,' added Cesare, sensing his opportunity.

After a moment's reflection, the chief spoke.

'A masterful plan. Caesar you set off now to intercept the Roman army. Ioannes, I would like you to accompany my party, with Maximus. The two of you know these hills and forests better than anyone. I need you to convince Hannibal.'

****

A night watchman drew open the entrance to Julian's tent and let Alessandro in.

Julian was already putting on his body armour and chest plate, in anticipation that they would be breaking camp at dawn. He had lit a candle on a table, illuminating a small group of votive figurines he had yet to pack. The shadows of Jupiter and other gods cast on the tent wall moved with the flickering flame.

'It's you,' Julian said, rubbing the last residues of sleep from his eyes. 'No need to apologise. You did me a favour.'

'I wanted to see how you were. To tell you I passed your message on to Flaminius. We are going to march south at the break of light,' said Alessandro.

'Good, I guessed we'd be moving. That was quite some punch. My jaw hurts, but thankfully the head is clear. No more wine for me until Hannibal is defeated.'

'Then we can share an amphora or two. Talk about professionalising the army. Our love of Umbrian women. Something we have in common, you know, outside all of this,' revealed Alessandro with a faint smile.

'Mine's Etruscan.'

'Close enough. See you at our next encampment.' Alessandro backed out of the tent and returned to his maniples.

Now that is a kindred spirit, thought Julian to himself, blowing the candle out before confronting the day ahead.

****

It was Massimo's turn. Giovanni had held his nerve and felt Hannibal had believed him.

'*Quid nomen tuum Romanum est?*' asked Hannibal. Although he had interpreters to hand, he spoke good Latin. Hannibal did not believe the young man in front of him was Tancredi, the descendant of a famed Etruscan leader. He would give him one more chance.

'To the *Romani* I am known as Maximus. It is an adopted name. But everyone at home knows me as Tancredi.'

Hannibal knew there was no love lost between Etruscans and Romans. Equally, the historical animosity between the two peoples had diluted over time. To the point where this young man would not be standing in front of him offering to betray Rome on this pretext alone. The real reason he was here, thought Hannibal, was to try and save his family and broader local community. Hannibal respected his bravery, and that of his companion.

Massimo and Giovanni had been asked this and many other questions by Numidian interrogators, after surrendering to an advance party of Carthaginians, a few hours into a walk west along the hills that bordered the lake.

'You go alone. I am too slow,' their chief had said, shortly after they left their village. He had been struggling to maintain the slowest of paces and collapsed in pain onto a bed of last season's oak leaves.

'Ioannes, you are my son, understand? Maximus, you are related to Tancredi. That's your cover. Never down, subservient, never in the eye while you are speaking to him,' were his parting words, as an attendant bent down to give him some water.

They had resigned themselves to being killed, but the leader of the mounted scouting party restrained his men. He wanted some local intelligence first. Furthermore, the latest orders from Hannibal, since it was known Flaminius was now eager to engage in battle, were to start befriending the local population.

When they agreed to accompany their chief, they had never actually expected to meet Hannibal in person. But here he was in front of them. He was not the terrifying, savage warrior he had expected. Rather he was refined and dignified, more as he imagined a statesman to be. He had fine facial features and a thin straight nose. Had he been wearing a toga, he could have passed as a Roman Consul.

'Why do you come to me?' was Hannibal's next question, looking at Massimo piercingly in the eye.

Massimo managed to hold his gaze. This is the question they had been waiting for. They struggled to control rapidly beating hearts. It was Giovanni who answered. He described their hunter-gatherer existence in the hills above Lake Trasimeno. He talked about his and Massimo's knowledge of the shoreline and the best places to fish. He spoke of their intimate knowledge of the terrain, every hillside and ravine, the woods and clearings, where the wild boar had their dens even where porcupines roamed at night.

As Giovanni spoke Hannibal's facial expression began to soften. Giovanni could detect that mentally Hannibal was traversing those hills with him. He was formulating a plan, one involving concealment and ambush. Just as they hoped he would.

'Why should I trust you?' Hannibal asked, his last question of the interrogation.

Giovanni and Massimo looked at one another.

'We have put our lives on the line,' said Giovanni.

'That is not enough. I want your families here. Then, you will both accompany me on a scouting trip.'

****

Flaminius ordered his legions to set up camp on a plain on the north-west corner of Lake Trasimeno. Here they were in sight of the Carthaginians further along the lakeshore, where the hills were closest to the water.

His moment of potential glory had arrived. Addressing the troops before sundown, Flaminius deployed the fine oratory which earned him his consulship, to infuse them with the same levels of optimism he clearly felt himself.

Many men felt otherwise. Even Alessandro now shared Julian's strong sense of foreboding.

'You know had Flaminius followed the Senate's orders, we would now be marching back to defend *Roma*,' Alessandro told Julian afterwards. 'Instead, he wants to go down in history as the Consul that defeated Hannibal; the General that saved *Roma*.'

'That's quite a change in your tune,' remarked Julian. 'Yes, and I would be arranging for my future wife to follow the long baggage train behind us.'

'Me too. I would go and look for mine and we would all travel down together. Do you know, she lives up among those hills somewhere?'

'You hadn't told me. You must be very worried for her.'

Alessandro did not answer, so Julian changed the subject.

'Has Flaminius sent scouts ahead to check for any Carthaginian positions in those hills? To see the battleground Hannibal has chosen?'

'No. He wouldn't take any advice.'

'What are you orders Alexander?' Julian asked, after a few moments.

'My maniples are near the vanguard. We are to break through the Carthaginian lines on the hillside and circle back to trap them.'

'Don't circle back. Go and find your new love.'

'Nice idea! What are your orders, Julius?'

'I am to help protect Flaminius with my men. In the middle of the marching columns,' said Julian. 'By the way, what's her name?'

'Livia.'

'Beautiful name.'

The two centurions shook hands before returning to their respective quarters.

****

As darkness fell Julian made his personal rounds of his two maniples. He spoke to his men either individually or in small groups. He tried his best to lift their spirits, with talk of marching to Rome victorious, the baggage train filled with Carthaginian weapons and other spoils they would share on arrival. The lure of booty always made his men fight harder. Furthermore, the knowledge that he had brought his maniples out of Trebia almost intact also gave them confidence both in him and in their ability to survive the day ahead.

Before retiring to his tent to make further offerings to his favourite gods, Julian walked to the edge of the encampment. He could see the camp fires of the enemy. Starlight was reflected on the lake and the outlines of the hills were clearly visible against the dark sky behind. Suddenly the sound of the crickets echoing off the hills seemed to stop. Julius had a strong sixth sense. He knew something was happening there, something had made those companions of the night go silent.

Julian told the perimeter guards to be extra vigilant and, resigned to his fate, retired to his tent.

****

While Julian stood looking towards the Carthaginian fires, Massimo led a group of scouts guiding the Numidian cavalry in the dark over the brow of the hill behind their camp. They then headed west on the reverse, north slope of the hills so that they could not be seen or heard from the lake shore. Massimo halted them at a point close to but above the Roman camp, where they regrouped and waited for the signal to attack at dawn. After the cavalry came the heavy infantry, the bearded Gauls itching for revenge after their setback at Trebia. They were guided by Giovanni, who stopped them behind the hill mid-way between the Roman and Carthaginian camps. Other units of light infantry were then stationed behind the hills nearer the Carthaginian base. Only the African and Iberian infantry remained behind, ready to set up battle formation in the early morning.

The ambush was set.

****

Dawn broke as the Roman troops began forming into three parallel columns. This would make it easier to wheel into battle formation, although not in time to defend any attack from the flanks. There were columns of light infantry in front to handle any skirmishes as the army marched near the lakeshore. Behind them were several maniples of *triarii*, including Alessandro's. The Carthaginian line could already be seen in battle formation rising some way up the hill from the lake.

As they marched along the shore the morning heat built quickly. A haze descended on the water, obscuring visibility. Julian could just make out the outline of two islands. Estimating the closest was just over a kilometre away, he formulated his escape plan. When all around him seemed lost, he would shed his body armour and swim for his life. Brought up on the coast, he was a strong swimmer. He would bide his time and go and find his new love.

The rising temperature triggered the serenades of the cicadas. Today they were of warlike intensity, as insects in their thousands joined the chorus across the landscape. As they marched the hills bordering the lake suddenly retreated to reveal a small triangular valley. This was it, thought Julian, this was where Hannibal had set his trap. Julian's trained ear heard an enemy signal, the sound of trumpets reverberating across the hills. The enemy attack had begun.

The Roman column halted and all eyes turned left. There was confusion all around him. Julian had the presence of mind to reorder his maniples in a makeshift phalanx around the Consul and his Praetorian guard. Within a few minutes, a screaming horde of vengeful Gauls were upon them. A strange and alien emotion began to envelope him. One he had never felt in combat. He imagined it was what his enemies might have felt in the past when they faced the might of Rome against them. They called it fear.

It was not the sights of the battle that troubled him. He had seen so many severed heads, stepped across so many detached limbs and body parts, splashed through endless pools of gritty blood as he advanced with his troops through enemy lines.

Nor was it the noise. Which in battle, was greater than thunder. Louder than the mountainside that slid just past him once after relentless rains. He had grown immune to the ear-piercing, metallic clashes of sword striking sword; to the thud of metal-tipped spears embedding in the chests of warriors; to the squelch of feet slipping on human guts and entrails; to the blood-curdling shrieks of the attackers and moans of those that fell.

What really unnerved him, was that for the first time, he was not able to move forward. Slowly, over a number of hours, Roman numbers dwindled as the mounds of corpses grew. Gradually they were driven backwards, leaving dead and mortally wounded men behind, towards the lake.

Julian had never retreated before.

Suddenly there was a collective cry of anguish, as Romans saw Flaminius being lanced by a Gaul on horseback. At that instant, Julian had lost control of his men. Soldiers all around him fled for their lives. Julian joined them, discarding his helmet, breastplate and sword- but not his dagger- as he waded into the light green tepid water among the tall reeds. He looked for the island and started to swim towards it, even though the waters were still shallow.

As he swam and his adrenaline subsided Julian suddenly felt a wave of exhaustion. He tried to block out the cries of thousands of men being cut down by their pursuers. Then, he heard a horse snorting heavily as it swam just behind him. He turned and saw a Numidian light cavalryman raising a Berber sword into the air above his head.

Julian instinctively recoiled and caught sight of a swallow. Skimming over the lake surface just out of harm's reach, it beckoned Julian to follow him to a better place.

****

Tensions were riding high in the small community above the battle site. Good to his word, Hannibal had the families released. The community was spared and the Carthaginian army had marched on towards Rome, leaving them to return to their fields and the lake that sustained them.

But those fields were filled with fallen soldiers that they would have to bury before next season's crops could be sown. The current year's crops were destroyed, either plundered or trampled into dust by the battle. Their lake was spoiled too, polluted by thousands of rotting corpses that formed islands drifting in the wind. The whole length of the northern shore was coloured red with Roman blood.

Worse still for Massimo, was that their plan had backfired. Their community was split into two. Livia did not even acknowledge his presence any more.

'I knew we could not trust him,' said Giovanni. 'He never tipped off the Romans.'

He was referring to Cesare.

'At least we all survived,' muttered Massimo.

Giovanni hated seeing his friend feeling so depressed.

'Look, whether we had helped Hannibal with the ambush site or not, someone else would. The Romans were destined to lose that day,' he said.

'And let's face it Massimo, you had already lost Livia to that centurion, well before Hannibal arrived. You know what she has done every day since being released? She has gone to see if her new love is among the dead.'

'I know. I know, but I will never lose hope.'

Chapter 4. Ornella
2020 A.D.

'Unlucky in love. That's me, Ornella. 26 and no boyfriend. Why?'

She had just showered and stood naked in front of a long mirror. One that was quite forgiving of her slightly plumb but curvaceous figure. She was not a bad height, not too tall or short. Just right. She had long brown hair that hung in wavy curls below her shoulders and hazel eyes which, when combined with a furtive smile, could lock a boy's gaze briefly.

Until that is, they saw the woman next to her. Lucrezia is why. Her best friend, whom she loved and begrudged in equal measure. Actually, she did not dislike her at all, just pretended to do so to stop her becoming too vain. But enough of Lucrezia for now. She had to concentrate on what to wear. Something sensible and conservative.

Her nurse's uniform hung on the door of her old wooden wardrobe, freshly ironed. She worked part-time in a hospital in Spoleto. Her family urged her to demonstrate real commitment and take a permanent job there, as she showed huge potential and they felt she should have aimed higher at college.

However, Ornella nursed another dream. That of entering the world of classical music. Not as a performer. She had played the cello at school and sang in the choir and knew she lacked the talent to seek a career in music. But perhaps in stage management or as a musical agent or maybe an events' organiser. She blamed this distraction on Gian Carlo Menotti, the composer who established Spoleto's classical music and performing arts festival in the late 1950s. Every year in early summer, her Umbrian town was basked in the musical limelight, filled with aspiring and famous musicians, music-lovers from around the world in burgeoning numbers, and lots of young *Spolettini* like her wanting to take part.

'Maybe I scare them off? Too extrovert; or too direct; bossy,' she said to herself, back to reflecting on her spartan love life.

She opened the cupboard and began pulling out a succession of her favourite dresses, dismayed at how low some of the necklines had become. Again, she blamed Lucrezia. 'The boys can't stop looking at your tits, Ornella. Show them off.' She was right about that. Her last boyfriend, how long ago, over two years, used to sketch them in a secret note-book. '*Ma, sono bellisimi*,' he would say, as he drew while they rested after making love. The thought sent a shiver of excitement through her body and she felt her nibbles respond, their silhouettes sharpening in her mirror.

Finally, she came to her festival outfit. The black jacket, black tapered trousers and white buttoned shirt she had worn the last two years as festival usher. 'That's it. Decided.'

She dressed quickly and was just locking the apartment door when she remembered. 'Covid. Damn it, forgot my mask.'

Her interview for the role of venue manager of *Sala Pegasus* was in half-an-hour. She had plenty of time to get there. As she walked up the hill she rehearsed her ideas for the performances at this venue, one of many used by the festival. She had learnt the programmes for the last three years and researched possible new artists to invite. She had even gone as far as reading about the venue, its name, story and place in the cosmos.

Ornella was ready.

****

Maria Celeste was online, scrolling through the matinee and evening performances across multiple venues in Spoleto on her laptop.

'This is not a user-friendly website,' she complained.

'Wait a moment and I'll help you,' said Sandra from the kitchen next door, opening a bottle of wine.

She was trying to narrow her search to piano recitals. One in particular caught her eye.

'Listen to this. My favourite Beethoven sonata, the Tempest. The third movement. Chopin's Heroic Polonaise, always popular. The Liszt transcription of Schubert's Ständchen.'

'*Che bello!* Lots of crowd-pleasers.'

'Topped-off by another piece by Schubert, the Ave Maria. I like the sound of this pianist. A romantic. If you are free the evening of 11th July, I'll book two tickets.'

Maria Celeste was so taken by the programme, she did not even need to read the pianist's name to know who it was. She beamed with pride.

'Go ahead. I'll book a table for two afterwards,' Sandra offered.

She ambled over to Maria Celeste and handed her a glass of wine.

'Ah, you are smiling at last. *Ecco*, from a bottle of *Trebbiano Spoletino* you love.' Placing her hand on Maria Celeste's shoulder she asked, 'Now tell me, what was wrong? You sounded so sad over the phone, I had to come to see you. Is it anything to do with that army officer? Have you heard from him?'

'Oh, it's nothing important. I just needed some company. I am fine now that you are here and we've chosen a summer concert,' she replied, tears swelling into her eyes. 'What's more, I have some good news for you.'

'*Davvero? Cos'è?*' Sandra asked, realising her friend was uncomfortable talking about what had pre-occupied her.

'I have won a place to do operatic training at the *Conservatorio* here in Perugia.'

'Mari, *non ci credo!*' exclaimed Sandra in surprise. '*Ma dimmi*, what other talents have you hidden away there? Will you lend me some?'

'But.'

'*Ma cosa?*'

'I'm not sure it's for me.'

****

It was mid-way through the festival and locals were out taking advantage of the early morning respite from the searing summer heat. From where they sat at the *Caffe degli Artisti* with their coffees, Massimo and Giovanni could see open air stalls stocked optimistically high with summer fruits and vegetables. Vendors chatted animatedly with their regular customers, relieved to see them emerging from shuttered homes. It would be a while before the festival visitors emerged from their hotels and rented apartments, after their late nights in Spoleto's surviving bars and restaurants.

There was a sense of collective relief in the air. A return to a semblance of normality after months of lockdown. Remarkably, festival numbers were almost at pre-Covid levels.

'What are you reading?' Massimo asked, looking at the paperback Giovanni had left on the table next to his coffee. 'What a grim cover. Looks like a Picasso.'

The cover was of a heavily stylised cow's skull with long horns, set against a background of blocks of purple, brown, black and greys.

'It's *La Peste*, by Albert Camus. I'm trying to read-up on pandemics in literature. Including first- hand accounts by people that survived plagues in the past. To gain insights on how humanity has been shaped by global pandemics.'

'Well, it seems like it's all about governments taking advantage to tighten their grip over us.'

'*Esattamente!* You know, it's uncanny, the similarity between the measures taken by authorities faced with plagues across the ages.'

'Quarantines.'

'Yes, a word first applied to the period ships were impounded on arrival at ports. Here in Italy.'

They fell silent for a while, reflecting on the good fortune of surviving lockdown without falling ill, along with their families and most of their friends.

'It's not over yet,' said Giovanni. 'The levels of immunity are much too low still. Luckily, science is coming to the rescue. We are all going to be vaccinated in the coming months.'

'I've heard.'

'Past generations were not so fortunate. The Spanish Flu outbreak after the First World War. An estimated 25 to 50 million dead. Then the bubonic plague,' Giovanni continued. 'Which struck in waves throughout the Middle Ages. So many millions died. Did you know, in the worst outbreak in 1347 to 1348 A.D. over half the populations of certain towns and cities in Europe perished in a matter of weeks?'

'Enough,' Massimo announced. 'You are depressing me.'

'Sorry, you're right,' Giovanni said apologetically. 'By the way, it's coming along nicely.'

'I should hope so. Only one more practice session to go.'

'Mas, you'll be absolutely fine. We all believe in you.'

'*Grazie* Gio, that means a lot to me.'

'I particularly like your Tempest sonata. What strength and power, beauty and grace all in one piece. It's like a dialogue between two opposites, between good and evil.'

'It's my favourite piece. Speaks to me from deep inside.'

'As for the Schubert. Ethereal.'

Giovanni seldom lavished such praise on his friend, but he felt he needed his support for his big night that evening.

Their conversation was interrupted by Massimo's phone, which lit up and vibrated loudly on the table between them.

'Don't be late,' the message read. 'Or I'll be angry.' He replied with a nervous face Emoji. The one with chattering teeth.

'It's Ornella. Quite the task-master she is.'

'She's chasing you for the final rehearsal? I must go too. Back to collect my parents. They are so excited I think the whole of Perugia knows you are performing tonight.'

'Ah, that explains why it's sold out!'

Giovanni smiled. As he stood-up to go and settle the bill, Massimo noticed Ornella walking past, smiling at her phone.

'Ornella!' he shouted. A little loud for that time of morning.

****

They managed to persuade Ornella to stay, and Giovanni promptly ordered more coffees.

'Five minutes,' she said. 'Not a second more.'

'Massimo tells me you were the one who discovered him.'

'Hardly. It was only a matter of time- I just got there first. I should be grateful to him, as he helped me get my position as manager of *Sala Pegasus*. Didn't you Massimo?' she said looking towards him, a little flirtatiously.

'It wasn't me. Wasn't it your story of Pegasus that sealed the interview; when they asked you why the venue was named after the white winged horse?'

'Let me guess,' Giovanni couldn't help interrupting. 'You told them that music was the bridle that tamed the flying horse. That the thunderbolts Massimo would play on the piano in the Tempest would placate Zeus?'

'Something along those lines,' Ornella said, a little thunderstruck by these quirky observations. No wonder Massimo kept referring to his friend as *il professore*.

Somehow the conversation turned to Pegasus the constellation and Ornella established that Giovanni shared an interest in astronomy with her best friend Lucrezia, which sent *il professore* off excitedly on another tangent.

'Lucrezia, I love that name! Reminds me of one of my heroines. Lucrezia Borgia, that mythical woman with more talents than she had affairs. Much maligned you know. All those unfounded rumours, of incest and orgies in the Vatican. Spread by...'

'I know. Everyone in Spoleto knows about that Lucrezia. She was governor of our town. In ...'

'1499,' he said. 'Of course you know about her, how silly of me.'

Giovanni had been cut short very firmly. He rather liked that. He needed someone like Ornella to keep him grounded.

'Anyway, our time is up. Look, why don't the two of you come to the finale performance this Sunday evening. I'll order the tickets and invite Lucrezia as well.'

'That is an excellent idea,' Giovanni replied.

'And dinner afterwards?' asked Massimo, cheekily.

'I'll see to that as well.'

Leaving Giovanni to pay the bill, Ornella accompanied Massimo down to *Sala Pegasus*, with its two bronze bells and tiny *piazza*. The streets and narrow alleys between restored medieval buildings were starting to fill with tourists.

She could not help thinking she was beginning an entirely new chapter in her life. 'But who do I like best?'

****

Massimo sat in what was once a vestry, his skin prickling with heat. The air was oppressively still.

'Ornella, any chance of an electric fan?'

His minder was engrossed in her phone. As she looked up, she noticed how most of his once ironed black shirt now clung to his chest and back.

'Let me check.' She stood up and walked towards the room opposite.

'I've already looked in there,' he said.

'*Ah, scusa*,' she replied, feeling a sense of agitation in his voice. He was on edge, understandably. 'I know where they keep a stock. I'll be back soon.'

Ornella stepped out of the open side door into the hot summer air outside. Her black outfit was bad enough. It was having to wear a dreaded mask in public that made it suffocating, she thought, as she strode through the streets of Spoleto towards another of the festival's concert halls. She looked at her watch. Twenty minutes to go. I could do without this added hassle. She was already feeling nervous, not only for the outcome of this performance she had organised, but also for her artist Massimo.

While waiting for her to return, Massimo could hear a growing hum in the nave. It was the sound of his audience talking in low, respectful voices. He resisted the temptation of taking a peak. Instead, he imagined Giovanni and his parents taking their seats among the pews of darkened oak. He pictured Livia, arriving late and breathless as she always used to. She had said she would try to make it, although Massimo somehow doubted she would.

'Here you go,' said Ornella, as she plugged a fan into a socket near his chair.

'That was quick. *Grazie mille* Ornella. Sorry for being such a grump earlier.'

'*Non ti preoccupare.*'

Massimo stood in the narrow stream of flowing air, his arms raised to catch the full draft.

'*Ma che bello fresco.* How long to go?'

'Ten minutes,' she answered. She must have looked at her watch a dozen times since leaving on her quest. 'By the way, I saw a couple of talent scouts outside, each holding a copy of your programme. They are intrigued to hear the musician with the mystery sponsor.'

'No pressure then!' Massimo joked. Mention of his benefactor made him feel uneasy and even more nervous. What if he -or she- was in the audience? Would he meet his backer's approval? Would he ever meet the person, or at least find out who it was who had changed his life so dramatically? For he was sure Livia would be in that audience had he stayed on some government scholarship in Perugia. They would still be together. But then, perhaps he would not have had the opportunity to audition for the festival in the first place?

He reached across for an overnight bag he had brought with him. He took off his shirt and dried himself with a small towel. There was another black shirt in the case, neatly folded. He put this on, in full view of Ornella. Politely averting her gaze, she still could not avoid seeing his well-toned muscles and slender physique from the corner of her eye.

'Now that must be the Horowitz touch,' she observed, seeing him fold an oversized bright-pink handkerchief into his shirt pocket.

Massimo smiled, 'You were listening. I thought I had bored you silly with all my Vladimir Horowitz worship.'

'You did.'

'Ah. Touché!'

Massimo had told her how this pianist, born in Kyiv, was the inspiration behind some of the programme. How Horowitz used to leave a large handkerchief on the strings of his Steinway to mop his brow during his concerts. Performances he gave well into his 80s.

Ornella looked into the concert hall. The *Sala Pegasus* was the smallest venue of the festival. Nothing like the grand setting of the *Piazza del Duomo* where inaugural and finale concerts were held. But she liked the intimacy of the medieval church, which created the atmosphere of a recital in a wealthy count's private chapel. Thankfully, she did not have to organise all the equipment for a digital broadcast, as they used to during lockdowns.

'Let's give it another ten minutes,' she suggested. 'There are still some empty seats.'

'*Va bene.*'

Massimo closed his eyes and tried to slip into his music. Instead, his mind floated back to his arrival from London, when Giovanni collected him from the airport; and to Livia. Would she make it? Maybe not: he remembered she was spending a lot of time looking after her mother Donatella, who was very ill.

****

Maria Celeste drove alone. Sandra had an important meeting come up which, with her eyes focused firmly on a promotion to museum curator, she could not afford to miss. Equally, there was no way Maria Celeste was going to forego the piano recital.

'*Mi dispiace*, Mari,' Sandra had said, with the long mournful face she pulled when sad. 'I was really looking forward to our concert and dinner together.'

'Me too. Are you sure you don't want me to accompany you?' Maria Celeste offered, half-heartedly.

The interview was to take place in the early evening several kilometres north, in Umbertide. The role on offer was to manage both the museum there and two others locally.

'Positive. You had your heart set on the Spoleto recital. You must go, for the two of us.'

'*In bocca luppo*, Maria Celeste said, hugging her friend as she left. 'Tell them about your figurine find and the job will be yours!'

'*Grazie, amore!*'

As Maria Celeste drove, it suddenly dawned on her that if Sandra won the promotion, she would probably have to move back to Umbertide. That for the first time since they met, they would no longer be neighbours. The thought left an unexpectedly empty feeling inside. Soon however, she began to enjoy the scenic landscapes surrounding her. It seemed the eye was rewarded every direction you took out of Perugia. Whether to the north, alongside the hills thick in oak trees that bordered Umbertide. To the west, to the milky-green waters of Lake Trasimeno. To the south, heading for Rome. Or as today, to the east, towards the *Sibillini* mountains, a starkly beautiful area of high plateaus prone to terrible earthquakes.

She drove along the valley beneath Monte Subasio, whose gently sculpted contours offered protection to Assisi at one end and Spello on a spur at the other. Assisi, with its cluster of medieval buildings of pink and white stone, dominated by the huge Basilica of San Francesco. Spello, whose time in the limelight, its famous flower festival, had passed as spring slipped into summer.

Then she passed near the Temple of Clitumnus, an ancient, sacred site near the source of the *Clitunno*, a stream of sparkling clear water that had inspired various poets such as Giosuè Carducci and Lord Bryon.

Arriving at her destination, she left her car just off the Via Flaminia. The car park was full of camper vans taking advantage of the new travel freedom. Huge concrete pillars supported the autostrada above, rising into the hills at the head of the river *Teverone*, a tributary of the Tiber. With her parking ticket clearly visible on the dash-board, she walked towards the first of a series of covered escalators. They rose steeply uphill, disgorging visitors in their hundreds at various Spoleto landmarks, such as its cathedral and at the top, a fortress and vast Roman aqueduct. It was busy: the world-famous classical music and performing arts festival was in full swing. The crowds slowed her progress and emerging at the cathedral, she had to run some of the way down to *Sala Pegasus* to make it on time, perspiring heavily in the heat.

A festival steward handed Maria Celeste a programme. Adjusting her eyes to the relative darkness inside the small church, she found what appeared to be a space at the end of one of the pews.

'Is this seat free?' she asked a quixotic-looking young man with long arms and a prominent nose.

He smiled, and moved slightly to make room for her.

'Thank you, I am Maria Celeste by the way,' she said, her voice muffled slightly by the light blue mask.

'Giovanni. *Piacere*. These are my parents. Antonietta and..'
She didn't catch his father's name. There were no hand-shakes, just nods of greeting.

Maria Celeste looked at the programme, noticing for the first time the pianist's name. Massimo Rondini. She had a hunch.

'Are you here to see your friend perform?' she asked Giovanni.

'We are yes,' he answered, looking surprised. '*Lo conosce?*'

'Yes, I believe I do.'

****

Time,' Ornella announced suddenly, snapping Massimo back into the present.

She smiled. As a gesture of reassurance, she took the liberty of squeezing his arm as he passed by into the concert hall.

Massimo smiled back, then walked onto the platform where the shining black piano stood waiting for him.

The audience welcomed the newcomer with a warm applause.

Massimo placed his pink handkerchief above the key-board, sat down on the piano stool and took a deep breath.

****

Massimo had just begun playing the Tempest, when many kilometres away in hospital, Donatella opened her eyes.

'*Amore*, you should have gone to the concert,' she said softly, heavily sedated.

'No *mamma*, I wanted to be with you. There is only one place I want to be right now, and that is with you,' Livia said, fighting back the tears.

Mauro had lost his struggle and cried freely while holding his wife's hand.

A nurse came into the room to check the drips and equipment. Donatella no longer had the energy to tell her not to bother. To remove all those tubes. To save the oxygen for other patients. Nothing could help her now. How cruel life can be, she thought. One day in remission. The next it had metastasized. A word she could never pronounce, let alone fully understand.

'Alessandro. Have you heard from him?'

'Yes I have. He sends you lots of love and says he's on his way. He finally received some leave from the army.'

'Oh wonderful. I always liked Alessandro. A kind person. Caring.'

'He is *mamma*. Very special.'

In fact, there had been no word from Alessandro. From his secretive posting.

'I tell you who else is on his way.'

'My brother?' Donatella said, with a momentary sparkle in her eyes.

'Uncle Giuseppe. Any second. We are so excited.'

'Giuseppe. How I cried when we sent you to stay with him, all those years ago.'

Chapter 5. Lucrezia
2020 A.D.

Late one night Ornella, found herself being shaken in bed.

'Wake up. Get up. Something's wrong with Lucrezia.'

'What? What's going on?'

Gathering her composure, Ornella saw one of Lucrezia's ladies-in-waiting standing over her.

'It may be the plague,' the troubled noblewoman from Rome answered. 'I've called for the physician.'

'The plague? It can't be. What are her symptoms?' Ornella collected her shawl and bedside candle.

'She has a fever, she writhes in bed like a serpent, bending and twisting. She talks aloud, frightened.'

'It could be her morning sickness, you know. She is several months' pregnant. What is she saying?

'One minute she's shouting at her brother, 'Don't touch me. How dare you. Get off me, leave me alone.' Then she is trying to protect her first husband. 'Run, quickly, he's going to kill you. Hide, come this way.' Repeated time and time again. Sometimes she speaks in the Tuscan dialect, others in French or Castilian, then a language I do not recognise, maybe Catalan?'

'Any buboes?' asked Ornella.

'No boils that I can see. But then, her night-gown covers almost everything.'

'Sounds to me as if she is having nightmares again. We'll see.'

Ornella walked in through a dark oak door. There was a large four-poster bed in the centre of the room. In the dim candle light she could see a large tapestry covering almost the entire wall to one side, depicting a hunting scene. A wild boar with a spear thrust through its chest while another was shown held by a dog, a hunter about to stab it with a knife. Behind on a hill stood a walled town, overlooked by a fortress. It was Spoleto.

A young woman, barely 19, lay serenely in bed. She had cascades of curly fair hair that stretched past her knees and was noticeably pregnant. The room was still.

Ornella looked closely at Lucrezia, then at the noblewoman.

'That's no fever. It's her nightmares, poor thing. Not surprising, with that evil brother of hers,' said Ornella. 'Not to mention her father. That awful man, our Pope Alexander.'

'I heard that,' said Lucrezia, waking from her deep sleep, startled to see two women standing over her. 'What are you two doing here? How dare you speak of my family in that manner?'

Before they had time to offer an explanation, Lucrezia addressed them both. 'Kindly leave my room. We have a busy day tomorrow.'

They excused themselves, left the room and closed the door behind them.

The physician arrived and they had a brief discussion in the corridor in low voices. He agreed not to disturb her, before asking, 'Is it true she is returning to Rome already? She only arrived a month ago.'

'Well, she says she is returning to give birth to her child in Rome. But I believe she was only made governor of Spoleto to get her out of the way. While the Borgias dealt with her husband, accused of siding with the king of France,' said the noblewoman. 'She is returning to try and protect him.'

At that point Ornella awoke a second time, bathed in perspiration. She looked around her dark room, trying to regain her bearings. Her bedside alarm clock brought her back to the twenty-first century. Large green digits told her it was 3:30 a.m.

****

Massimo called Giovanni as soon as he heard about Donatella.

'Gio, I've just received the news.'

'Me too.'

'I can't believe we missed the funeral. How's Livia?'

'Coping, I think. I'm going to see her in a couple of hours. You should come too.'

'Not so sure about that. What if Alessandro is there? It could be awkward.'

'Get over it Mas. You should come, whether he is there or not.'

'No, I'm staying put. She's not asked me anyway.'

'You will at least make the memorial service, won't you? It's a week after your Spoleto festival ends.'

'I'd have to extend my stay?'

'Or fly back from London- one of the two.'

'It's in Spello, I presume?'

'No. Now here's the surprise. According to her will, she wanted a service of remembrance in Gubbio. Apparently, that was her ancestral home.'

'Gubbio? Funny, my family had ancestors from there. In the 19th century. In the tin-glazed pottery trade.'

'I'm sure if we looked into it, we'd find family links throughout Umbria.'

'And beyond. How's Mauro?'

'Heart-broken. Going to put the shop up for sale, I'm told.'

'Gio, will you be back in time for the finale? We have dinner booked afterwards with my minder and a friend, remember?'

'I'll be there, Mas.'

****

Ornella and Lucrezia were walking uphill to the closing concert. The early evening heat was stifling and they were regretting the decision not to take the escalators.

'Before I forget, *ecco il tuo biglietto,*' said Ornella. 'And a copy of the programme.'

'*Grazie amore.* You treat me like a baby sister.'

'You are, almost. You did remember your face mask didn't you, *piccolina?*'

Lucrezia was no *piccolina*. She was almost six-foot tall and had legs that reached the heavens.

'*Certo, sorella.*' Lucrezia replied, glancing at the programme. 'Ah, it begins with the intermezzo of Pietro Mascagni's *Cavalleria Rusticana*. My absolute favourite'

'Mine too.'

As they approached the historic centre of the town, they found themselves among growing crowds in evening wear. Immaculately dressed men, predominantly over fifty but younger classical music enthusiasts too in tailored suits or blazers with the occasional tie. Women wore elegant long dresses with revealing backs, some holding jackets or shawls to ward-off any late evening chill. Many had travelled long distances for the event, up from Rome or down from places like Ravenna on the Adriatic and Bologna. There were foreigners too, but heavily outnumbered by the home audience.

'I had another of my crazily vivid dreams last night,' said Ornella.

'Another one? What was I up to this time? In the first one I was having lots of affairs, while married to *il Duca di Ferrara.*'

'This one was in an earlier marriage. While she was governor here. We learnt about Lucrezia Borgia in school, but never in so much detail.'

'It must have been that meeting with your pianist and his friend. Sent your mind spinning, Ornella. Tell me more about Massimo and Giovanni. That's much more interesting.'

'Lucrezia, patience. You will find out soon enough.'

'Do you fancy Massimo?'

'I do, but not in the way you might think. I value him more as my discovery as a pianist. And anyway, he is still in love with his ex.'

'That's no good then, is it? What about Giovanni? You told me he is intriguing, fascinating even. Tall and handsome too.'

'*Il professore*, he is tall and lanky. Not handsome in a conventional sense. Interesting, most certainly. You could chat all evening about your shared hobby.'

'Hopefully not all evening. But tell me *amore*, do you like him?'

'Lucrezia, what difference does it make if I do?' Ornella said. She had long ago resolved not to let Lucrezia's relationships interfere with their friendship.

'But I am trying. Really I am,' Lucrezia replied.

'Trying what?'

'To be more aware. And understanding. A better friend.'

'Lucrezia, you are who you are. You can't help yourself. It's just you and you will always be my best friend, just as you are.'

'But I could be more self-aware.'

Ornella just smiled to herself and said nothing.

They walked a little further, passing the *Caffè degli Artisti* where a group of stage-hands were having drinks, their work finished for the day. A few recognised Ornella and waved.

'Ornella, why didn't we come here first? You could have introduced me to your friends. I feel shy meeting them on my own.'

'You'll manage.' Ornella smiled as she clipped the festival staff badge onto her black jacket, before reaching up to kiss Lucrezia on both cheeks. 'See you after the performance. You look stunning by the way.'

Lucrezia was wearing a strapless off the shoulder black and white dress, with a broad waist band that accentuated her figure.

'Love you too.'

While Ornella joined fellow workers back-stage receiving instructions for the evening, Lucrezia found herself standing next to a ceremonial military guard. He was one of two stationed either side of the narrow alley at the entrance. Hands in white gloves rested on the hilt of an inverted silver sword while white cords and halters criss-crossed a heavily starched blue uniform. She skipped past to avoid embarrassment, as she knew him. An early flame.

She walked down ancient shallow steps bordered by shuttered homes with balconies that had the best views of the concert, the equivalent of box seats at a theatre. As the flight of steps broadened, rows of two safari-style metal and canvas chairs on either side grew in increments to fill the open space that became a large *piazza* leading to the stage and Spoleto's proud cathedral behind.

Her row had only three seats on either side of the central aisle. Clever Ornella.

'The acoustics are the best. You'll be in a funnel of music in a most magical setting. Just you wait.'

She sat down in the middle one and unfolded a fan, more to keep herself occupied than cool, although the breeze it created was refreshing. She was early, feeling awkward waiting for the auditorium to fill and her two chaperones to arrive.

Looking up, Lucrezia noticed she had some company after all. Groups of gregarious swifts performed their aerial dances and screeched with excitement at the abundance of insects to be caught on the wing.

Gradually, people began to materialise and she saw Ornella leading elderly couples to their seats near the stage. Musicians appeared from nowhere to check their music stands and tune their instruments. Behind, Christ watched the growing crowd from within a large byzantine mosaic by Solsternus, surrounded by rose windows and guarded by a tall bell tower with a peaked roof. Luckily, there had been no sculptures of winged horses for Napoleon to steal when he set up his administrative hub in Spoleto.

Suddenly there they were. Two young men with broad grins. One tall, fair in an off-white linen suit and blue silk shirt. The other dark, with a closely-trimmed beard, blazer and white shirt.

'*Sua eccellenza la duchessa?*' enquired Giovanni, bowing while taking her hand to his lips.

Her shyness evaporated as Lucrezia slipped effortlessly into her other persona. She became her namesake in the prime of life, holding one of her poetry, music or classical literature soirees surrounded by intellectuals and European high society in the court of the duchess of Ferrara. Irresistibly aloof and quite alluring.

****

The four of them sat at a table on a wooden platform surrounded by medieval buildings in the small but intimate *Piazza Santa Agata*.

'*Eri bravissimo* Massimo,' extolled Lucrezia.

'*Grazie*,' he replied, a little uncomfortably. He had been very unhappy about his performance. The mistakes in the Polonaise. The nerves that muffled the Tempest.

'Ornella told me all about your stunning performance. I so regret not being there. I was stuck at work.'

That was true. She had been showing a client several properties in the hills surrounding Umbertide all day, returning home white with dust at eight.

'Ornella is paid to say good things about me,' he smiled, looking at her.

'*Non è vero*! I told Lucrezia what one of the agents confided in me afterwards. Salzburg is next, then Vienna, followed by the Royal Albert Hall,' said Ornella, blushing slightly.

'I think it is time to propose a toast to Massimo, said Giovanni, raising a glass filled with *prosecco*. '*A* Massimo! Our very own virtuoso pianist.'

Four glasses clinked in unison.

Always keen to deflect attention from himself, Massimo raised his glass again.

'And I would like to toast Ornella, for having faith in me. For the hugely successful series of concerts she organised at the *Sala Pegasus*.'

'Ornella!' They chanted, before emptying their glasses.

While the waiter filled glasses with a *Sagrantino* from Montefalco, Lucrezia turned her attention on *il professore*.

'Ornella tells me you are a doctor. Which field?'

'Anaesthesia.'

'The only medic I know who can put you to sleep just by talking,' quipped Massimo. 'You'll be lucky if you count past three.'

'Not to worry, I will let you know if I get bored,' Lucrezia replied with a smile.

There was no danger of any boredom. He was so well read and entertaining. In no time they were engrossed in each other's company, ignoring the others, almost as if they were alone at a table for two.

As the meal progressed, Massimo was increasingly unhappy with how the pairing had evolved. Not that he was not enjoying Ornella's company -he most certainly was- but it did not fit with his master plan. Which was for his friend to get to know Ornella, while he would be reunited with Livia.

Ornella was just right for Gio, he felt. He needed a tether. Someone firm and pragmatic; bold and decisive. Clever too. He imagined Ornella holding her ground intellectually, while Giovanni's intelligence swirled about her like a large gaseous cloud, ready to ignite at any moment.

Ornella was understanding and empathetic as well. She certainly sensed Massimo's nerves and had helped calm him before the performance. She was warm and could be flirtatious, too, when needed; just like Livia. What a dreamer he was, Massimo acknowledged, to think he could draw Livia back into his life.

'Tell me about Livia,' Ornella asked suddenly, as if she were reading his thoughts.

Their exchange suddenly became awkward and stilted. Ornella had inadvertently taken them down a conversational and emotional cul-de-sac. It was not helped by the fact Massimo was returning to London the following day.

The momentary awkwardness ended when their waiter appeared, carrying a large plate. The words *Auguri Massimo* were inscribed in sweeping lines of red coulis and in its centre stood a cupcake with a solitary candle.

'Giovanni, you remembered!' said Massimo, having forgotten it was his birthday.

'It wasn't me, it was Ornella who organised this,' he said, reaching into his jacket pocket for a small gift he had for him.

'Ornella, how did you know?' Massimo asked.

'Ah, that is my secret,' she said, as the waiter brought the bill.

They all looked at each other. No-one wanted the evening to end.

'Anyone care to join Ornella and me now for negronis at my apartment? I have a guitar there and we still need to sing *buon compleanno* to Massimo,' suggested Lucrezia.

'That sounds like a plan,' answered Giovanni, smiling broadly.

****

The two couples made their way down to Lucrezia's apartment. It was located in a newer part of Spoleto, away from the tourists and music scene.

Massimo appointed himself barman. Ornella watched him pour precise measures of gin, vermouth and Campari with an expert eye. He topped the mixture with a splash of *prosecco* and added two cubes of ice to each glass. She picked-up two of the glasses and placed them on a small table next to Giovanni and Lucrezia on her narrow balcony.

Giovanni was pointing at a constellation above Spoleto, while Lucrezia leant her cheek on his arm for better directional guidance.

'Looking for stars again Lucrezia?' asked Ornella with a tinge of envy.

'I believe I found one,' Lucrezia whispered in her ear. Whereupon she took *il professore* by the hand and led him to her bedroom.

'What about the guitar?' he said, pretending to resist.

'That can wait.'

Ornella's night did not quite follow the same script. Another negroni each later, coupled with the effect of the week's emotional cocktail, Massimo collapsed on the sofa and fell fast asleep. Ornella covered him with a throw, took off her black slip-on shoes and lay next to him.

She heard the distinctive hoot of a tawny owl through the open veranda doors. The haunting sound had travelled down the mountainside, declaring the night now his. She conceded and soon fell asleep, with Massimo by her side.

****

It was a Sunday and Ornella joined Lucrezia on a walk behind Spoleto, a short circuit that passed the magnificent Roman aqueduct that once supplied the town with fresh mountain water from the Apennines.

A year had passed and Ornella's dream of a fresh start in life had faded. At night, she no longer journeyed back into Renaissance Italy. She heeded her family's advice and now worked full time as a nurse. Contact with her festival protégé had withered. Massimo still lived in London and the word was he worked as a music teacher at a well-known girls' school in London, while waiting for calls from his agent. As for Lucrezia, she asked for a transfer to the Perugia office of her estate agency to be close to Giovanni, only to find he decided to retrain as a radiologist and spent most of his time in Milan.

'I still don't understand why you moved in with him,' Ornella said. 'Other than the convenience of not having that long commute to work.'

They were not talking about Giovanni, but about Lucrezia's new boyfriend she had met on a dating App. He was known as Cafaro. Her friend's dependence on men was so strong, she spent life bouncing between relationships. Lucrezia remained deep in troubled thought and did not answer.

'In fact, whatever did you see in him in the first place? Other than the handsome looks of a male model. He should have gone for modelling. But construction?'

'He tried.' Lucrezia was at least listening. 'Anyway, he's good at his job. Won lots of contracts for his firm.'

'Have you ever wondered how?' Ornella said. She had perhaps overstepped the mark, but there was no response, so she continued. 'I have never trusted him. That fake staccato laugh. His gesticulations so wild you have to duck when he talks.'

That last comment made Lucrezia smile briefly.

'Actually, Ornella I am scared,' she said after a while. 'It was when I told him my company wanted to send me to London, to spend some time in the head-office of our new owners there. You should have seen the look in his eyes. As for that filthy temper.'

'He is obsessed with you. Probably has been since you first posted that photo. Anyway, tell me all about London. It sounds really exciting.'

It was a welcome change of subject for the two of them. They completed the circuit and walked back down to Ornella's apartment, as Lucrezia had rented hers out.

'You should look up Massimo while you are there.'

****

Massimo read an unexpected message on his phone one day.

'*Ciao* Massimo. *Ricordati di me*, Lucrezia?'

Of course he did.

'..I'm in London this week on business...'

Impressive. She must be doing well.

'Would you be free for a drink on Thursday?'

'How did she get my number? Giovanni? They only dated a couple of times; he'd have forgotten it by now. Must be Ornella. What an idiot I was that night,' he thought to himself.

He started tapping out his reply.

'*Ciao* Lucrezia. How nice to hear from you. As luck for would it, I have a spare ticket for a Royal College of Music's production of Rigoletto. Any interest?'

She replied instantly with a heart symbol, which made his skip a beat.

Massimo was looking forward to his evening at the opera.

****

Lucrezia had not wanted a lift to the airport from her boyfriend. But Cafaro was insistent and, having been perfectly charming and considerate the whole week prior to her trip, she did acquiesce in the end. He had even been boasting among his circle of friends about her meteoric rise in the firm and how proud he was, while reminding her several times a day how much he loved her.

That was her problem. Cafaro did love her, quite obsessively. He had cut her off from her own friends and social circles so clinically, that Lucrezia had grown utterly dependent on him emotionally. It had not helped that Ornella and her other friends were immersed in their own lives and busy schedules. But at least now, she realised she was isolated and vulnerable. All she had to do, was break up with him. It was that simple. Easy.

Cafaro fussed about her while she packed and, to avert any suspicion, she selected clothes that would not draw untoward attention, including a loose-fitting tracksuit with trainers for the flight. She also made an emphatic point of leaving her perfumes behind. However, she did pack the four best outfits she wore to her office in Perugia, with striking footwear to match.

'My work clothes,' she said, with Cafaro nodding in apparent approval.

They drove through two sets of stone gates out of Perugia, winding their way down the steep hill on which the ancient city was built and onto the dual carriageway that headed past the regional airport and on towards Assisi. The traffic was quite light, having missed the earlier rush-hour, and a redolent blue sky above held the promise of yet another languorous summer's day in Umbria.

Not so in London.

'19 degrees with blustery showers,' she said in heavily-accented English, reading the BBC weather App she had downloaded for the trip. 'Why do they use such affected language? Why not say the truth: cold and rainy?'

'*Quegli inglesi*,' he replied dismissively, shrugging his shoulders and pulling a comic face to join in the mockery. He actually knew very little about the UK, although he harboured a grudging admiration of the lost British Empire and Queen Victoria and secretly supported Liverpool.

'Sorry I am missing the *Ballestra*,' Lucrezia said, trying to sound contrite.

He had packed his competition crossbow and medieval costume, which together with his suitcases, took much more room in the boot of the car than did her luggage.

'Me too. You know, I think San Sepolcro has a good chance of beating Gubbio this year.'

Of course he'd say that, now that his home-town had reached out to him and invited Cafaro back onto the team.

'Good. Send me lots of photos won't you, *amore?*' said Lucrezia, finding the word love hard to say. It was totally disingenuous after all. But she just could not find the strength or courage to break with him.

At this point she noticed a change in mood in Cafaro. He seemed to bite his lip while his knuckles turned pale as his hands gripped the steering wheel. His earlier smile vanished and when he looked across at her, it was with dark, empty eyes.

Fortunately, at this moment they found themselves in a stream of traffic entering the airport. He stopped the car near the entrance and she was able to gather her belongings and maintain the pretence of being his caring girlfriend long enough to kiss him goodbye.

'*Ciao, amore. A presto.*'

'*Ciao* Lucrezia. Enjoy London.'

Lucrezia did not know, as she settled into her window seat about an hour later, that Cafaro meanwhile was sipping a coffee at a petrol station reading the exchange of messages he had seen earlier and copied from her phone.

'*Ciao* Massimo. *Ricordati di me*, Lucrezia?'

'Of course I do! Lovely to hear from you.'

'I'm in London this week on business. Would you be free for a drink on Thursday?'

Cafaro stopped reading. It was too painful. He had seen the exchange a hundred times already. Who was this Massimo? He dialled a number of a contact in the trade he thought might be able to help.

'*Pronto*,' a gruff voice answered.
'Cesare, *ciao*. *Sono* Cafaro...'

Chapter 6. Cafaro's Revenge
1861 A.D.

Steam was drifting past the carriage window next to Sandra. A flat landscape rushed by in brief glimpses, appearing between billowing white clouds that alternated with the black fumes of burning coal.

Maria Celeste had fallen asleep, resting her head on Sandra's shoulder. Sandra meanwhile, was enjoying a deliciously warm feeling inside. It might have felt intimate even, were it not for the presence of another passenger opposite, an elderly gentleman named Ferdinando. The train juddered suddenly as the driver applied the brakes, jolting Maria Celeste awake. She sat bolt upright, slightly embarrassed.

'Sorry, I must have drifted off to sleep,' she said, adjusting her bulky ankle-length dress. 'Have we arrived at Modena?'

This town in the Po valley marked the end of the line from Milan- or so they thought- the beginning of a long bumpy ride in a horse-drawn carriage. Small orchards of apple and pear trees jostled for room in between fields of rice. In the distance, Maria Celeste could see a ridge that marked the edge of the valley. Beyond that lay the range of mountains that separated the cold north from the warmth of the Mediterranean. The Apennines. She was looking forward to the abrupt change in vegetation, to seeing the olive trees, the pointed cypresses of dark green and fields of sunflowers. They meant home.

'I don't think so,' Sandra replied, noticing Maria Celeste lost in the view. 'Maybe there was something on the tracks. There are always people and animals wandering along the railway, carts that cross it.'

'I've decided which arias I want to sing after the *Palio*.'

'*Finalmente* Maria Celeste. *Che bello!*'

'Excuse me for interrupting,' said Ferdinando, 'but I heard your name.' His long, twisted moustache and bushy sideburns made him look very contemporary. 'Are you by any chance the soprano who played *Violetta* in *La Traviata?*'

Maria Celeste blushed slightly.

'The papers said you were *spettacolare*. You did Verdi proud. *Bravissima*. Where are you performing next?'

'*Grazie signore*. We are joining the impromptu Reunification of Italy celebrations in Gubbio. They coincide with their bi-annual crossbow competition against San Sepolcro.'

'*Il Palio della Ballestra*. I hear the contest will be in traditional medieval costume this year to mark the special occasion. I've been to the other famous *Palio*, the horse-race in Siena, but never to Gubbio. I wish you well. Please don't let me interrupt your conversation,' the gentleman said, before immersing himself back in a leather-bound book.

'He's been waiting all journey to speak to us,' observed Sandra quietly.

Maria Celeste noticed the book was the Divine Comedy, by Dante Alighieri. As if reading her mind, he looked up again.

'I believe this book features one of your ancestors. *Cante de' Gabrielli da Gubbio*, wasn't it? Dante got his revenge after being exiled by him, by casting Gabrielli as a demon in the poem Inferno.'

'That's my co-star you are talking about. The mezzo-soprano that plays Flora,' said Maria Celeste correcting him.

'*Mi scusi*. She is the Gabrielli, *non Lei*. Well at least there were some *buona gente* in her family. Like the knight Girolamo who helped take Jerusalem in the First Crusade.'

'You are well-informed,' said Maria Celeste. She had told her co-star she would pass by her family seat when she was in Gubbio.

Oh dear, thought Sandra, I wish he would shut up. Maria Celeste, please do not be drawn into yet more history. Fortunately for Sandra, they both obliged and the carriage remained quiet for a long while.

'Schubert's Ave Maria.'

Sandra looked at her friend quizzically.

'One of the arias,' announced Maria Celeste.

'I should have guessed!'

'I keep thinking about the oil painting we saw at the reception in Milan,' said Maria Celeste, a few minutes later.

'*Il Bacio*? I know you do.' Sandra wished she would let go of her loss. Julian. At least she had found out who it was.

They had spent some time in front of that canvas, while sipping champagne. A man in a brown cape, red tights and pointed feathered cap held a young woman in his arms. The woman had long wavy dark brown hair and wore a floor length silk dress of light powder blue. They were lost in a long, deep kiss. The fingers of one hand touched her left cheek, while the other held his right shoulder tightly, as if to stop him leaving. He had his left foot on a staircase, suggesting his departure was imminent.

'*Il Bacio*, did I hear? That painting by Francesco Hayez?'

'Not that man again,' moaned Sandra under her breath. Audibly this time.

'I heard it is an allegory for the unification of Italy. The man represents the Kingdom of Sardinia, including the regions of Piedmont, Savoy and Sardinia, and its allies, the *Ducati di* Toscana, Modena and Parma. The woman represents *Le due*

Sicilie, the former kingdoms of Palermo and Napoli controlled by the Spanish Aragon and Bourbon dynasties for so long.'

'Long live our new *Re Vittorio Emanuele*. Long live our hero, *Garibaldi!*' the gentleman declared enthusiastically.

'Not forgetting the *Conte di Cavour*, our first prime minister,' added Maria Celeste. 'After all, he persuaded Garibaldi to lead the fight.'

Thankfully for Sandra, the town of Modena came into view. Fields gave way to warehouses and new factories which she imagined were stacked high with wooden casks filled with balsamic vinegar. They waited for the train to jerk to a halt then stood up to reach for their luggage.

'Are you alighting here?' asked the gentleman in surprise.

'Yes. Aren't you?'

'You know the line now continues to Bologna.'

'No, we didn't,' said Sandra, suddenly feeling most unprofessional. But then she had so much to organise. The train journey from the opera house in Venice to Milan for the exhibition at the Pinacoteca di Brera, where they met Francesco Hayez, then the onward trip to Gubbio.

'Don't you worry. Our coach is waiting for us here anyway,' said Maria Celeste.

'What a relief,' Sandra exclaimed as the porter gathered their luggage on the platform. 'No more pestering.'

'At least he was well-informed.'

'Too unctuous for my liking,' said Sandra, stopping at the telegram office. 'Could you wait here with the porter briefly? I must send a message to Gubbio with your music choices for the programme.'

'Where would I be without you, Sandra?'

****

Vincenzia knocked on Cafaro's door. There was no answer. She banged it repeatedly, but not too vigorously, as she did not care to hurt her hands. As a seamstress, her livelihood depended on them.

Finally, she lost her patience.

'Cafaro, your costume is ready,' she shouted, as loudly as she dared.

This provoked a response from a window opposite.

'Cafaro, open your door. Before this woman drives us all crazy,' shouted an ill-tempered neighbour.

A man walking up the street joined the mockery, 'Cafaro! *Scemo. Apri quella porta.*'

He was a fellow team member. A rival marksman and no friend of his. Noone on the San Sepolcro side understood what Lucrezia saw in Cafaro. Apart from his being the winning bolt in the last contest against Gubbio.

Shutters started opening up and down the alley, inquisitive heads straining to see what the commotion was all about.

'Vincenzia, come in. *Che stronzi*,' said Cafaro, closing the door behind her.

'You owe me an apology,' she said, looking flustered.

'I do and I am sorry. I was busy waxing my crossbow and polishing my boots.'

He sounded genuinely contrite, which was a wise precaution as Vincenzia was Cesare's sister and Cesare was *gonfaloniere*, head of San Sepolcro's communal office. It was important to be in Cesare's good books.

'Thank you for bringing my costume,' he added.

'*Provalo*. No more adjustments please, we are running out of time.'

He went into an adjoining room and shed his clothes, leaving them in a pile on the dirty floor.

'Your house is in a real mess,' she said in a raised voice. '*Non c'è* Lucrezia to look after you?'

He was trying on a sweater of coarse grey wool. He supposed it was designed to look like the chainmail he would have worn into battle in the Middle Ages.

'I've been too busy to clear up,' he replied, while his fists inadvertently tightened by his side. What business was it of hers anyway, to pass comment on his relationship with Lucrezia?

Next came the mustard yellow stockings. On one thigh were sewn a ring of brown diamond shapes while the other bore jagged edges of dark brown.

'It's all very, what's the word?' he paused, thinking.

'Fetching. That's our very own Piero della Francesca for you. He was our inspiration.'

'Him again.'

Lastly, came the sleeveless mustard yellow tunic with multiple slits beneath the girdle, onto which a felt purse was sewn. He was particularly proud of the *quartiere* emblem, a blue shield with white stars on the front of his tunic, as it broadcast that he was crossbow champion not only of San Sepolcro, but also of his local district.

'*Ma che bello*,' said Vincenzia, admiring her handiwork moments later. She was very happy with the design. 'I would say it is perfect,' she declared. 'Not bad for only two fittings.'

Cafaro paid Vincenzia the final amount due and she turned to leave promptly.

'Three more team members to fit,' she said, as he looked at the sack she carried. 'Good luck this weekend,' she said.

'*Grazie*,' he replied, without even looking at her.

He was afraid Vincenzia might have guessed the real reason he did not answer his door. That he had needed time to calm himself after his fit of rage. Time to restore some order to the room, to pick up pewter plates and mugs and the furniture he had thrown or knocked over in anger.

He had discovered Lucrezia had been unfaithful. One of the drummers from the Gubbio team was to blame, Cafaro had been told. He was going to get him.

He felt his pulse rising again and sought calm by waxing the stock of his crossbow and greasing its metal working parts, for the second time. He picked it up and rested it on his left shoulder, as he would in the procession. He imagined using it in anger. He could hear the loud thud of the feathered metal-tipped bolt hitting a person at a distance of thirty-six metres, the competition distance. The bullseye was not much larger than a human heart and it had been a while since he had missed the bullseye.

He remembered what he had been taught about crossbows as a child. That they had been the weapon of choice of medieval citizens, free men who could be called upon to defend their towns at any time. Those used in battle would have been much lighter and easier to handle than his tournament model, which was more like an artillery piece, it was so heavy. Crossbows did not require the same degree of strength or training as handling longbows, but they were much slower to reload. Their maximum rate of fire was around three bolts a minute, a third of the number of arrows a longbow could unleash in the same time. By the time he added this level of detail, Cafaro would have inevitably lost the interest of anyone still listening, but he soldiered on regardless.

Once again, his thoughts led to Lucrezia. He took a small knife from his room and began sewing it with its leather sheaf onto the inside of his right boot.

He also needed a plan.

****

'Ornella, let me walk you home,' said Giovanni. 'I insist.'

'*Dottore*, that is kind of you. I am used to walking back in the dark,' she answered. 'This is too early for you anyway, surely.'

'No, I am finished for the day too. I can think of nothing I would like to do more, than to walk with you.'

Ornella turned bright red. Why is Giovanni showing so much interest in her?

'Not even drum practice with Massimo and the boys?'

'No, not even that. What's more I've been meaning to tell you about Florence Nightingale.'

'Oh, about her new college of nursing, in London?' she remarked.

'Yes, exactly that. The world's first.'

That's what impressed him more than anything about her. Her ability to surprise him. But actually, the more he came across her in the hospital, the longer the list of reasons why he liked her. It was more than like. Every time he saw her, or felt her presence in the room or passageway his heart skipped a beat and his chest burned. He had even lost his appetite, sparking concern from Antonietta and derision from his fellow drummers.

'Here, let me help you with your coat. The evenings are still chilly.'

As they left the hospital, another patient was being unloaded from an ox-cart. Another farm machinery accident, most likely. A lost hand or foot. Broken bone perhaps.

'Are you sure you shouldn't stay *dottore*?'

'We have coverage, don't worry. And call me Giovanni please. No more *dottore* outside the *ospedale*.'

'Sorry, you are right. It's only since I came to work here in the hospital.'

'Now, nursing. The London college. It will happen here. Rome or Milan will be next to offer formal training.'

'I'd say Florence would be the most likely. After all, that was where she was born. Named after her place of birth,' said Ornella.

'*Mamma mia*! Ornella!' he exclaimed. 'Where did you learn all this?'

'It's become my passion, nursing. My calling. Just like Florence's,' she said. 'There is only one problem.'

'And what is that?'

'I am not leaving home,' she answered. 'It was bad enough when my best friend moved to San Sepolcro. I miss her.'

Giovanni felt a little uncomfortable at the mention of Lucrezia. It triggered thoughts of their first night together, when he had been overwhelmed with desire for Ornella's friend.

'She's coming back to Gubbio, isn't she?' he said. 'That's what the drummers are saying. Had enough of that boyfriend.'

They spoke about Lucrezia and their shared concerns for her and suddenly they were standing a little embarrassed outside Ornella's family home. A narrow, terraced house of dark grey stone that leant conspicuously over the alley below.

'Giovanni, thank you. I'd invite you in, but the house is full of medieval costumes and seamstresses.'

'Like every other house in Gubbio,' he said smiling. He wanted to reach out to her to show his strong feelings for her. A kiss or embrace. Or something physical. Instead, he whispered in her ear.

'Ornella, if you want that qualification, I will follow you.'

'*Anche a Londra?*'

'Especially London.'

As she closed the front door behind her, Ornella leant against the coats that hung there, motionless.

'Just in time *amore*, your dress is ready to try,' said Antonietta, as her mother hovered in the background.

'Antonietta! What a surprise. Your son has just walked me home,' Ornella said.

'Did he now?' Antonietta replied.

'About time,' mumbled Ornella's mother.

****

'I'm ready for battle!' said Giovanni, his ears ringing loudly.

'Feeling fired-up?' Massimo replied.

'Most definitely. I'm invincible right now.'

The fifteen drummers had broken up into groups in the *Piazza Bruno*, to take a short break from their final rehearsal for the *Palio*. All were dressed in the red and white livery of Gubbio and all had marching drums in matching colours. They played as a unit for several minutes, raising the tempo and volume until they reached a crescendo louder than the clapping thunder of an electric storm. Just as their ancestors would have done, to rouse the troops and lift morale before battle.

While Massimo wandered off to a fountain for a drink of water, his drum still slung from his shoulder, Giovanni walked up to a group of women surrounded by suitors. They were the 'nobility', the last of the long parade that would walk to the marching cadence of the drums up to the *Piazza Grande*, where the *Palio* took place. There was much excitement among them, as they admired each other's medieval costumes for the first time in public.

He headed straight for Ornella.

'That costume looks beautiful on you,' he said, feeling uncharacteristically tongue-tied. It was Ornella's beauty he wanted to compliment, not that of the dress.

Ornella wore a white linen shirt beneath a low-cut autumnal brown dress drawn together at the front with leather straps. Over the dress, Ornella wore a long, open sleeveless cream gown embroidered with the outlines in dark brown of roses, fastened with one simple silver clasp.

'*Grazie*, Giovanni,' she replied, while admiring his.

'I haven't seen Livia. In fact, we have hardly seen her since her mother's memorial service. Isn't she in the parade this year?' he asked, while looking around the increasingly crowded square. The trumpeters had started to arrive, along with some of the crossbow men with their striking lilac and black outfits.

'*Ma certo.* Wait until you see her costume! I think she has gone to see if Alessandro has made it back from *Sicilia* in time. She said she was going to look for him among the flag-throwers rehearsing in the *Piazza Grande.*'

Almost everyone in town knew Alessandro had joined Giuseppe Garibaldi in his war to unify Italy. The Expedition of the Thousand, as it was now called.

At that moment, Massimo joined them after walking back from the water fountain, where he had been speaking to a group of Gubbio crossbowmen.

'*Ciao* Ornella. Don't you look gorgeous!' he said as he hugged her tightly.

'Why thank you. I think you and Giovanni are the most handsome drummers in Umbria.'

'Such a diplomat, as always,' Massimo joked. 'Can I have a quick word with you Giovanni?'

'Gio.' He said sternly, after Ornella had re-joined the nobles and their partners, 'I've been warned that Lucrezia's boyfriend is going to get his revenge after the *Palio.*'

'But you told me nothing happened between you and Lucrezia.'

'That's not what Cafaro believes. He's an obsessive tyrant, that man.'

'Don't worry. You can count on my help, Massimo.'

'I am not worried about myself. Who is going to protect Lucrezia?'

****

'Alessandro!' Livia shouted, so loudly that almost everyone in the *piazza* stopped to look around, including Alessandro. Which was unfortunate, as his and 23 other colourful display flags were at that moment suspended in a peaked cone high above the *piazza*. It was the climax of their rehearsal. All the

Sbandieratori caught their flags as they fell to earth, all except Alessandro.

There was an audible gasp in the *piazza*. The flags were symbols of purity and should not touch the ground. But more than that, flags were indispensable for communicating in battle, their bearers among the most important soldiers in the field. They developed the art of flag throwing to avoid their capture by an advancing enemy. A flag fallen was a battle lost.

Waiting for her cue, confirmation that the show was over, Livia ran headlong towards Alessandro to embrace him.

'*Sei tornato*! My Red Shirt is safely back!' she said, with tears swelling in her eyes.

Alessandro didn't say a word. He just hugged her tightly and began spinning round and around. Until her legs and long maroon velvet dress with its golden embroidered front were carving a circle through the air. Just as his flag had done, minutes earlier.

****

Maria Celeste looked out of her bedroom window onto the busy scene below. A number of bystanders had gathered in and around the *Piazza Grande* to watch the final preparations for the following day. Beyond the *piazza* there was a ruffled sea of tiled roofs, punctuated by a couple of church towers. Behind them lay a wide verdant valley that along with wool trade and Gubbio's specialty in *maiolica*, or tin-glazed pottery, made it one of the wealthiest towns of Umbria in medieval times.

There was a knock at her door and without waiting for an answer Sandra entered and joined Maria Celeste by the window.

'Will you join me and our hostess on a walk? It is such a beautiful afternoon,' she said enthusiastically.

Lengthening shadows cast by the Gothic buildings across the piazza heralded a cooler time of day. They invited the visitors to explore the maze of narrow streets bordered by homes of white stone that had turned dark grey with age.

Maria Celeste did not answer. She was caught up in her own thoughts.

Sandra tried to embellish the invitation. 'She wants to take us for a stroll in the English garden that her husband created for her up the hill behind. We are also stopping by the home of Federico da Montefeltro, *il Duca di Urbino*. You know, *il Duca* painted by Piero della Francesca, complete with broken nose.'

'I do.' The duke of Urbino was the hero of Gubbio that overthrew one Maria Celeste's co-star's tyrannical ancestors. 'But I think I will just sit here and relax. It was a long morning. Please apologise to our hostess.'

It had been busy. Long hours standing, watching and waiting for the final rehearsals to come together. The visit to her co-star's ancestral home by one of the town's gates, *Porto Metauro*, had depressed her. The building, with its five arched entrances and arched windows above, was in need of repair. The street had been renamed, as if the locals wished to erase the family from history.

'I obviously can't persuade you then. See you later for the concert rehearsal.' Sandra left the room, closing the door emphatically behind her.

Maria Celeste continued to observe the world beneath the window sill, her chin resting on folded arms.

Carpenters had finished constructing a wooden stage on the curved stone steps that splayed like a fan down from Gubbio's iconic *Palazzo dei Consoli*. The stage was the *Palio*'s centrepiece, where the crossbows were fired from stands that to her resembled stencilled horses drawn by children. Some workers were applying finishing touches to a grandstand bordering the *piazza*, while at the other end of the range three men fixed the target to a wooden board on the wall of the town hall.

She remembered seeing an image of a target being carried to the judges after the last bolt had been fired. There were so many bristling feathered darts stuck in and around the bullseye, it reminded her of a porcupine flashing its quills.

Gathered off to one side of the Town Hall, were the seats, music stands and conductor's podium that would be set in place the evening of the *Palio*. 'That's me, down there, in twenty-four hours' time!' she thought to herself. Thinking a brief inspection might calm her nerves, she decided to go outside after all.

'*Viene con me*. I'll show you how they work,' said an archer, who had been making sure everything was in order.

'I understand why you need these stands on which to rest the crossbow. They are so heavy,' she said, struggling with the weight.

'*Esatto*! Take the seat straddling the rear of the stand and I'll pivot the crossbow on the pillar at the front.'

'This crank to one side, that's for loading the weapon presumably,' she said, as he pressed the long lever used to ratchet back the taught bowstrings of sinew and animal hides.

'That's right. Now place the stock of the weapon on your right shoulder. Nestle your arms on the elbow rests. Your left arm should be steadying the crossbow and the right folded so that your thumb touches both your shoulder and that metal lever.'

Maria Celeste seemed to be no stranger to this sport, knowing instinctively what to do.

'The key to good marksmanship lies in the breathing,' he said. 'You have to slow your heart rate with a series of long slow breaths, before pressing the trigger ever so gently while exhaling.'

'The other secret is knowing how to adjust the sights for the curved flight of the dart. As well as for any wind,' she added, while picturing the raised eyebrows of her instructor.

She looked through the small peep hole of the sights at an imaginary target and started to squeeze the lever.

****

'Gio, what's the matter with you? How can you switch-off like that, mid-sentence?'

'Oh, sorry Mas. Where was I?'

'Alessandro. You managed to speak to him today about the 1,000.'

'Garibaldi's expeditionary force. I asked him about the battle at Calatafimi. Yes. He was not very forthcoming.'

'And Livia. They are back together, aren't they?'

Giovanni drifted-off again, his eyes lost in the smoke that filled the tavern. It was more of a rhetorical question, anyway.

The waitress appeared, clutching two tankards of frothy beer. It was their third round.

'Laura, just the person I need,' Massimo gleamed. 'Giovanni won't talk to me. *Vieni, siediti!*'

He patted the empty seat next to him.

'I have to work, darling. Maybe later?' she winked. 'A bit of an odd-ball, is our Gio. Aren't you sweet-heart?'

'*Io?*'

'Yes you,' Laura replied, squeezing Giovanni's right cheek before turning to take an order from some trumpeters still in costume at the table next to them.

They had enjoyed a brief dalliance after dancing that night. But that was all. It was some time ago.

'Mas, I think I am smitten,' said Giovanni.

'Now that's where you've gone. It's Ornella, isn't it?'

'She now works in the same hospital, you know. I get to see her bewitching smile almost every day. Yes, it's Ornella. I want to marry her.'

'My, that's a bit sudden. Hold those horses! Anyway, I doubt you'd get approval from her father- let alone her.'

'And I'd have all the drummers and trumpeters of Gubbio play at our wedding,' Giovanni said, paying no attention to his friend. 'I'd hire a coach to take us on honey-moon by the sea. In Le Marche.'

'Sounds like you've thought it through,' said Massimo. 'Tell you what, if you invite that soprano to sing, I'd even offer to be your best man. Did you see her at our rehearsal today?'

'The Verdi opera star? That modern-day goddess? Not a hope she'll accept. Anyway, Mas, I have an idea,' Giovanni said, turning to Laura, who had lingered at the trumpeter table. 'Save the table and three chairs for us, we'll be back.'

'Don't trust you. Settle up first and I might.'

Giovanni paid the bill and the two of them walked out into the night air.

'Where are we going?'

'To Ornella's. But first we need to collect our drums!'

'And costumes too, how about it?' responded Massimo, starting to share in his friend's excitement.

Ornella's shutters were not the only ones to open that night. But hers were the first, and she did join them at the bar, dressed in her medieval costume, after the rousing serenade.

****

'*Cazzo. Che vento malvagio.*'

He relaxed the pressure on the trigger. The thermals in the valley were drawing air down Monte Insino, causing unpredictable winds for the contestants.

'Don't worry Cafaro. You've plenty of time,' said his spotter.

He had been squinting for so long his vision was starting to blur. It was bad enough there were already so many bolts in the bullseye it was hard to pick its epicentre.

'*Tranquillo.* Concentrate. Inhale. Exhale.'

Twang went the bowstring, followed a second later by the thud of his dart hitting the bullseye.

'Just off centre, four o'clock,' said his spotter.

'*Cazzo!*' Cafaro scowled once more.

He stomped off the stage and went to hide among his teammates. At least he could now focus on his revenge. He had managed to stop Lucrezia from attending the *Palio* to keep her out of the way. His three paid accomplices were mingling in the crowd, ready to strike. And there was his target, Massimo, already joining the crowd in the stand along with other drummers.

****

Alessandro was biding his time, waiting for his moment.

So Massimo stepped forward instead, looking rather starstruck.

'*Meraviglioso*. It was a privilege to hear you sing.'

Sandra, who was standing by her side, was becoming used to this adulation. She knew precisely why. That tall but delicate frame, her dark shoulder-length hair, the heavenly blue eyes. As for that soprano voice: it made her feel proud. She, Sandra was the one always by her side, in whom Maria Celeste could depend as a loyal friend and potentially, if Maria Celeste wanted, so much more.

'*Grazie tante*. I enjoyed your drumming earlier. It was really warlike, it quite frightened me,' said Maria Celeste, finding herself drawn to this man again. To avoid being noticed, she turned to Alessandro.

'*Auguri per la Sua medaglia. Posso vederlo?*'

Alessandro showed her the bronze medallion.

'It was totally unexpected. The major's speech, my award, the fireworks,' he said, not really enjoying being the focus of attention again.

'You so deserved it,' said Maria Celeste. 'You and Garibaldi and all those men who realised the dream of so many of us since Rome fell. Remember the rallying call of *Papa Giuliano II*, '*Fuori i Barbari*'.'

'Yes I do. But today's *Vaticano* still needs to come on side,' Alessandro reminded her.

'*Il Papa* will fall into line, just you wait,' Maria Celeste declared. 'He will give up his *Stati Pontifici* to the new *Italia*.'

'Let's hope so,' said Alessandro, before adding. 'Maria Celeste, I have something to tell you.' There could only be one Maria Celeste. It had to be her.

'Go on.' She was intrigued.

'It's about Giuliano. I fought alongside him. He became my friend. More than that, he was my hero.'

She turned very pale and covered her face with both hands. Finally, news of Julian.

Sandra took Maria Celeste by the hand and started to lead her away.

'Thank you, Alessandro,' the soprano said, looking back. 'Please, join us at the reception. The *Palazzo Ranghiasci*. Bring your friends.'

****

Cafaro was still in a vesuvian rage when he returned to San Sepolcro the following evening. Where had Massimo disappeared to? Normally all the competitors celebrated together afterwards in Gubbio's bars. Not this year. *La maledetta Unificazione. Il maledetto concerto.* They ruined his plans.

Lucrezia should have known better than to have stepped into his house later, thinking he might have calmed down. She knew he suspected infidelity.

'How was it? Did you win?' she asked, her voice tremulous.

'Of course not! How could I concentrate? All I could think about was you, *scopando* that drummer boy.'

'Cafi. How many times do I have to tell you? Nothing happened between us. Nothing. He means nothing to me. Can't you understand?' she pleaded.

'You're lying. And don't you 'Cafi' me, *stronza*. *Che puttana che sei!*' he shouted.

Riding his horse back from the contest, he had spent many hours thinking what he would do to punish her. He would carry out unspeakably horrible things to teach her a lesson, not to betray him or cross him or even question him on any matter. To ensure her complete subservience. He had beaten Lucrezia into submission so repeatedly and for so long in his mind, as his horse laboured beneath him, that on arrival he began to feel sorry for her. Nearing his street, he even resolved not to touch her. Especially not her beautiful face. People might suspect. He would just frighten her. Assault her verbally. But he would have to reach deep within himself to keep his composure. To be able to simply walk away.

Which is what happened. Unbelievably. One minute, Lucrezia sat cowering in a corner while he poured invective about the room. The next, he simply turned around and left his house, slamming his front door shut and leaving her alone, shaking uncontrollably with relief.

But Cafaro forgot to tell his accomplices to stand-down. And so it was, that a few months after their relationship ended, Cafaro's gang of three petty criminals assaulted Lucrezia as she walked home from evening mass.

Chapter 7. Buona Sera Signorina
2022 A.D.

Massimo stood among a throng of people in a large *piazza*, at the heart of Perugia. To one side of the open-air stage, he faced the majestic *Duomo di Perugia*. Behind him to his left was the gothic town hall, the *Palazzo dei Priori*. Sculptures of a griffin and lion reached out over the stone-balustraded balcony and broad shallow stairs at its entrance. The whole scene was suffused with a warm light that reflected off the ancient white and pink stone.

'We have met before, haven't we?' said Massimo, standing very close to her. It was hard to make yourself heard above the music.

Finally, finally a dint of recognition. It was about time, she thought.

'Possibly,' replied Maria Celeste, enigmatically.

'You are an opera singer. A soprano. I am sure I've heard you perform,' he insisted.

'No, I teach English. Here at Perugia university.'

'I am mistaken. Sorry…'

'Don't be,' she said, drawing even closer.

'Are you alone?' Massimo found himself saying. He had been watching her for a while in the crowd and there was no obvious partner. She looked a few years older than him, but not many. 'You are most welcome to join us, if you like.'

Maria Celeste looked at his group of friends, just feet away. Like her, they had been swaying gently while enjoying the jazz. The band were doing an excellent impersonation of Louis Prima and many in the crowd joined in. The lead vocalist was swaggering across the stage dressed like a Chicago gangster, microphone in hand.

...*Buona sera, signorina, buona sera, it is time to say goodnight to Napoli...*

'*Grazie*, but I am waiting for someone,' she replied.

'Pity,' he ventured. 'I'm Massimo by the way.'

'*Lo so.*'

He looked at her in surprise.

'I was at your debut in Spoleto,' she said.

...*In the meantime let me tell you that I love you...*

'*Esatto*,' the penny finally dropped. 'You came up to me afterwards.'

'Yes, I did. Oh look,' Maria Celeste said suddenly, pointing towards the fountain that was the centrepiece of the *piazza*. 'My friend has just arrived. There she is waving at me.' It was Sandra.

Buona sera, signorina kiss me goodnight.

'*Ciao* Massimo,' she said, before stepping away, to be swallowed by the crowd.

Massimo re-joined his friends, looking a little bewildered by his fleeting encounter with this beautiful woman.

'*Ma che scemo*! You scared her away,' said Giovanni.

Giovanni was holding hands with Ornella while Livia and Alessandro stood arm-in-arm in front of them.

'Seems like it,' Massimo replied. His voice was now hoarse from trying to make himself heard.

It hurt inside to think he had let her slip away so easily. One second there she was, inches away from him. The next instant, she was gone.

'I didn't even get her name.'

****

There was a short break between gigs in the main *piazza*. A small stream of jazz fans started to flow out of the enclosure onto *Corso Vannucci*, the main pedestrian thoroughfare of central Perugia lined with restaurants, bars and shops.

'Let's go to *Piazza Matteotti*. There is an all-girl band we should see. The lead vocalist is also a phenomenal clarinet player,' said Livia, looking at her wrist watch. 'They start in just over half-an-hour.'

'That gives us time for a *gelato*,' suggested Ornella.

All agreed to try a new *gelateria* just outside the main walls, down a long flight of steps that led through a southern city gate, hoping it would be less crowded. High above to one side stood the imposing walls of what remained of a fortress, the *Rocca Paolina*. It had been built by a Pope over the ruins of a whole neighbourhood once owned by the ruling family of Perugia, the Baglioni. It wasn't wise to take on the Papacy in those days, Giovanni thought.

'Started writing the best man speech yet?' he asked, handing Massimo a cone with a lemon and basil gelato.

'*Lasciami in pace!*' he snapped back, but in an endearing way.

'And don't forget to let me read it first,' asked Ornella, using a small florescent green plastic teaspoon to taste her dark chocolate and fig ice cream. 'I don't trust you.'

'*Dai!* Lay off you two,' he said.

'Aww, he's feeling all sorry for himself. *Poverino* Massimo. You look so forlorn.' Giovanni was having fun now.

'Hey, that's not fair,' piped-in Livia. She and Alessandro remained quiet throughout this conversation. They would hold back their announcement for a while, so as not to steal the limelight from Giovanni and Ornella. Furthermore, Livia still was not entirely sure how well Massimo would take the news.

Ornella decided to try and give Massimo some hope.

'Giovanni, remember that woman you sat next to at the *Sala Pegasus?*'

'Vaguely. It seems a long time ago.'

'Wasn't she the same person?

'Yes, that's right,' Giovanni remembered. 'She introduced herself. My mother was quite struck by her. Kept on mentioning her name afterwards. Maria Celeste. A name from the past. Galileo's eldest daughter was a Maria Celeste, you know. Used to communicate avidly with her father by letter from her nunnery.'

'Well then, it seems as if you have at least one fan Massimo!' said Ornella, admiring her fiancé's encyclopaedic knowledge.

'Maybe two by next week,' said Alessandro.

'Alessandro is my new friend,' declared Massimo. 'At least he can make my recital, unlike you lot.' Against all odds, a genuine friendship was slowly developing between these two men. It was Livia that broke the ice, inviting Massimo to join them sailing on Lake Trasimeno. Where Alessandro kept a dinghy, a 470.

'You lawyers have it easy, compared to us medics,' said Giovanni, looking at Ornella.

'*Basta!* It's time for more jazz,' announced Livia.

She had a conflicting photographic exhibition, but Alessandro promised to break from his law studies to hear Massimo play. After all, he had come all the way from London to perform. What's more, Alessandro would not miss an evening of piano recital in the resplendent *Sala dei Notari*.

As they walked back up the steps, Ornella took Massimo aside.

'Have you been in touch with Lucrezia since she moved to London with her company? She doesn't communicate with me any longer. I am really worried.'

'I am too. I'll try again, when I return.'

****

Massimo was flustered. He still found it hard to believe that Maria Celeste had come to his recital. He had trouble focusing on the menu. All the choices became a blur as he struggled to stop himself from looking up. He managed to focus on one word, *ragù*. 'What do you recommend?' he asked.

'My favourite is the white *ragù*. I think I will order that and a salad,' said Maria Celeste.

'Me too,' said Massimo.

'Will you choose the wine?'

'Are you happy with red?'

'Would love some red; and some *acqua frizzante*.' Her voice was rich. Her accent though, it was not from Perugia. She sounded northern. From Milan perhaps?

Massimo regained some composure and chose a Montefalco Sagrantino. They did not stock his favourites, but the Arnaldo Caprai would do.

Maria Celeste leant forward so that her face was no more than a few inches from his. '*I turisti sono tornati*,' she whispered.

Massimo looked around for the first time since sitting down. There were blond couples and men in shorts. Orders were taken in English but accents varied from German, Polish and Dutch amongst others.

'That is good news. Travel is so much easier again.' Massimo observed. His eyes looked up at the dark high walls of the medieval buildings above them, separated by the narrowest of alleys, where the restaurant placed its outdoor tables. Members of the public had to weave their way through a maze of tables to get through, which added to the bustling atmosphere of the warm evening.

'I loved your concert,' said Maria Celeste, trying to bring Massimo back.

He blushed and thanked her.

'Especially that encore. So soft and melodic and enchanting. I felt I was at a Viennese debutant's ball.'

'The Valse Sentimentale? I enjoy playing Tchaikovsky. He was so passionate.'

This woman opposite stared at him with those celestial blue eyes. He could not believe his good fortune.

'My only disappointment.'

'What was that?' he cut her short.

'No Schubert. The Ave Maria you played in Spoleto.'

'Really? I can remedy that.'

Massimo got out his phone and started tapping a message. He received a reply almost immediately.

'*Vedrai*,' he said, gleefully.

The red wine and water arrived, along with a brown paper cone filled with freshly baked bread. Massimo asked for some olive oil. As the waiter poured the deep scarlet wine, Massimo began to tell Maria Celeste about his interest in Umbrian wines, those from Montefalco in particular.

After dinner, Massimo led Maria Celeste by the hand up the stairs of the town hall to the *Sala dei Notari*. He was relieved one of the large ancient metal-studded oak doors was ajar. The lights in the heavily frescoed concert room were also on and the lid of the Steinway was open. Just as he had asked in his message.

Massimo started playing Ave Maria. Maria Celeste stood so close to him they were almost touching. After the opening bars, he suddenly heard this sublime soprano voice. Unexpectedly, but on cue. Just inches away. He knew instantly he had heard that voice before. His fingers froze above the keys and Maria Celeste continued singing the aria *acapella*, while he looked up at her.

'I thought you said you were a teacher?'

****

Maria Celeste drew her Fiat Panda up behind another car parked at the road's edge, under the shade of a line of umbrella pines. It was Livia's.

'*Perfetto*,' said Massimo, giving her a kiss on the lips.

To the left, he saw the flat greenish water of the lake shore. Cormorants bobbed to the surface, shaking their long, pointed heads, before diving again in search of elusive prey. Tall reeds stood still in the shallows, concealing herons poised to strike unsuspecting sand smelt. Dragonflies entwined in couples danced erratically above the water while swallows swooped down from blue skies devouring lake flies. In the distance, midway across the silver mirror stood an island silhouetted against the glare of the morning sun, with a tower at one end rising above pointed cypresses and a fringe of oak trees.

'No sailing today,' shouted Alessandro as he spotted Massimo. 'Typical, always on a weekend.'

The air was heavy and still. What a contrast to Massimo's last visit. Then there were dark skies, white horses and halyards clanging frenetically against the masts of sailing dinghies that lined the shore. He had been out on the trapeze then, skimming inches above the water to keep the boat flat and fast. Exhilarating.

'That's the temperamental Trasimeno for you,' retorted Massimo. 'Look who has agreed to join us!'

'*Dai, favoloso. Benvenuta* Maria Celeste.' Alessandro had met her briefly at the recital the previous evening.

Livia, who was crouching low taking photos of the natural spectacles surrounding her, suddenly stood up and waved.

Just then a large motorbike growled its way into view, stopping just next to Massimo and his new friend. They took off their streamlined helmets, stepped out of matching black leathers and gave Maria Celeste hot and sweaty greetings.

'How about renting some kayaks instead?' suggested Alessandro as he approached them. 'We bought a cool box with drinks, fruit and *panini*. We could share a picnic on the island.'

'Brilliant idea,' said Giovanni. 'I even brought my fishing rod with me.'

'Excuse me,' Ornella corrected him, while giving him a sharp tap on the bottom. 'I carried his rod, while precariously trying to hold on, thank you.'

No one had noticed that Maria Celeste had quietly slipped away to stand in the shallow water by the reeds.

'Wait for us!' shouted Massimo.

She turned around and smiled at them.

****

Massimo was back on a plane to London, composing a letter to Perugia's *Conservatorio di Musica*. He would come back to live in Umbria, teach piano and try to break into the concert circuit.

He drifted off to sleep with multiple images vying for attention. Walking beside her along rows of pink oleander flowers beneath the island's poplar trees. The soft cool water dripping down her paddle onto a white shirt, with her straight back and long hair just in front of him. Livia's engagement, announced as they sat under holm oaks at a bar afterwards. He would be seeing Maria Celeste again very soon, in just a few weeks.

Chapter 8. The Sagrantino Harvest
2022 A.D.

Sandra collapsed next to Maria Celeste on the white sofa.

'*Finito!*' she said, feeling pleased with herself.

'That was lovely of you. Washing-up is not my strong point.'

'What a mess you make MC. I even had to wipe *polenta* off the ceiling.'

'Really? I was distracted, sorry. You only have to turn your back on it for a second and it erupts. Like Mt. Etna.'

'Oh, I forgot my glass of wine,' Sandra said, returning to Maria Celeste's kitchen. 'You are an amazing cook you know.'

Sandra returned to find her friend engrossed in a guide book. 'Are you reading about Sicilia? We promised ourselves a trip there,' she said with a glint in her eye, before leaning over for a closer look at what was occupying her friend's attention. 'Montefalco? Here we are celebrating my promotion and your mind is on your weekend with Massimo.' The glint vanished. '*Quando arriva?*'

'Sandra *scusa*, that was selfish of me,' said Maria Celeste, sitting up to reach for the property magazine on the coffee table. 'Let's continue looking at apartments.'

This was going to be a big change for Sandra, moving back to Umbertide from Perugia. But she could not decline the offer to manage three museums in the area. It was Sandra's turn to rest her head on Maria Celeste's shoulder, as they looked through the magazine on her lap together.

****

'Massimo, turn around.'

Maria Celeste's handsome boyfriend stood in front of several rows of vines. Behind were the oak trees amongst which her little Fiat Panda was parked and to the right on the hilltop, the roofs and large white water-tower of Montefalco. She took several photos then joined him for a selfie, smiling cheeks pressed closely together.

'Has the grape harvest begun?' she asked.

'Yes, I believe so.'

'*La Vendemmia Sagrantino*. Your favourite wine,' she said.

'Umbrian wine, yes.'

The summer sun had done its work and over the next few weeks different grape varieties would be picked as they ripened in a carefully orchestrated sequence, with those destined to become *Passito* dessert wines possibly the last, left to sweeten as they dried on the vine.

'Have you noticed the rose bushes at the end of every row?' she said. The flowers had gone but the orange rosebuds and thorns were unmistakable.

'I think they were originally planted as a sort of early warning system. The roses attract aphids and other bugs away from the vines. They were also considered to be more susceptible to disease than the vines, giving growers time to treat them. These days I think vintners regularly spray their vineyards with copper sulphate to ward-off any pests before summer begins. But they still look nice, when in flower.'

'What about pests like you?' she said, provocatively.

'Me, a pest?'

He took her hand and with interlocking fingers, they walked deep among the vines.

****

'So, this is your idea of a wine lesson,' she said afterwards.

He smiled.

Looking up, she saw bunches hiding shyly among the broad green and yellow leaves. The grapes were much smaller than she had imagined.

'The purple ones. Red wine I presume.'

Massimo did not answer. His was a very different view that he had no wish to change one bit.

'Funny, on this other row the grapes are smoky green. White wine? Some have turned a light umber'.

Still no answer. She squeezed him tightly and together they rolled over so that their views were reversed and she was looking at Massimo's head resting on the thin grass. To each side of his smiling face, lay a miniature world that was oblivious to her presence. A small beetle with a shiny green back scuttled past another which had red spots along its black wing cases and fluffy black antennae. Ants scurried around searching for seeds.

'Now you are going to tell me. What grape varieties are those?' She tried again.

'I need my glasses.'

'You're hopeless,' she said, standing up and reaching for his hands to pull him to his feet. 'I'm hungry. Let's skip the winery and go straight to the restaurant,'

'But it's only 11:30!'

'Alright, the *cantina* it is.'

****

'How did you know that?' Massimo asked with disbelief.

Maria Celeste was driving the two of them through a soft landscape of gently rolling hills that were covered in neat rows of vines.

'Your school. I just do.'

She knew he was at the Royal Academy. It was in the Spoleto programme. But school in Umbertide? What else did she know about him? This secretive side of Maria Celeste made her even more sexy in Massimo's eyes.

He was in love. Not just physically attracted to her. Besotted. In a way he thought beyond impossible after Livia. Of course, she knew about Livia too. But she never probed. Maria Celeste was too discreet for that. Nor did he, about her lovers. Not now, at least. It was too early in their voyage of mutual discovery. Although he needed to do a lot more discovering than she did, it seemed.

'*Allora*, it's my turn,' he said, while relishing the sight of her profile as she stared ahead through the windscreen. 'You have to reply instantly. Like those stars being quizzed on *Rai Uno*.'

'Try me,' she said, invitingly.

'History or art?'

'Not both? Well, history then.'

'History or music?'

'It's history again, sorry Massimo.'

'That's fine with me. Except you'd make a finer soprano than teacher of the past.'

'I teach modern languages,' she reminded him.

'I know,' he acknowledged, smiling. 'But seriously, you belong in a Verdi or Rossini opera, not in a classroom.'

'That is very generous of you. Maybe, one day.'

'Roman or Renaissance?' What he had wanted to do, was to complete her sentence. But again, it would be premature to suggest they perform together.

'Renaissance.'

'Baglioni or Oddi?'

'You know about these rival families? Which do you think?' she asked, turning the question on him. It might have been construed as a bit condescending, but Massimo was oblivious at this stage. She was perfection, so far as he was concerned.

'Oddi, I suspect. I'm right, aren't I?' he said, noticing the slightest hint of a smile. 'Piero or Rafaello?'

'Massimo, that is rather unfair. They are my two favourite artists. Della Francesca. No, Rafaello.'

It was most unlike her to prevaricate like that.

'Sure?' he asked, while she nodded in confirmation. 'Handel or Schubert?'

'Back to music, are we?'

They were so busy talking, that they missed their turning to the winery.

Maria Celeste back-tracked and having found the correct route, drove along a narrow road that dipped and rose and wound its way through an unfamiliar, undulating countryside. The only traffic they came across were tractors, their trailers filled with grapes.

A short while later they arrived at their destination, a complex of buildings on top of one of the two hill tops from which the winery derived its name. Everything was so pristine, neat and tidy it was hard to imagine it was a working farm on which grew not only vines, but also olive and hazelnut trees. The panoramic view, which encompassed the surrounding vineyards, a smattering of hilltop villages and the distant mountains was almost breath-taking.

The owner emerged from their office to greet them.

'*Buongiorno*,' he welcomed them with a warm, engaging smile. He had slender athletic looks, blue eyes and a hint of greying hair.

'We have our own personalised tour. How special,' remarked Maria Celeste, expecting to be part of a larger group.

'Do you produce organic wines here?' she went on to ask, as they walked near a roof covered with solar panels, proclaiming the winery's environmentally conscious credentials. She did like the idea of reverting to natural wines using early wine-making techniques with native ambient yeast and few if no additives. Low intervention wine production, Massimo had called it. 'We have resisted so far,' he answered. Like most wine-makers, he still added sulphur to control the fermentation process and used his preferred yeast cultures rather than relying on the grapes' natural yeasts. 'I think they are over-hyped and arguably, over-priced,' he said, while leading them into the largest room of the winery. 'But we are experimenting with various beans and other crops between the rows of vines that help replenish the soils with nitrogen.'

'This is the cooking room,' he announced, as they stood staring at huge pristine steel cylinders on stumpy legs. The fermentation vats were well over a storey tall. 'Where we turn juice into wine.'

Massimo and Maria Celeste were each handed a wine glass, into which was poured a sample of two-week old *Vermentino* from the vat closest to them. It was grape juice. This was followed by a month-old sample of *Trebbiano Spoletino* wine from a neighbouring vat. It tasted like a young wine.

'Here the added yeast has had time to work, converting the sugars in the grapes into alcohol and carbon dioxide,' said their guide. 'The longer the fermentation, the less sugar left behind and the drier the wine.'

Further down the room they tried a one year-old *Sagrantino*. It was almost ready to be blended with Sangiovese and other red grape varieties to be sold as Rosso di Montefalco after a short stint in oak. They also tried a *Sagrantino* of the same age that would spend several years ageing in oak barrels, before being bottled and sold as the area's premium quality wine.

'In the case of the white wines, we quickly separate the juice from the skins after crushing before fermentation begins. The reds are fermented together with their skins, allowing the wine to draw out not only the colour, but also the tannins that extend the wine's life and allow it to grow in character and flavour.'

The owner went on to explain how during fermentation temperatures rose and needed to be carefully monitored so that the young wine was not spoiled. He showed them a touch screen pad used to control temperatures by pumping water through the outer jackets of the vats. He also pointed to a row of small plastic bottles each with a different coloured-lid, in which samples were collected to be tested in a nearby laboratory for acidity, sugar and alcohol levels.

They passed a covered area where the harvested grapes were brought in to be crushed in specialised machines, before being led into a room filled with very large oak barrels, each containing red wine of a different vintage. Here his demeanour changed. His smile disappeared and he looked intense and serious.

'Welcome to the art room,' he said, provoking a slightly puzzled look from Massimo.

He took two tulip glasses from a nearby table and poured a sample of a deep scarlet wine from the nearest barrel, before handing one to each of his visitors. 'More sampling?' I am already feeling a little giddy,' said Maria Celeste. She, like Massimo, refused to waste the wine they had tasted in the fermentation room by spitting it out on the beige-tiled floor, with its narrow drainage slit.

The owner filled a third glass for himself, and began inhaling the wine's powerful bouquet in silence. The others followed his example.

'Tell me, what is the secret of making good wine?' Maria Celeste asked.

'I've been waiting for this question from a visitor for a long time,' the wine-maker said. 'By secret, you mean the art of wine-making, presumably?'

'Yes, exactly.'

She was not really that interested in the process, or the science. The 'cooking', as he had called it earlier.

Massimo had told her a bit about the science as they drove across. About learning from nature. Knowing your soils and how to pamper the vines that grew in them. Understanding climate change and the new diseases it brought. Judging weather patterns and knowing when to harvest. Gently massaging the reds as they matured in their oak barrels, sampling them regularly for their appearance, smell and taste before deciding when to bottle each vintage.

'The art of fine wine-making, is to make wine that you love,' the winery owner replied. 'Oh, and learning from your mistakes,' he added, almost as an afterthought.

He proceeded to give them both an impromptu lesson on wine appreciation. Starting with how to hold their glasses ('use the stem, don't hold it by the bowl'); when to open a bottle ('take the cork out early, it lifts the wine'); how to decant it ('pour vigorously, it brings the wine out more quickly'). They talked about appearance and colour, the importance of scent and of course, the taste.

An assistant appeared to remind the owner of his lunch appointment. He excused himself profusely and the assistant took over, accompanying them for the remainder of their tour.

She led them upstairs to the bottling room, next to a storage area with stacks of pallets each piled high with bottles. The final stop was the shop. Here the full range of wines produced were temptingly displayed and where yet more sampling took place.

'Will you drive, Massimo?' Maria Celeste asked as their tour came to an end, while he placed three cases of wine in the boot of her car.

****

'Massimo, this place is a gem.'

'I thought you'd like it.'

While he spoke to his friend, the restaurant's sommelier for advice on the wine list, Maria Celeste was taking-in the scene around her. They had a table for two under a large square umbrella shade at the edge of the central *piazza*. Tastefully restored renaissance buildings encased the square, including the civic hall with its ground level arches and the town's *quartiere* flags above. From her seat she could look down one of the four alleys serving the *piazza*, out over the green *Umbra* Valley and onto the Apennine mountains behind.

The two men were reeling off names of wines, vintages and descriptive adjectives. Still happily feeling the effects of the morning's tasting, she did not need any more wine. But she would not discourage their animated discussion.

'Sorry. We've decided, finally. A white from the *cantina* we have just visited. A red from a family-owned winery we should see next time. Have you looked at the menu?'

'I was waiting for you, so we could choose together.'

He held one hand over hers, as they studied the menu. She reached her second hand across to envelope his.

'I quite like the sound of the *cappellotti* with duck filling and truffle shavings. Followed by the fillet of sliced beef sliced on a bed of *radicchio*, topped with *gorgonzola* and *pistachio* sauce.'

'Me too. What about the *antipasti*?' Massimo asked. 'They are delicious here.'

'Isn't that too much?'

'Maybe.'

A young waitress with a striking aquiline nose came by to take their order and Massimo stood up to hug her. Then another attractive woman walked to their table to greet them both, in her early thirties. She was heavily pregnant. To add to the growing fan club, the chef appeared wearing baggy white trousers and a floppy net that contained a mop of grey hair but not her pleasure at seeing Massimo, '*Che piacere come sempre. Ma quella ragazza…*'

She was at a loss of words to describe Maria Celeste.

'Massimo, you seem very popular around here. Is this where you bring all your admirers?' Maria Celeste said as the two sat alone.

'Girlfriends? Only you.'

'I find that hard to believe.'

'The pregnant lady, she's the manager,' he said, changing the subject. 'The chef is her mother. They are an award-winning team.'

After a short while, the sommelier returned with two glasses of *prosecco*.

'On the house!' he announced. 'Maria Celeste, it is a pleasure to meet you. You are every bit as beautiful as Massimo told me over the phone.'

He promptly left to attend to another table, to be replaced by the waitress who presented two dishes in front of them.

'Compliments from the chef,' she said.

At this point Maria Celeste started turning red. Alarm bells rang inside her. At the back of her mind something had told her to expect a surprise during this visit. To prepare her answer.

The waitress carried on, pointing to the dish closest to Massimo, 'This is *bruschetta* topped with *burrata*, anchovies and red onion.'

But she dismissed it. It was too soon. He hardly knows me.

'You also have a dish of finely sliced *prosciutto* cooked in *Sagrantino* wine and served with home-made bread. *Buon appetito.*'

Oh dear. What am I going to say? Can he really love me? What will Sandra think? She warned me he was just infatuated with the soprano in me. Do I love him? I am too old for him, surely? Her heart was pumping.

'Are you alright Maria Celeste?' Massimo noticed something was wrong.

'Oh, I am fine. I just need some water. That was quite a morning we have just had.'

'The restrooms are past the kitchen inside if you need to freshen up.'

'Good idea. I'll be back shortly.'

When she returned, Maria Celeste saw Massimo drawing in a sketchbook.

'You are a dark horse. I didn't know you liked sketching?'

'More than wine, you know,' he replied.

'Can I see?'

'Let me just finish this latest one.'

'Now you have me intrigued.'

After a couple of minutes, Massimo put his pencil down and closed his sketchbook.

'Let's eat,' he said. 'It was very rude of me to keep you waiting.'

****

On their return to Maria Celeste's apartment in Perugia, they fell in a heap of exhaustion on her sofa. But within moments they were making love in her bedroom, as they did intermittently throughout the night and following day. In between, they slept and laughed and teased one another; grazed on some cold food in the fridge; and played on the upright piano in the sitting room.

All of a sudden, it was Sunday evening. The following morning Massimo would be returning to London.

'Let's go for a walk before it gets dark,' suggested Massimo.

'Good idea. I have a bad case of the Sunday blues.'

They each put on a sweater to ward off the evening cold of late September and Massimo picked up his knapsack.

Let's go to the *Oratorio di San Bernardino*.

'Good choice. We might even catch evening mass.'

'I'd like that very much,' said Massimo.

Twenty minutes later they sat on a bench next to the *piazza* which overlooked the *Chiesa di San Francesco al Prato* and the smaller *oratorio* closer to them. There was a large open space of grass, where a very athletic couple were doing some gymnastics training. Massimo and Maria Celeste sat holding hands, looking rather sad.

'Massimo.'

'Yes.'

'Are you going to show me your sketch-book?'

'You hadn't forgotten it?'

'*Certo di no.*'

Massimo reached for the dark green book in his knapsack and handed it to her. She opened it on the first page. There was a pencil drawing, with the clear outline of Perugia's *Palazzo dei Priori* in the background and a crowd of people in front. Only one person was drawn in any detail, a tall slender woman.

'Umbria Jazz?' she said.

She turned to the next page. This time a large hall with frescoed vaulted ceilings. Another crowd, with only one person in detail. Across the page, that same person standing next to a piano, singing. Overleaf, the straight back of a woman holding a kayak paddle, water dripping down onto her white sleeves.

'Oh Massimo, this is very touching,' she said, losing focus as a watery film filled her eyes.

She continued the story. Next, she was standing in a vineyard, with Montefalco behind and on the facing page, a lot more detail. It was the beginning of a portrait of her, against a background of tables and chairs.

'Yesterday's restaurant? This is incredible.'

'Carry on. Two more to go.'

The next one startled her.

'It's the two of us sitting here. On this very bench. With the *oratorio* beside us. How did you manage that?' Tears were now falling down her cheeks.

'One more to go.'

There was no drawing on the next page. Just the question.

Maria Celeste, mi vuoi sposare?

Chapter 9. La Madonna Azzurra
1508 A.D.

The big earthquake struck the small settlement at *la torre di Santa Giuliana* during the day. Women were working the fields or fetching water in pails from the nearby spring. Men idled under large oak trees or tended the sheep on the hillsides. Children played as the elderly watched from the shade of the church and tower. Inside the church, a priest was giving religious instruction to an altar boy called Giuseppe.

The air pressure built and ear drums began to hurt. Domesticated animals became agitated. Dogs barked. The priest recognised the signs.

'Giuseppe, run. Quickly, to the entrance.'

The next instant the earth beneath them rumbled, then it started to shake, violently from side to side. As he ran away from the apse towards the western entrance, Giuseppe was thrown off balance and fell to the floor in front of *la Madonna Azzurra*. So-called, as she was draped in delicate mantle of light blue.

A minute later stillness returned and for a moment there was utter silence. Giuseppe heard the moans of the wounded. Children began to cry. He could not believe he was still alive. As the dust fell, it revealed the *afresco* of the Madonna. She too had survived and looked at him impassively from her large hazel eyes. The demure and serene demeanour was unchanged, as if nothing had happened.

But then he noticed the goldleaf from the large halo behind her head was missing. He turned towards the apse and to his horror, the Madonna behind the altar had simply vanished. The red Madonna and her infant Jesus. The whole fresco had tumbled to the ground. A large area of the southern wall of the church had collapsed, as had parts of the roof it supported.

Beneath the rubble, Giuseppe saw the out-stretched arm of the priest.

Meanwhile outside, a whole slice of the upper reaches of *la torre* had fallen and crushed some of the buildings beneath it. The tower too was wounded.

That night a star exploded in the sky. Far away. So far, it would take a very long time to be seen from Earth.

****

'Who is this man?' her father asked. 'Why have I never heard of him, or of his family?'

It was several decades since the big earthquake.

'He has no family, *papà*,' Maria Celeste answered. 'He was orphaned at a young age. In the early 1490s.'

She had been dreading this moment. An ebbing Oddi family fortune combined with persistent pain from a sword injury sustained when he was young had turned him into a solemn, cantankerous man.

'What is his occupation? Where does he live?'

'He is an artist. He lives with a doctor and his wife and their children in Perugia.'

'An artist,' her father replied, in a patronising tone. 'We have no need for an artist in the family. We can call on the best when we require one.'

'You are right *papà*. But Massimo is still very young, full of promise. He just needs to find a good patron. Look, I have brought you some of his sketches.'

'I am not interested in sketches. I want to see the frescoes, altar pieces in oil. Like the altar piece your cousin commissioned Raffaello to paint for the Oddi chapel in Perugia,' he said disdainfully.

'But *papà* he trained with Raffaello in Perugino's Umbrian school of art,' said Maria Celeste, thinking this might rouse his interest.

'A pupil of Perugino's? Really? Why has he not risen to fame then, like Raffaello?'

'Massimo worked with Raffaello on the frescoes in the *Sala del Cambio*,' Maria Celeste persisted.

'Ah, that commission of Perugino's in the *Palazzo dei Priori* by the wealthy money changers guild. The bankers. That sounds impressive, my dear. Except when you know- and Perugino told me this in person – that he ended up doing almost all the art-work himself. His pupils were not up to his standard. Apart from Raffaello, of course.'

Maria Celeste had stood under those painted vaulted ceilings only recently. She thought it the most beautiful work of art she had seen. All those allegorical figures drawn by chariots harnessed to horses and other creatures such as geese and griffins and dragons. They represented the celestial bodies of the Moon, Mars, Mercury, Jupiter, Saturn with the god Apollo at the centre. The pupils had worked on the surrounding grotesque decoration, which she liked as well.

'Tell me, Maria Celeste, do you know what Raffaello is working on now?'

He has clearly made up his mind, she thought. Raphael was about to start work in the Apostolic Palace at the Vatican. Commissioned by none other than the new Pope Julius II. The pontiff she hoped would restore the fortunes of the Oddis in their longstanding rivalry with Perugia's Baglioni family. The Pope that had replaced Pope Alexander VI, head of the scheming Borgia dynasty.

Maria Celeste looked down at her feet in silence. Nothing would convince her father to change his mind at this point. There had to be another approach. 'I do,' she said finally.

'Well then, tell that suitor of yours he can ask me for your hand in marriage if I approve of his first commission.'

'Thank you, *papà*. I will.' She left the room and the heavy oak door was closed behind her by a footman.

****

Livia watched the growing cluster of workmen in the valley below with much excitement. She had a commanding view of the *la torre di Santa Giuliana* and its church *la Chiesa del Piano Di Nese*, along with most of the valley from her terrace in the fortified hamlet above.

'Alessandro, have you seen? They are finally going to start repairing the damage from that earthquake all those years ago. Look at the scaffolding going up,' she said in her cheerful, animated tone. 'Uncle Giuseppe was right.'

'We never doubted him, did we, my darling? Giampaolo also told me the restoration had been approved on my last visit to Perugia. Both the tower and the church.'

Alessandro was garrison commander of the line of defensive towers running north of Perugia towards Ghibelline territory. He reported to Giampaolo Baglioni, the leader of Perugia.

'Financed by *il Papa*, presumably,' said Livia.

'Yes. Like the well in the courtyard. As a reward for the community's long-standing support of the *Vaticano* at the north-eastern frontier of the *Stati Pontifici*,' Alessandro observed. 'Soon we won't have to walk so far to mass in future.'

'True, but I will miss the *badia*. That is our real spiritual home.' The *Badia di Monte Corona* was where they were married. Located near the Tiber on the other side of the mountain, it took over half-an-hour to get there on horseback. Almost three times that on foot.

'Are you writing to the Oddis, as we agreed?' Livia asked, seeing him with quill in hand as she walked into the family room next to the terrace.

'I am. Help me compose the letter. I am very nervous about this. What if the letter is intercepted by the Baglionis?'

'It won't be, my love. I will hand it directly to Maria Celeste on Sunday.'

Livia had met Maria Celeste again after Mass the previous Sunday, who had confided she was very concerned for her and Alessandro.

Everyone knew the Baglionis were traditionally Ghibellines, that they enjoyed a sense of independence from the Papacy. Suddenly they faced a new Pope intent on extending his secular powers. One who favoured the Vatican's long-standing supporters, the Guelphs- such as the Oddis. Although Giampaolo Baglioni quickly swore allegiance to him, Maria Celeste felt it was only a matter of time before Julius II struck, placing Alessandro and his family in jeopardy.

'Alessandro, will you see to the children's lunch? There is *pecorino, torta bianca* and *dei fichi* on the kitchen table,' asked Livia some twenty minutes later, aware the little school across the courtyard would soon be finishing for the day.

'And where, may I ask, are you going?'

'I am going to see Uncle Giuseppe.'

'Take a guard with you.'

'Darling you are so thoughtful and protective. I'll be fine without, promise,' she said, kissing him fully on the lips before walking down some steps and into the courtyard.

The *Borgo di Santa Giuliana*, not to be confused with the tower further down the valley bearing the same name, was a small but surprisingly noisy settlement. Some two hundred people lived in cramped conditions in a cluster of stone buildings. The hamlet was located on a flat spur of land that rested on precipitously steep cliffs. The approach by track was protected by a high wall, with a square tower on one corner and a round one on the other. There was a line of wooden sheds and barns just outside this wall, where the livestock was kept in times of safety.

Livia walked down a short alley, into the gatehouse where and across the open drawbridge. As she walked back along the spur before taking the footpath, Livia saw the many rows of olive trees in the fields beyond them. Facing west to take full advantage of the hot afternoon sun, the fruit had ripened well. Soon the villagers would be harvesting the olive crop, shaking the trees and gathering the olives in nets on the ground below.

It would be a short walk down a path to one side of a ravine, passing through woods of oak. The path was lined with *ginestra* bushes that long ago had shed their fragrant yellow flowers. Instead, it was the turn of the brambles to display their bounty of luscious blackberries. She would have to be careful not to catch her robe on the thorns. The path had overgrown through lack of use, but this was sure to change once the reconstruction was completed and the church once again attracted its full congregation from across the valley.

Soon she was walking beside a small cemetery and down into an open area, with a view of the stone church and behind it, the top of a tall tower. Father Giuseppe stood outside, clipping sprigs of rosemary off a large bush. He was stooped and very measured in his movements. It had been a tough life, remaining here in the country among the poor that worked the land.

Always loyal to his parishioners. Dreams of becoming a cardinal were long gone.

'Brought you some lunch, *zio*,' she said, holding a bundle consisting of the same simple food Alessandro would be offering the children after school.

'Thank you, my darling Livia,' he answered. 'My life has improved one hundred-fold since you moved in up the hill.'

'As has mine, being close to you.'

'Will you stay and have lunch with me?' he asked.

'I'd love to. I brought enough for the two of us.'

'Wonderful. At least we have a bit of quiet- the workers have their lunch about this time too, you know.'

They sat on the steps outside the church overlooking the valley and Livia offered her uncle a piece of freshly-baked bread accompanied by a chunk of cheese.

'Oh, my favourites. Clever girl. I suppose you are not a girl any longer, forgive me.'

'Unfortunately not.'

'Remember those flowers I gave you on your first trip here.'

'I do. Yellow broom and dog-roses.'

'How is your husband Massimo?'

'It's Alessandro, not Massimo.'

'Ah yes. May the Lord forgive me. I get so confused these days.'

****

'Massimo,' said Ornella, 'A letter had just arrived for you. It looks like the Oddi family seal.'

'A leaping lion? It must be from Maria Celeste,' he said excitedly.

A moment later, the seal broken and letter unfolded, all the joy disappeared from his face.

'I am sorry Massimo,' said Ornella, guessing its content. She gave him a hug, bending delicately over her large bump to reach him. Her third child was due any day.

'I knew it. I need to prove myself first.'

Giovanni felt Massimo's frustration and sorrow transmitting through the walls into his practice. He had no patients, so opened the door from the adjoining room. 'Let me guess. Her father is blocking this. We are not nobility, it is as simple as that.'

'I've been reflecting on this for a while,' said Massimo. 'There are too many artists and too few patrons in this region. I am going to travel north. To visit cities recently retaken from the Venetians by Pope Julius, such as Bologna and others in Romagna.'

'What is Maria Celeste going to say to that? It could be months before you find work, and years before you return. She won't wait for you,' said Ornella, clearly opposed to the idea. 'Anyway, the north must be full of aspiring painters from Umbria and Tuscany like you. That Luca Signorelli has swept-up all the commissions around here.'

She's right, thought Massimo. Always is. Who is to say Maria Celeste would still be waiting for him when he returned. Time was not on her side.

'What's more, it's so dangerous up there,' said Giovanni. 'With our new *Papa* on the warpath against foreign powers, striking alliances with and against enemies you can't trust that seem to fall apart before the ink has had time to dry. The French for instance. The Republic of Venice.'

Massimo could see husband and wife rallying against him. Concerned for his prospects of marriage. For his safety. He had a trump card to play however, to bring at least one of them on side. 'I could also visit the duchy of Ferrara,' he said, almost casually.

Lucrezia! Now that changed everything for Ornella. 'Only if you convince her to come back!'

Ever since receiving that letter from her best friend, after her long disappearance, Ornella had selfishly wanted her to return. 'You are my saviour,' the letter read. For having introduced her to Lucrezia Borgia while Ornella served her during her governorship of Spoleto. The role model, now married to Alfonso d'Este duke of Ferrara, for whom her dearest friend now worked.

'I can try. I can forewarn her that *il Papa* is planning to recover Ferrara next, to lead the battle in person. Isn't that right Giovanni?'

'According to Alessandro, yes. But playing the devil's advocate, do you think she would want to see you again Massimo? Won't it just re-open the wounds of what happened to her? Maybe she wants to remain in the new life she has created for herself, try to leave the scars behind?'

'What if *il Papa* turns on the duchess herself,' Massimo countered. 'Along with those that work for her? Isn't she the sole surviving member of the Borgia dynasty in Italy Julius vowed to destroy on the day of his election?'

'Oh, I think she was forgiven long ago. But yes, you have a point. While you are there, who knows, she might even be able to help you win a commission. It seems from reading her latest letter, that she is a well-ensconced member of the duchess's team.'

'That's it,' Massimo declared. 'Thank you for support and advice. If Maria Celeste agrees, I will head north as soon as I can.'

'Let me write to forewarn Lucrezia,' Ornella offered.

****

After Mass at the abbey, Livia took the steps down to the lower church. She went to light a candle, near the altar where she once stood saying her vows, Alessandro by her side.

'I was hoping I would see you here, Maria Celeste,' she whispered. 'I have something to give you.'

'A letter?'

'Yes, let's talk outside.'

They finished their prayers before a rack of flickering lights and stepped outside into the bright sunshine. The early autumnal morning air was still crisp.

'I'll make sure this gets into my uncle's hands.'

'Not your *papà's*?'

'I am not on the best of terms with him at the moment,' said Maria Celeste. 'He is prohibiting my marriage. Massimo is still unknown as an artist.'

Livia stood silently, absorbing the news.

'What if I can help get him some work in our valley?' she said, after a few moments.

An hour later, they both stood in front of the abbot. The abbot was a man of middling height who was an able administrator that had an unusual appreciation for art- so long as it too, followed the rules.

'Yes, we are looking to commission a new altar piece at the *Chiesa del Piano Di Nese*. The priest favours a painting in oil on wood panels, which is the trend these days. I am more of a traditionalist. Does your friend have experience in frescoes?'

The abbot listened to Maria Celeste as she described his *curriculum vitae*.

'It is hard to find the best artists these days,' he said, after she finished. 'The new Pope is exorcising the memory of the Borgias, repainting the whole of the Vatican it seems. Raffaello is there. Michelangelo has started painting the Sistine Chapel. Luca Signorelli is so much in demand, he has a list of commissions in Umbria and Tuscany that will keep him going into his 80s. Then there is my dear friend Piero della Francesca, who sadly is no longer with us. He would have been my top choice.'

The stark reality was that the abbey could not afford any of those artists.

'By all means,' the abbot continued. 'Ask Massimo to come and see me. He should visit the *chiesa* first to present his ideas. They will need to complement the blue Madonna in the nave near the western entrance.'

'One more thing, my ladies,' he said as they turned to leave, almost as an afterthought. 'I will need a written reference.'

The two women stood outside again, walking past the abbey's bell tower. Livia was overflowing with excitement. 'The reference, your family know Raffaello don't they,' she said, thinking of the Oddi Altarpiece she had seen in Perugia. 'Finally, you'd get to see Rome, your lifelong dream! What is more, while you are at the Vatican, you can greet Michelangelo!'

Maria Celeste was already planning which of the household staff she would take with her and what she would pack for her journey.

****

Massimo was walking north, heading for the *la torre di Santa Giuliana*.

Luckily, Alessandro had intercepted him with news of the potential local commission just in time. Before he left Perugia for the much longer journey to Ferrara in the Po valley.

'It is just under a day's walk from Perugia,' Alessandro had said. 'But I think you should leave before dawn and let the pole star be your guide. After sunrise simply follow the line of tall stone towers. The church is next to the first of two towers once you have crossed the Nese. It should still be a dry river-bed at this time of year. Local shepherds will help direct you if in doubt. Now, are you sure you don't want protection from one of my men?'

'I'm sure, thank you.'

Massimo had lost count of the number of defensive towers he had seen since leaving home. Imposing stone giants on which fires would be lit in sequence to warn Perugia of an encroaching enemy army. He could see their silhouettes at night and hardly needed Polaris's guidance. He regretted not having accepted a guard. Although the short journey had been without incident, the company would have been comforting.

In the early afternoon, as he walked down into a valley with two towers, he heard a distinctive chorus of bird song. It was a flock of bee-eaters. There were so many it was hard to follow any individual as they soared, sliced and pirouetted through the air, catching insects in long straight beaks. A group of swallows joined the feast and soon there were a hundred or more aerial acrobats filling the air.

Autumn had arrived and the birds were congregating, feeding energetically ahead of their winter hibernation. He did not know where they spent the winter. Whether they went underground or slept in caves.

To add to his excitement, Massimo spotted a buzzard soaring effortlessly along the ridge of the steep hill to his left. Its calls echoed across the valley and as if responding to its summons, a whole family of the gliders appeared above him.

He wondered whether they had a nest among the outcrops and cliffs of white limestone that protruded from the forest of oaks. That ubiquitous stone from which much of medieval Umbria was built. The same white stone of the tower that suddenly loomed above him.

An inquisitive crowd of all ages gathered around him. Including a priest that emerged from the church that might become his place of work and home for the next few weeks.

****

Massimo and Livia sat apprehensively in a drawing room in the abbot's quarters, along with Father Giusppe. They decided to keep the appointment, even though Maria Celeste still had not returned from Rome. They were missing the precious reference.

The abbot was handed a scroll of large pieces of parchment, on which Massimo had drawn his ideas for the fresco above the altar. Massimo clutched a leather book containing sketches of earlier work on his lap.

They waited for him to untie the ribbon, but the abbot held the scroll unopened in his hand. 'Tell me about the blue *Madonna*. Describe her to me,' he asked.

'I am pleased you asked me about her, *vostra eminenza*. I am in awe of the blue Madonna, of how she survived that earthquake. She is a miracle,' Massimo said, starting to describe his impressions. 'Where do I begin? Well, she greeted me as I entered the nave and her gaze followed me as I walked up to her. Her large hazel eyes are set in an exquisitely gentle face. They invited me to pray to *il nostro Signore Gesù* through her.

Her head is inclined slightly to the left, the discreet angle accentuating her demure and serene demeanour.'

'She wears a long maroon robe over which is draped a light blue almost diaphanous mantle. The cloth covers her head and most of her fair hair. As if needed, her divinity is accentuated by a large halo behind her head- although the goldleaf is missing. Seated on a wide throne, the *Madonna* is cushioning *il Gesù bambino* on her lap, her left hand supporting his lower back. The child has a small vivacious fluttering bird resting on his hand- a sparrow perhaps? It seems too small to be a dove. A string, fastened to the bird's foot, is held delicately between the *Madonna*'s thumb and middle finger. There are angels peering down from either side while holding the throne aloft and geometric patterns and bands of light umber frame the image.'

'I don't know who the artist is. Perhaps your archives here at the abbey have a record?'

The abbot did not reply, so Massimo continued.

'Well just to finish, the fresco is in the style of *Madonna* enthroned, which has Byzantine origins. My best estimate is that she would have been painted around a hundred years ago. Between 1400-1430 A.D.'

The abbot raised his eye-brows briefly, hopefully impressed with Massimo's knowledge.

'What about your plans for the altar?'

'Can I show you my sketches, *vostra eccellenza?*'

'I will look at them shortly. Please describe your vision for the fresco first.'

'*Certamente vostra eccellenza.* I would paint a Madonna Enthroned, as in the case of the blue *Madonna* in the nave. But my composition would be a *Sacra Conversazione*. I would position two saints on either side.'

'Which saints?' interrupted the abbot.

'Well, from left to right my figures would represent *Santa Lucia*; then the church's patron saint *Santa Giuliana*; the *Madonna e Bambino* in the centre; *Maria Magdalena* to the right and finally, one of Perugia's patron saints, *Ercolano* perhaps.'

'Whose likenesses will you use?'

'Your reverence, given the importance of the Oddi family in the local area, I had in mind likenesses drawn from that family. But I will do as you wish, your grace.'

'I see. Livia tells me you plan to marry into that family. That makes sense,' the abbot remarked dryly.

At that moment a page entered with a letter. 'This is marked urgent, *vostra eccellenza*.'

As the page walked past them to hand over the envelope, they both saw an outline of a pouncing lion on the seal.

Massimo's heart almost missed a beat as the seal was broken.

'Tell me about the style and decoration.'

'Well, your excellency,' Massimo continued, re-gathering his composure. 'My sketch envisages adding two windows above in which angels play musical instruments, one a lute and the other a lyre harp. I would chain the devil and have him held underfoot by Santa Giuliana. All would be set in an arabesque background.'

'Stop there,' the abbot interrupted again. 'It seems as if Raffaello considers you very worthy of this commission.'

****

'Have you ever been in love Lucrezia?' asked the duchess. The other Lucrezia.

'I don't believe I have,' she replied.

She was sitting at the duchess's feet, while the duchess combed her dark hair.

'Believe me, you know when you are.'

'Then may I ask, is it possible to love more than one person in a lifetime?'

'Only you are allowed to ask me that,' the duchess said, acknowledging the unusual bond of friendship they now shared. 'I am not so sure that one can.'

'Perotto. You loved him, didn't you?'

'Yes I did. At least I thought I did. But I was so young and desperate for love.'

'The poet Bembo then.'

'You are observant, Lucrezia. Not alone in thinking so, I imagine. Well, I suppose it does not matter. Alfonso does not care. He is too busy having his own affairs.'

'Those letters.'

'From Pietro Bembo? You haven't read them, have you?'

'Of course not. But one day someone will. He will call them 'the prettiest love letters in the world."

'There goes my Delphic high priestess again,' the duchess sighed. 'But now it's my turn. Do you know where you will find the love you seek?'

'Not among the musicians, poets, academics or artists that visit your court?'

'No, back in Umbria. I can see one waiting for you, although he does not know it yet. And you miss your home, don't you?'

'Not really. Too much pain still.'

'Lucrezia, we have to put our pain behind us in order to move forward. In my case my despotic father and brother. In yours, that monster, whose name I have chosen to forget,' the duchess said, before changing the subject. 'Now that artist friend of yours who was supposed to come by. Whatever happened to him?'

It was not just their names. They both had emotional trauma in common. Abuse. Both had lost children. The duchess two daughters to miscarriages, while Lucrezia had had an abortion. A few months after she was raped by that gang. A procedure in a dark smoke-filled room while surrounded by the practitioner's infants that almost killed her. She was told later by a physician that she would never be able to have children of her own. Other points in common included the same name; and a deep necessity to be cherished by men, although Lucrezia had not had any man in her life since Cafaro.

'Massimo? I have no idea. I have not heard anything since receiving that letter from Ornella. Perhaps something happened to him on the journey?'

'Well, let us hope there is a positive reason. Perhaps something detained him,' said the duchess, searching for a reason, 'Such as winning a commission locally? But tell me about Ornella. How is she and her physician husband?'

'Both well, thank you. They are expecting a third child any moment.'

'Ornella was so good to me in Spoleto. Well, you both were. I was in such a state. Heavily pregnant. Worried about my second husband, whom I was convinced my brother wanted to have killed. She was so calm. Even came to my bed-side to wake me from the terrible nightmares I used to have. I still feel guilty remonstrating her for saying awful things about my family while she thought I slept. She was so right.'

'What do you think about our new Pope?' Lucrezia asked.

'Julius is a bit of a warlord, to be frank. But not scheming and deceitful like my father. I am a bit worried that we are heading for a war between the Pope and the French and that Ferrara will be on the front-line.'

'What will you do?'

'Continue doing what I have done for years now. Holding court. Making Ferrara a magnet for literature and poetry. Swear allegiance to whoever takes control. Continue having children. All the more reason for you to go home.'

Just then there was a knock on the door. The wet nurse appeared carrying the duchess's youngest child Ippolito.

'See you later,' the duchess said. 'Think about it. Going home. Might be safer for you there.'

****

Massimo sat on the stone steps that led up to the church next to *la torre di Santa Giuliana*. He was looking nervously at the ridge over which the buzzards had welcomed him all those weeks earlier. He had not seen them since.

An entourage could arrive down Monte Corona behind him at any moment. Judgement day had arrived. He prayed they would like his naïve style, the bold chromatic colours, the festive nature of the figures in their contemporary dress.

He was racked with self-doubt. As he had been for much of the long process.

He thought back over the long hours agonising over the *giornati*, the sections of the fresco he had to complete each day so the paints could fix before the plaster dried. His constant worry about theft. That gold. The blue lapis lazuli, whose provenance was somewhere along the silk route in the orient. Doubts also about the pigments that he ground into fine powders. Did he have enough sinopia? It too came from far away. From near the Black Sea, he was told. He needed this bold red pigment to draw the outlines of his composition before applying the plaster. Fortunately, there was no shortage of lime white, which he would mix with *sinopia* to produce flesh colours. Or of the locally mined raw umber in its various shades, including the reddish-brown of burnt umber.

'It is very beautiful.'

A soft, pure voice enveloped him from the church behind.

'Might that be the *Madonna azzurra*?'

'No, it's only me,' answered Maria Celeste.

He sprung to his feet and they hugged, for a very long time.

'It's been so long,' he said. 'Where is your *papà*?'

'He doesn't need to see it. The letter from Raffaello was enough. Shall we get married here? Now?'

'This instant?' Massimo looked around to see Father Giuseppe and a gathering assembly.

'Why not? We have plenty of witnesses,' she suggested.

'And a best man,' came a shout from among the crowd, as Giovanni emerged.

'Maria Celeste, how did..' Massimo said, lost for words. He spotted Ornella holding her baby daughter, while the twins stood fidgeting beside her. Then Alessandro and Livia appeared, with their three children.

Chapter 10. The Bronze Figurine
2026 A.D./ Around 550 B.C.

It was a Saturday and both Massimo and Maria Celeste had a free day. Although they did have to be back before seven in the evening, when some of Massimo's best students were giving their first piano recitals in Perugia's *Palazzo dei Priori*. They drove north to Umbertide, to visit one of the three museums managed by Sandra, with whom Maria Celeste had lost contact since getting engaged.

It was not surprising, really. Especially as Maria Celeste had not invited Sandra to the wedding. The excuse was that it was very impromptu and low key. Which was true. It had all come together very suddenly and there was a long list of aggrieved friends and even some family that were excluded. In Sandra's case though, Maria Celeste secretly hoped she would understand the real reason. That not being invited, was an admission of the illicit emotions and strange physical sensations she had begun to feel when Sandra was around. That she was not going to let this upset her and Massimo's big day.

Today's excursion therefore, unbeknown to Massimo, had a hidden agenda. It was to see her friend again. And of course, to introduce her husband. Massimo only knew her as 'the woman who pulled you away' at the jazz festival. Maria Celeste was convinced they had met but could not remember where. 'It's your fuzzy memory playing tricks with you again,' he had told her.

'Massimo, let's take the scenic route and exit here,' said Maria Celeste, spotting the turning to Pierantonio.

'*Un ottimo idea-* we can drop by the abbey where Livia was married.'

'You read my mind,' replied his wife, grinning.

They crossed the Tiber, then turned onto a country lane that wound its way around the base of the eastern side of Monte Corona. The fields beneath them were mostly brown with fat furrows of ploughed earth, the tobacco leaves long ago harvested.

'Massimo you know I had a dream which featured that *badia* recently. You were trying to become an artist.'

'Really? Maybe I should – the classical circuit is so tough.'

'Aw Massimo, you are always putting yourself down. You'll make it, just you wait. Maybe we should try together- a duet? What do you think?' She squeezed his knee as he drove.

'What troubled me about the dream,' she continued a little later, 'was that you also struggled in art. I had to sleep with someone to help get you a commission. It was horrible.'

This caught his attention.

'What, you didn't, did you? You would never do that, would you?'

'*Certo di no* Massimo,' she said, squeezing his knee harder.

'That was horrid. It's given me instant heart-burn.'

The abbey drew into sight, with its imposing bell tower and parallel lines of mature umbrella pine trees. Massimo left the car near a side entrance and Maria Celeste followed him through an unlocked ancient wooden door into a large crypt.

Inside it was very dark. As her eyes adjusted she could see numerous arches supported by columns. She suspected they were originally Roman. The crypt itself was probably 11th Century.

While Massimo took some stairs to the upper church, Maria Celeste remained behind to light three candles next to a side altar. She had not been a religious person, but this had started to change following her miscarriages. Looking up to the decorated vaulted ceiling she saw the four vows repeated by countless brides through history. Humility, self-denial, sweetness and obedience. Before their wedding, Maria Celeste had told Massimo she would not utter the last one. It was not in her nature. She might also struggle to be sweet to him. But she would try.

****

Massimo read out loud from a pamphlet, while they stood next to the Deposition by Luca Signorelli.

Signorelli's style met with widespread success in the Valle del Tevere, where he was able to assert a preponderant influence that left very little room, for example, for the large band of Perugino's followers working in the rest of Umbria.

'Was this who you slept with?' Massimo tried a joke, but it was a lame one.

'Massimo, *lasciami in pace*. It was only a dream. I wish now I had never told you about it.'

They had found the *Museo di Santa Croce* in Umbertide, just to one side of the *Piazza San Francesco*. The woman at the ticket office ignored them at first, as she was absorbed in her mobile phone. Maria Celeste caught Massimo admiring her short dyed blond hair, brown eyes and thin arms with well-toned muscles. She was still bronzed from the summer sun, even though it was now November. She was attractive.

'*Ciao* Sandra,' Maria Celeste said, rather meekly.

Sandra recognised the voice instantly. 'Maria Celeste!' Sandra looked up and jumped out of her chair, reaching across the reception desk to embrace her friend. Realising this was a bit ambitious- the desk was too wide and piled high with brochures- she sprinted around for a proper hug.

Maria Celeste had played-out many possible reunions in her mind, but not this one. She must have been forgiven. When they eventually disentangled, both women were clearly blushing.

'*Dio mio*, where have you been all this time? And this handsome young man,' Sandra said, turning to Massimo. 'This must be Massimo.'

'Pleased to meet you, finally,' said Massimo, as he kissed her on both cheeks. 'I've heard so much about you and your museum.'

'Ah yes, the museum. I am so happy you have come to visit,' Sandra said, a little lost for words.

'Sorry I didn't phone you beforehand. We just thought we would surprise you,' said Maria Celeste.

'Well that you most certainly have! How have you been? Still teaching in Perugia?'

Another couple appeared and stood behind them. Sandra's facial expression changed as the professional curator in her took over. Outside, through the glass doors, she could see other customers entering the museum courtyard from the street.

'Oh, I think we have just lost our guided tour,' said Massimo.

'See, you should have booked Mari,' Sandra said as she returned to her post on the other side of the desk and began tapping away on a key-board.

Mari. That was a new one for Massimo. He had lots of names for her, depending on the context. Ranging from her full name when he was serious or demanded attention. Maria, when he felt lazy. Miss Mary, a name that sprung from nowhere, to embarrass her, especially when spoken with a laboured Italian accent. And *Cielo*, that he thought a term of endearment but which for Maria Celeste was the brand of a nondescript wine, which riled her. But Mari? That was sick.

'*Ecco*, your tickets and an information leaflet for each of you,' Sandra announced, sounding very formal. 'They will give you free access to two other museums nearby if used in the next two weeks.' She motioned them towards the gallery containing works by the early Renaissance painters such as Signorelli, then added, 'Give me a moment to see to these other customers, then I will open the Etruscan exhibition for you.'

'Ah, that is what interests us the most,' said Massimo.

A short while later, they both headed up a narrow staircase and began reading the placards about the Etruscans and their historical neighbours to the east, the *Umbri*. There was also a summary of the archaeological dig on Monte Acuto.

'Did you know the *Etruschi* at their peak occupied lands from Emila-Romagna in the north down to Napoli in the south,' announced Maria Celeste, paraphrasing the written text. 'As well as Corsica. They were the masters of the Western Mediterranean until the 5th Century B.C., when they came up against the *Greci* to the south. Then along came the *Romani*, who inflicted a series of defeats culminating in the battle of Sentino in 295 B.C.'

'The *Romani* then did what they did best,' she said digressing, 'borrowing anything useful from the culture they had subjugated. In this case the art of *afresschi*; painted pottery,' she tailed off.

Massimo meanwhile, was already in the next room.

'Apparently it was *Umbri* that had settled Monte Acuto, not the *Etruschi*. It was a sacred site the *Umbri* used to make votive offerings from around the sixth century B.C.,' he said, adding his own discovery.

Maria Celeste joined Massimo and saw him staring at a glass case filled with bronze figurines. There were simple male and female figures, as well as representations of wild boar and some domesticated animals such as horses.

She joined him, squeezed his hand and kissed his cheek.

'Come on, let's go and climb that mountain', she said, after admiring the figures for some time. 'Let me just say goodbye to Sandra on the way out.'

'Did you enjoy the exhibition?' Sandra asked, a few moments later.

'We loved those figurines. They were beautifully displayed. So tempting to just put one in your pocket!' said Massimo.

'Believe me I almost did, when I was involved with the dig.' Sandra replied, before turning to Maria Celeste. 'Give me a call sometime. Soon.'

'I will.'

****

Massimo parked the car in a lay-by, next to a wooden signpost with a large map showing the main walking trails of the area. The car had done much of their work. It took them winding up a ridge, about half-way up to the summit, before the road passed the mountain and turned right to follow the watershed of the Nese and Niccone valleys. For much of the short drive from Umbertide they could see the large iron cross and mobile phone masts at the summit.

Leaving Perugia that morning, having planned to make this climb, they had loaded the car with hiking trainers, their waterproof mountain jackets and small backpacks containing warm clothing, water and snacks. While it was sunny, the air was distinctly cool and a switch to easterly winds was forecast. These were notorious in winter months, for lifting moisture off the Adriatic and dumping it as snow across the mountains of Le Marche and Umbria.

They walked hand in hand, side by side at first, ascending a woodcutters' trail that led along open ground and through a gate into a forest of pine trees. The ubiquitous red and white trail symbol, parallel rectangles of white and red, painted on the side of the occasional tree trunk or rock, assured them they were on the right path. Pine needles cushioned their steps and occasionally Massimo kicked a large pine cone into the undergrowth.

'We lost on Thursday, by three goals to one,' Massimo said, after sending a large cone tumbling down the hillside.

'I know, you told me,' Maria Celeste replied.

He had been playing for a local side in Perugia since shortly after he left London. Thursday evening football, followed by pizza and beer with his team-mates was the highlight of his week. Maria Celeste meanwhile occupied herself with Pilates sessions, sometimes preceded by a workout in the gym.

They heard rustling amongst the trees above them and looking to the right they saw two middle-aged men in dark green jackets walking down the slope. Both carried wooden walking sticks and both had very worn satchels that balanced on their hips. One had what looked like a thin straight trowel fastened to a wooden pole attached to his waist, while the other held a similar tool in his hand.

'Truffle hunters?' whispered Maria Celeste.

Massimo and Maria Celeste greeted them enthusiastically.

'*Salve. Buongiorno.*'

One managed a grunt in response while the other gave them a hostile glance.

'Truffle hunters are more secretive than Freemasons,' said Massimo.

'I wonder where their dogs are?' asked Maria Celeste, just as they heard bells ringing up the slope. Within seconds two scraggy dogs with small bells attached to their collars rushed past them.

'*Vieni qua;* come here!' shouted the hunters.

The dogs ran in broad turns, noses to the ground, ignoring their owners.

'Their bags looked quite full, didn't they?' Maria Celeste wished they could have seen those rough dark chocolate-coloured balls, the size of oak apples.

'I wouldn't be surprised if they had €1,000 of winter black truffles between them,' said Massimo. 'Not a bad return for a beautiful morning's walk with your dog!'

'Massimo. Why don't we get a dog? Maybe a retired truffle dog, so we don't have to train it?'

'I'd rather have a puppy. Why miss out on that playful stage? But even if we did have one, imagine what would happen if we were caught looking for truffles by guys like those. They'd protect their truffle rights with their lives.'

'Now that's a chilling thought. When I think of truffles, I think of delicate shavings sprinkled generously onto bowls of homemade tagliatelle, or used as garnish on a plate of sliced beef, *filete di manzo.*'

'I think of them as an aphrodisiac.'

'Massimo, later. You have a one-track mind.'

They arrived at a fenced area with more wooden boards displaying some of the same placards they had just seen at the museum. The twin track of the woodcutters' road ended and split into footpaths, each signposted with its destination and estimated walking time.

They took the path to the summit. The pine plantation ended and in its place were small oak trees with thin trunks and what looked like hazel trees and field maples. Their branches were almost bare at this altitude, leaves strewn in bundles where the wind could no longer reach them. Pink autumn crocuses poked through the ground next to tufts of tall brown grass, in defiance of the approaching winter.

Just next to one cluster of crocuses, Massimo could just make out the tip of what looked like a large brown capsule protruding through some lead mould.

'*Un porcino*!' he exclaimed triumphantly, as he bent over and gingerly picked a mushroom off the earth from the base of its heavy white stem.

'*Bravo* Massimo. They always sprout in groups, let's keep looking.'

They spent the next few minutes examining the undergrowth, finding another three *porcini* in the vicinity.

'*Eccoci*. Dinner is sorted,' she said. 'Sliced and fried in olive oil with garlic.'

'To be served on your home-made *tagliatelle* sprinkled with chopped parsley.'

'Home-made? What cheek!'

After this exciting diversion, they continued their climb. Further up trees were small and sparse. The slope was strewn with white boulders and smaller scree, so that it became increasingly hard to follow the path. The wind picked up and soon they were in cloud, with white snow flying past, stinging their red faces.

****

Maria Celeste was cold.

'Shouldn't we turn back? We can try again some other time,' she said.

'Another time? We are running out of time,' Massimo answered. He too had to shout to be heard above the howling winds around them. 'We won't get lost, I promise.'

Her husband was normally quite cautious. But not here, on this mountain, which he knew so well and whose spirits spoke to him. Including those of his parents, which she believed. She too had been separated from her parents although, as she had never heard their whispers, she presumed they were still alive.

A sudden gust hit them, a white wall of driving horizontal snow which Massimo spotted from the corner of one eye. He braced himself and reached for his wife's hand, but was not in time to stop her falling and scraping her knee on a rock as she slipped in the treacherous wet snow.

'Are you all right, my love?'

'I think so.'

'Let's rest here a while, until this blows over.'

They sat down in the lee of a large rock and huddled together. Massimo drew his arm tightly around Maria Celeste then blew air warmed by his lungs onto her uncovered hands, while snow settled on in wet clumps on their fur skins.

'How's the knee?'

'Throbbing a bit. But I'll be fine. How far to the top?'

'Almost there,' he said, mustering a smile. 'And our precious bundle?'

She felt for the small animal skin pouch about her waist and pressed to check its contents were safe. As she had done many times on this long walk up from their settlement next to the Tiber.

'Still there. What about the grain?'

'Safely stored.'

This was the gift for the priest.

As they sat, Maria Celeste cast her mind back to the hot days of summer. To when this adventure began.

'Could have done with your help, you know. We might have been ready to make this trip earlier. Before the snows arrived,' she said, while starting to shiver from the cold.

'I know, I am sorry. But who was to predict winter would be so early.'

'What's more we are going to go hungry.'

'I'll make up for it one day, sorry.'

To be fair, it was Maria Celeste who believed most ardently in the powers of the votive offerings. Massimo remained mischievously sceptical, and only really started to have faith in what they were doing when they strapped on their felt lined winter boots for the journey. In any event, he distrusted the priests and metal-workers whose lives were enriched so visibly by these customs.

He preferred to communicate with the forest spirits. It was free after all.

Maria Celeste therefore travelled alone to commission the metal worker near their settlement. He was a most untrustworthy man who drove a hard bargain, knowing that after a long dry summer, the demand for votive figurines would rise. He could set his price.

'Where's that husband of yours?' he said heartily, after they had exchanged greetings. His face was a scorched red, as were his arms and hands that pumped the bellows of the furnace. 'Heard he is doing good, trading with the Etruscans. Your house must be filled with urns and plates and fancy stuff.'

'He is not doing badly, thank you,' she answered, realising this was not a good way to open the pricing negotiations. 'It's tough for everyone these days, as you know.'

'At least we are not skirmishing with them much nowadays. I remember when he and I were doing business together. He supplied the wooden spear handles, while I fitted the metal tips. Arming our Umbri boys for battle.'

'You are right. We may all be hungry, but we are not at war.'

'How many will it be, my love?' asked the foundry man, the pleasantries over.

'Three.'

'Three! My, you must be in trouble my darling,' he said. 'What will they be?'

'Mars, a boy and a girl,' she said.

'Having trouble starting a family, are we? Or maybe your children are sick? As for Mars,' he continued. 'Everyone's asking for him these days. Hoping for protection of livestock and a better harvest next year. He'll cost you more.'

'How much?' Maria Celeste asked, frowning.

'For you my dear, a special price,' he said. 'One of this season's lambs.'

'That's daylight robbery,' Maria Celeste replied aghast, wishing Massimo had come with her to help negotiate. 'How about two hares?'

'Try the smelter down-river,' he said dismissively.

She turned to leave.

The metal man may have had the upper hand, but did not want to lose the business altogether. Nor was he going to tell the potential client, that he would be recycling an old bronze weapon he had found, rather than smelting new metal. Copper and tin were in short supply.

'Look, I'll cast an extra one- four in total- in exchange for a lamb. A healthy ewe. Final offer.'

'Alright,' she replied, after a few moments.

'What's the fourth to be. A cow? Lamb?'

'Another girl.'

Maria Celeste returned to the metal-worker a few days later as agreed, dragging a reluctant young ewe on a lead.

'Sorry, love. They're not ready yet. We've a backlog.'

'What? Came all this way with payment. Wait until I tell my husband.'

'You can tell your husband, but won't make any difference. We ran out of bronze. Come back after the next full moon. You can leave the lady sheep. A down payment.'

'What a nerve!'

She felt like slapping him in the face but instead, lost for words, she turned around and stormed off, pulling her bleating cargo behind her.

Massimo did join his wife on the next visit, with the precious exchange strapped to his back. They could not afford any more delays, as winter approached and the ritual site could be closed on a priestly whim. Especially if the weather was harsh. There was no sign of the owner, which was a relief as Maria Celeste had rehearsed what she would say to him and it was not pretty. Instead, they stood watching the smelter's young and dextrous apprentice as he modelled the votive offerings out of bee's wax, wrapping them in a clay mould and setting them to dry near the furnace. Once dried, he poured molten bronze from a small ladle into the top of each figure, before cooling them in water...

****

'It's getting lighter,' Massimo said, breaking her train of thought. 'Let's get going.'

Looking up, she noticed a break in the cloud. The mid-afternoon sun appeared, to reveal the summit covered in streaks of snow. As the grey mists receded she could see far into the distance in all directions. She could even make out her village below, next to the river Tiber.

The wind dropped and as they climbed the final stretch to the summit she saw a plume of smoke. The terrain levelled out to reveal a fortified settlement, with its embankment and a stone building at its centre. In ancient times it was a military outpost used to control the valley. Now in her more settled era, it was the local *Umbri* community's place of worship.

She could see that a family of hungry wild boar had been feeding the night before, turning over the earth with their snouts in search of bulbs, grubs and roots. The snow had gathered downwind of the lumps of earth, creating a landscape that reminded her of fish scales.

As they approached the entrance to the west, they saw a tethered cow with its owner standing nearby.

'He must be very wealthy, to afford such a conspicuous sacrifice,' said Maria Celeste.

'Maybe not. He might just be very desperate,' Massimo responded, teasingly. 'For a new wife for instance.'

'Massimo, sometimes your sense of humour fails you,' she said. Their mutual frustration with each other had surfaced once again. It was a growing shadow, trailing behind their everyday lives. Moments later, the high priest greeted them and ushered them past a room with a large rectangular stand built of stone slabs, still red with the blood of the last sacrifice. The three channels carved into the stand struggled to drain the coagulated liquid. He led them to an open space where a deep trench had been carved into the rock. This was where they would drop three precious bronze offerings, while the priest invoked Feronia the goddess of fertility, Minerva and Mars.

Maria Celeste kept the fourth figurine. It was a girl and it was to be her secret. She wanted something to worship, in private.

****

When they returned to the car it was almost dark. Aching legs and cold feet tingled as warmth seeped back into their veins.

'How's your knee?'

'Bruised I suspect. But no pain, thankfully.'

'What a relief,' said Massimo as they took off their jackets and walking boots. 'Hope there's no traffic. Two hours until the recitals.'

'Plenty of time, Massimo. What an adventure! Mother nature threw everything at us, didn't she? Driving snow as we climbed. A blue sky and sun to greet us at the summit.'

'*Anche porcini* for dinner!'

'*Non stasera*. Now put your foot down.'

Fastening her seat-belt, she felt a hard object in her fleece pocket.

'Where did that come from?' asked Massimo, looking at a finely polished bronze figurine in Maria Celeste's hand, moments later.

'I have no idea.'

'Maybe Sandra slipped it into your pocket, to surprise you,' Massimo ventured.

'Could be. I'll ask her.'

He started the engine and they began the drive home, winding down the hillside towards Umbertide. 'But I wasn't wearing my fleece in the museum, was I?' she said, rhetorically.

Chapter 11. La Peste Nera
1347 A.D.

Alessandro took his seat among other junior members of the *priori* in the *Palazzo Dei Priori*. There was an almost deafening din as members of this, the highest governing body of Perugia, assembled for one of their regular meetings.

Friends and allies embraced or shook hands warmly as they met. By stark contrast, greetings of members of the opposition were solicitous and contrived.

Alessandro had much to learn about the cliques and cabals amongst the *priori*, but he had known of two main factions since he was young. The first was political. It divided the chamber between those who believed Perugia should be allied to the Pope, whose symbol was the lion, and their opponents who strongly believed in Perugia's independence. Their symbol was the griffin. Among them hid the politically astute, whose allegiance shifted with the most favourable winds.

The second faction split the *priori* in accordance with their backgrounds. Members of the chamber were broadly-speaking, either the nobility or the common people, represented mainly by members of various guilds. At the moment, the griffins and the nobility were in the ascendant, which made Alessandro feel somewhat uneasy. He aimed to keep his cards close to his chest.

The presiding officer read the preamble in Latin, following which the meeting was convened. The official proceedings began with a senior *priori* reporting on the progress on routine municipal business approved at the last session. Including interruptions from the floor, this lasted for some time, during which Alessandro reflected on the agenda for the rest of the meeting.

'*Portale Maggiore.*' This was the new main entrance to the *Palazzo*. The *priori* would express their gratitude to its benefactors, the butchers' guild. He wondered what privileges they would be given in return. What he liked most about the doorway, were the sculptures of two lions and two griffins. Perugia's political ambivalence carved in stone monuments.

'*Cola di Rienzo-* tribune to the Roman people.' Alessandro still found it hard to believe, that a few months earlier the *priori* had voted to send ten ambassadors in support of this rebel, Cola di Rienzo, who had taken control of Rome with the view of unifying Italy. The Pope in the meantime, based in Avignon, could do little to counter this until he persuaded the French king to invade Rome. While it seemed to him a fine idea, to reunite Italy, he felt Perugia would be made to pay the price of this misjudgement.

'Mystery disease at Messina.' This really caught his eye. Why be reporting on an illness so far away, in Sicily?

****

'Buongiorno Alessandro, nice to see you,' Ornella said while giving Alessandro a hug. 'Come in. How was your first meeting of the *priori*?'

'Very noisy, which is normal I suspect. Is Giovanni in?'

'I think he is next door,' Ornella said, leading him past the family room where their three young children were playing, into Giovanni's practice.

'Would you care for something to drink?' she asked, as she turned to leave the two men alone.

'A glass of ale would be nice.'

'Make that two,' said Giovanni. 'Thank you, *amore*.'

Alessandro looked around the room. There was a narrow wooden table covered with a light woollen cloth and a sideboard with jars filled with leeches. On the wall behind Giovanni had proudly pinned his Physician's graduation certificate from the University of Bologna, dated 1344 A.D. Awarded after ten years of attending medical lectures and studying astrology and philosophy.

The most treasured of Giovanni's books were in a cabinet with a locked door. They were writings attributed to the followers of Hippocrates and Galen, on which medical practitioners still relied. As far as Alessandro understood, these blamed illness on an imbalance between the four elements and the four humours.

'Tell me, what are the celestial bodies saying right now?' Alessandro asked, looking at the astrology chart on the wall.

'They are quiet. The aspects of the planets are benign.'

'That's a relief.'

Alessandro turned to the other side of the room, to see shelves crowded with pestles, mortars and jars of dried herbs and liquid potions.

'Looks like Ornella's apothecary practice is doing well.'

'She is busier than I am. Taken over our back yard with her herb-garden. You know, she does have amazing results. Between you and me, her patients seem to recover faster than mine.'

'But blood-letting pays the bills, doesn't it? It is what the rich pay for. All you are missing is the barber-surgery practice and you cover all the medical fields under one roof.'

'I'm working on it- our twins are showing an interest in the macabre.'

'Like all boys. They can always seek an apprenticeship with my neighbour the barber-surgeon.'

'So, how did it go?' asked the doctor. 'Make any new friends?'

'Not yet.'

'Any revelations? Interesting motions? Controversial decisions?'

'Seemed quite routine. However, there was something serious discussed, which I need to raise with you.'

'Tell me.'

'There has been an outbreak of disease in the south. They say it arrived on a *Genovese* ship that berthed at Messina last October. When the port authorities realised most of the sailors on board were dead and that the survivors were seriously ill, they tried to refuse it entry. However, several men managed to make it to shore and within days illness spread through the town and surrounding countryside.'

'Where had the ship sailed from?'

'The Black Sea. Apparently, the *Genovese* were at war with the Mongols. The disease hit the Mongol army, who set about catapulting their dead into a port controlled by the *Genovese* to break the siege.'

'What precautions did the *priori* agree to take?' Giovanni asked.

'None. Cesare and his kind made sure of that. Except that it was agreed a leading physician would be asked to report on the disease at the next meeting.'

A short while later, after Alessandro had returned home to Livia and his family, Giovanni made a note in his diary.

'*October 1347 annus domini. Epidemic begins in Sicily. People dying in the streets. Symptoms include large buboes, black fingers and toes, high fever, vomiting blood. Spreading so quickly, could be airborne, passing from person to person.*'

****

'Ornella, please. Listen to me,' begged Giovanni.

There had been another meeting of the *priori*, where it was reported the epidemic had arrived by ship in Pisa, just a few days' journey away. It was now January.

'The people of Perugia are going to need my skills every bit as much as yours. You know that.'

'And the children? Livia's not taking any chances with hers. They are leaving for the Oddi castle near Trasimeno tomorrow. Alessandro says Perugia's gates might be shut any moment.'

'Alessandro is staying behind, presumably. No. I have made up my mind. We will be no safer from the disease at Maria Celeste's country home than here. You know how thousands died in the Sicilian countryside. *Amore*, I am sorry. If you stay, we all stay.'

Giovanni knew it was a lost cause. Ornella could be extremely stubborn. Selfishly, he preferred to have his family with him. He found it hard to understand how Alessandro could wrench himself from his.

'What about our staff? We should let them choose to leave if they want.'

'I've already spoken to them,' Ornella replied. 'They will probably leave, to stay with relatives in Spello.'

That night Ornella hugged Giovanni tight in bed.

'I'm scared,' she said.

'So am I.'

'Only God can save us.'

'Yes, I believe so.'

****

Panic had set in among the *priori*.

It was March and word had reached them that the epidemic had arrived in Florence. Now it was only a matter of days before it was among them in Perugia. If it wasn't already in the air. Giovanni was certain that messengers bore more than just news. They helped the plague, *la grande pestilenza*, to spread.

A meeting was hastily convened at the *Palazzo*. Numbers were down as many had already fled. They invited the Bishop of Perugia, four physicians including Giovanni and two undertakers. Instinctively, everyone in the gathering kept their distance. There was no back-slapping. No hand-shakes. No smiling faces. Just anxiety and thinly-disguised fear.

'It is God's punishment,' announced the bishop, heightening the alarm. He went on to say some prayers and blessed the *priori*.

After the bishop sat down, they listened to reports from the presiding officer on the progress from Pisa into Tuscany. They heard about the measures taken in Florence the previous autumn. The cleaning of streets, enforced isolation in homes, the banning of prostitutes and sick travellers.

Giovanni was then called to report on the symptoms and treatments applied by physicians in Pisa and Tuscany. Even the hardiest of *priori* turned white as sheets as they listened to the long list of symptoms. There was some light relief as he described some of the treatments, such as taking baths in vinegar or rose water, or applying quartered pigeons to lanced buboes. The greatest shock of all was hearing about the high mortality rate. That half the populations of some towns in Sicily had died- in the matter of a few weeks.

'Thank you. Now let's turn to civic matters,' announced a visibly-shaken *condottiero*, the head of Perugia's governing body. 'How do we control this beast?'

They debated whether to close the gates; whether to ban public gatherings; the boarding-up homes of the sick; how to gain control of and ration the town's food and water supplies; the collection of bodies; digging of mass graves; the stock of burial lime.

After five hours, the *priori* agreed on a list of emergency proclamations and municipal prohibitions to be enforced through Perugia.

'Should have done this long ago,' said Alessandro, as they walked to their respective homes afterwards.

'Not that those precautions helped the people of *Firenze*,' Giovanni observed. 'So many are dying, there is already a break-down in law and order.'

'You're right. What is the latest news from Massimo? Is he still locked-up in *Firenze* with fellow artists?'

'I've not heard anything.'

'He should have never taken that commission.'

****

Three weeks later Alessandro walked home feeling very despondent.

Hardly any *priori* had attended the last meeting. People were already dying of the plague in Perugia and there was hardly anyone about in the streets. He still had not heard from Livia. To add to the bleakness it had snowed a heavy, slushy snow. It never snowed in April. Why now? He slipped on a steep slope and landed on a patch of waste-water, thrown only moments earlier from a window four stories above. He cursed. The dark narrow alleys had become menacing, slippery vipers waiting to strike at the unwary.

Arriving home, he shed his wet cloak and set about lighting a fire. He sat down and suddenly felt a wave of exhaustion. He must have fallen asleep, as he awoke to see the fire had faded into red embers, surrounded by white ash. He shivered with cold and felt nauseous. Realising these were some of the early symptoms described by Giovanni, he felt under his armpits and between his thighs for large boils. Luckily, there were none. He had heard buboes could swell to the size of oranges, before bursting into streams of puss and blood.

Buboes or no buboes, Alessandro knew what followed next. With no time to waste, he lit two candles which he placed on his desk. He took his quill, dipped it into the inkwell and began writing on pieces of vellum and parchment. He wrote very short letters to Livia, one to his son and one to each of his two daughters. It took him a long time to compose them and even longer to write them in his faltering hand.

He restoked the fire and sat back down in the armchair, with only the glowing hearth for company. During the night he woke up several times vomiting and in the early hours of the morning, he coughed up blood. He went into a delirium and had the sense of floating in and out of reality. One moment he saw black fingers gripping the arm rest he thought might be his. The next those hands were catching flying flags to the sound of beating drums, with Livia watching him from among the crowd. An image of his fire re-emerged and he was back at home.

Suddenly, a soldier appeared in the room. He was carrying a metal helmet under his arm. Its transverse crest of white feathers reminded Alessandro of his friend, the fellow centurion from the Battle of Lake Trasimeno.

'I thought you might need some company Alexander,' he said.

'So, you made it through Hannibal's lines after all, Julius. How is your head?'

'My jaw still aches. But I forgave you long ago.'

****

'People have only just started dying in Perugia, but already the priests are too terrified to approach the sick to listen to confession. Or to administer last rites. Even doctors are refusing patient visits,' said Giovanni.

He and Ornella were in his practice, talking about how to handle the imminent wave of patients.

'I think we should do the same Gio. There really isn't anything medicine can do to save the sick. It's hopeless. We need to save ourselves and our children. God will forgive us. Giovanni please, let's board-up the practice and sit tight.'

Ornella had had quite a change of heart since the plague arrived.

Suddenly, there was some frenetic knocking on the door to Giovanni's practice. It was Alessandro's barber-surgeon neighbour.

'Giovanni, please come quickly. There has been no response from Alessandro's house for two days now.'

'Alessandro? Gio, you must go,' insisted Ornella, forgetting what she said moments earlier.

She was still distraught when Giovanni returned, a couple of hours later. It had been hard to hide her distress from the children.

'Did you find Alessandro? How is he?'

'Ornella, Alessandro has died. We found him slumped in a chair, dressed only in his underclothes.'

He continued talking, while keeping his distance.

'I tried to arrange for him to be buried in the cemetery and not the mass graves. We had his clothes burnt and the house was being boarded-up by carpenters as I left.'

'I am so deeply sorry *amore*, but I am going to live in isolation here in my practice, to protect you and the children from infection.'

Giovanni cried that night, as he was trying to get to sleep. Ornella sobbed too. She would now need to look after the children on her own. But at least they were under one roof together. They could talk to one another through closed doors.

****

That winter seemed endless to Livia. The cold was as relentless as the plague that stalked them. From her window on the first floor of Maria Celeste's family home, she had a view up the mountain behind. The window through which she watched a daily tussle. The fight between cold fronts from the east that draped the mountain in a white blanket of snow at night; and the warm sun that set about its removal the following afternoon.

For a long time there was no word from Perugia. Then came news of her uncle, Don Giuseppe, the first of the family to be taken from them. It was in a letter from a priest at the hospice that had cared for him since mental incapacity took hold. Shortly afterwards, she heard about Alessandro.

'Can we go for a walk today, *mamma*?' asked her youngest daughter, interrupting Livia's dark thoughts.

'What's the point of being in the countryside if we can't even play outside?' complained Vittoria, her middle daughter.

'How many times do I have to tell you? It is safer here in isolation. Let me read you another story.'

'Not another one, *mamma*,' they groaned.

'If I get the plague, I want to die on that mountain,' said her 12 year-old son suddenly.

'*Tesoro*. Don't ever let me hear you talk like that again. We are safe here. None of us are going to die. Do you hear me?'

'I heard you.'

'*Mamma*, can you read us *papà's* letters again?' asked Vittoria.

'No Vittoria. *Papa's* letters always make me cry,' said her younger sister.

Their daily tribulations followed much the same pattern for weeks on end. Until one day, spring arrived. With it, came a knock on the door of their apartment.

'Come everybody, let's go outside,' announced Maria Celeste. 'It is time to pick cherries!'

'Yeah!' they all cried, this time with delight.

As the children skipped along on the way to the cherries, they passed rows of olive trees in full flower.

'Did you know, these trees were here at the time of the *romani?*' said Maria Celeste.

The trees had grown very broad, in many cases splitting into multiple trunks, all sharing the same roots that tapped the fertile earth.

'They were planted by the owner of a *villa romana* that was built here,' she added.

'How do you know that?' asked Livia's son.

'Look carefully and there are signs everywhere. From some of the decorated stones in the walls of the castle. They would have been carved by *romani* stonemasons and reused by our builders. And look,' she said, while bending down. 'This bit of clay tile is *romano*. Pushed to the surface by the winter frosts.'

'Amazing,' said Vittoria. 'Now what about those cherries you promised us?'

As they walked Livia began to feel the plague had missed them. She even began thinking of returning to Perugia, to restart their lives.

Over time, life took on the semblance of normality. She and her children went on long walks on the mountain, often led by Maria Celeste who knew it so well.

Then in late May some of the cattle, sheep and other livestock began to fall sick. They were released into the countryside by farm workers, who themselves fell ill. Livia's son complained of headaches and dizziness. Panicking, she accompanied a servant down to the nearest village to call the local physician. When they returned, he too had disappeared.

Livia's son was eventually found, on a path up to the summit of the mountain, in a sheltered area of beech trees near a small quarry. His body had been partially eaten by animals and crows. They could see large buboes under his arms and some of his fingers and toes were black.

In all the commotion, no one realised that Livia's youngest daughter had also fallen ill. She died within three days of her brother's disappearance.

****

Spring had also arrived in Perugia. But apart from warmer temperatures, no-one noticed the change in season. The world had turned upside down. The poor raided the homes of dead nobles. They wore their clothes and ate their food. It was every person for him or herself. Death was so common, hardly anyone wept for those lost.

One day Giovanni's household ran out of luck. Ornella and her daughter developed the early symptoms of the plague. They shut themselves in a room in the house. One of the few remaining municipal workers came and painted a red cross on their front door. Within a few days, Ornella and her daughter both died.

Giovanni waited and waited for body collectors, listening for the jangles of the bells on the ankles. But they never came. So he carried his wife and daughter's bodies wrapped in blankets outside the city walls, to dig their graves with his own hands.

On the way, he tried to scare off the dogs and black crows feeding from piles of corpses in the streets.

****

'Is this the physician's home?' Lucrezia asked a passer-by, an elderly woman.

It was late August and the disease had ended.

'Do you mean the house belonging to Giovanni and his twin sons Stefano and Paolo?'

'Yes.'

'What a tragedy hit that family. Have you heard? Lost his wonderful wife and treasure of a daughter. Miracle the boys survived. Like you and me. Why was I spared? I would have exchanged mine for one of theirs.'

'And I would have too,' Lucrezia said. 'For Ornella.'

'Was she special to you? Oh, I am sorry my dear. You know there's hardly a good soul left in Perugia. Just all those beggars made rich from charging fortunes for digging mass graves. God bless you.'

Tears returned and rolled down Lucrezia's hollow cheeks as she quietly slipped a letter under Giovanni's front door. She then stood up and, raising her flowing maroon dress with her left hand, gently floated over the cobble stones down the winding alley towards one of the city's many gates.

PART II

'Far other scene is Thrasimene now;
Her lake a sheet of silver, and her plain
Rent by no savage save the gentle plough;
Her aged trees rise thick as once the slain
Lay where their roots are; but a brook hath ta'en
A little rill of scanty stream and bed
A name of blood from the day's sanguine rain;
And Sanguinetto tells ye where the dead
Made the earth wet, and turn'd the unwilling waters red.'

GEORGE GORDON, LORD BYRON
Childe Harold's Pilgrimage Canto IV, 1812 A.D.

Chapter 12. Wild Asparagus
1349 A.D.

Paolo opened the front door. His father had told them never to answer the front door when he was out, but he felt he was old enough to now. He was tough and was going to be a barber surgeon when he grew up. As was his twin brother Stefano. Noone and nothing was going to stop him answering the knock on the door.

'Paolo, what did *papà* say? Don't let anyone in! What are you doing?' shouted Stefano, as he approached him down the hall.

Stefano was brave like his brother, but not foolhardy. He knew gangs of brigands and looters still roamed the streets, day and night.

A tall, slender lady stood smiling before them. She was graceful like Maria Celeste. But auntie Celeste, as they knew her, had no wings. This lady had wings. Of this both boys were certain. So sure, they were prepared to swear with their hands on a bible in front of *papà* afterwards.

They both stood open-mouthed in the doorway, for what seemed an eternity.

The angel spoke first.

'Is your father at home?'

Both boys were too tongue-tied to respond. She may have spoken in a northern dialect, but they could both understand her question. Eventually Paolo re-gathered his composure.

'Are you the lady who wrote the letter?' he asked.

'I did write to your father, yes.'

'We've all read the letter you know,' said Stefano, wading in so as not to be left out.

'Stefano, come on. We are still learning how to read. It's *papà*. He reads it out aloud to us almost every day at breakfast.'

'Does he now?' she said, with eyebrows raised. 'So, if you are Stefano, this handsome young man next to you must be Paolo. Two handsome young knights. I am so pleased to meet you,' she said, with a delicate curtsy.

Both boys turned red in the face and were left speechless once again.

'Would you like to come in?' offered Stefano eventually, against his better judgement as they knew never to let a stranger into the house. Even an angel. '*Papà* is at a meeting in the *Palazzo*. But he should be back soon.'

'Stefano, how can you say that?' said his brother.

'Meetings of the *priori* can go on forever, I know Paolo. You must be proud of him,' said the angel.

'We are. But most of our friends' *papàs* that survived the plague are now *priori*. All the old ones died,' said Paolo.

'Please tell your *papà* Lucrezia came to say hello,' she said softly, keen not to be drawn into that subject of the pandemic, which pained even winged messengers from heaven.

Later that evening, the boys found themselves having to defend their claim they had been visited by an angel. Giovanni tried to introduce some intellectual rigour into the discussion, as he always did with his boys, whatever the subject. It was important to have an informed point of view. To base your opinion on facts, not conjecture. But in this case, he decided to tread delicately. He would not deprive his boys of their angel. He too, needed one in his life.

'How did she know you were a *priori* then?' Paolo argued. 'Unless she came down from heaven.'

'That's a good point. Except, as you know, word gets around. And there is that list inside the *Portale Maggiore*.'

'But we both saw her wings, didn't we Stefano?' Paolo said, changing tack.

Stefano nodded vigorously.

'Those wings, were they folded by her side?' their father asked.

'N..' began Stefano.

'Like a swan resting yes,' said Paolo, speaking over his brother. 'Except, when she left us.'

'Yes, when she turned to leave,' Stefano agreed, finally synchronising with his twin. 'She spread her wings.'

'And flew away. Were they white, like those of a swan?'

'Yes,' they replied, looking rather meek and sheepish at this point of the interrogation.

Actually, they were more cream-coloured, but that detail could wait.

'Look, I believe you both,' he assured them. 'Now, what did I say about opening that door?'

Both boys looked at their feet in shame.

'Next time, make sure you know who is on the other side. One of you needs to look down onto the street from above. Agreed? Alright, time for some supper.'

A while later, after a very simple dinner prepared by a new servant girl that lived nearby, he put the boys to bed. As they did every night, they knelt in a circle and recited their prayers while holding hands, taking it in turn to say prayers for their mother and sister in heaven.

'Did the angel give her name, by any chance?' Giovanni asked, after kissing them goodnight.

'Lucrezia,' they replied. 'Good night, *papà*. We love you.'

'Sleep well my brave knights.'

'The angel called us knights as well,' said Stefano.

'Handsome ones,' added Paolo.

About a week later the cardinal household rule was once again put to the test. There was a thump on the front door, which this time rather frightened the twins. It was far from the gentle knock of an angel.

'I'll go upstairs and see who it is,' offered Stefano.

'How about we both go, to be doubly sure. Then we both run down to open the door,' suggested Paolo.

They ran upstairs and opened a window that overlooked the narrow alley below. Peering out, they saw a man next to a small horse, a woman and a small girl.

'Who is it?' they shouted.

'Livia and Vittoria,' the woman said, looking up.

'We've brought you some wild asparagus,' said Vittoria. 'And some flowers.'

****

'We are almost ready to leave,' announced Maria Celeste. 'Have you collected your favourite flowers Vittoria?'

There would be no time to gather them the following morning as they planned an early departure, before the sun rose.

'I have, but *mamma* says they may not last the journey, didn't you *mamma*?' Vittoria said.

Livia was in another world, trying to fit the last items of clothing into the leather hide bundle. That world was a very dark place into which she allowed herself to retreat whenever there was an adult around to entertain her daughter. Many times she openly admitted to Maria Celeste, that only Vittoria kept her from falling off a precipice into the darkness.

'If you take a small vase from the kitchen and fill it with water they might,' Maria Celeste suggested. 'I'll ask our cook to set one aside for you.'

'Oh thank you Maria Celeste,' the little girl said, reaching up to give her a hug.

'Show me what you have picked.'

Vittoria ran to the room next door and returned with a huge bunch wrapped in a wet cloth.

'What have we here then? Yellow *ginestra*, red poppies and what else do I see?'

'Dog-roses and cornflowers. All *mamma's* favourites too, aren't they *mamma*?'

They were going to be a present for Ornella and Giovanni.

Noone in the room knew that Ornella had died, along with her daughter. But then, no one knew whether any of that family had survived either. Vittoria firmly believed they were all still alive and she could not wait to play with the children again. She dearly missed her brother and sister.

'Yes darling, my favourites too,' Livia said, emerging from the underworld to hug her daughter.

They were the same as those Vittoria had placed on her brother and sister's graves that afternoon, as they all said their goodbyes.

'I promise I will be back every year to talk to you,' Vittoria had said while she cried.

'That would be lovely,' said Livia. 'But you know, you can talk to them any time you want. They can hear you wherever you are.'

'Not just at bedtime prayers?' Vittoria had replied, before turning to Maria Celeste for affirmation. 'Really, is that true?'

'Of course, darling.'

They had given up waiting for Massimo's return from Florence. Livia feared the worst but Maria Celeste somehow knew he was alive and was convinced he would be back home in Perugia waiting for them.

'You must stay with us in Perugia,' Maria Celeste kept insisting, every time Livia mentioned how she could not bear the thought of returning to the house where her husband Alessandro had died.

'I'm going to sell the house,' Livia announced once. 'Gather our belongings and find somewhere new to restart our lives.'

Livia felt very awkward about the idea of staying in her former boyfriend's home. Not that she saw herself as a threat to their marriage. She did not think she cared for him romantically -at least, not in the way she used to as a teenager. It just did not feel right. After so much time apart, Massimo and Maria Celeste needed the space to be together, she reasoned. Then there was another perfectly rational voice inside her. One that spoke of her ambivalence towards the relationship between Massimo and Maria Celeste from the very beginning.

The reality was that Maria Celeste had not given these concerns a moment's thought. She in any event foresaw that Livia's stay would be temporary, that she would in time join a convent, as so many widows were now doing. Perhaps, if Massimo had not survived the plague, she too would end up in a convent. The two of them would become nuns together.

Moonlight suddenly bathed the room. Dogs began barking in the yard beneath the castle and the geese joined the alarm.

'I bet you that's Massimo,' said Vittoria.

All three of them hurried down to find Massimo in the central hall surrounded by castle staff. Maria Celeste's parents also emerged from the adjoining drawing room. There were cries of joy and hats were thrown high into the air in celebration. Noone had the heart to tell him about the recent losses (although he said he had known of Alessandro's death for some time), so as not to spoil the reunion. For about half-an-hour everyone in this spontaneous gathering milled about hugging each other and crying and laughing. Wine was brought up from the cellar and offered to all, from footman to count and countess.

Maria Celeste then intervened. She took her husband by the hand and started to lead him up the staircase, turning around on around the fifth step.

'I can't risk having anyone catching the Florentine flu,' she announced.

'A bit late for that!' replied a footman, who was on his fourth cup of red wine.

'See you at dinner,' her father called after her, winking. Which was most unlike him.

Livia meanwhile bent down to cover her daughter's ears from any further comments of a suggestive nature.

The couple did not make it to dinner, which hardly surprised anyone. All assumed the departure to Perugia was to be on hold.

Later that night, while Vittoria lay huddled next to her mother watching the moon's descent towards Lake Trasimeno she heard a moaning sound so loud, that it set off both the dogs and geese for a second time since uncle Massimo arrived.

The following day the couple did not emerge for breakfast, nor lunch even. There was an ominous quiet. A footman with a heavy hangover was sent to Maria Celeste's turret to wake them.

'Noone there, ma'am,' he said on his return to the dining room. 'Candles burnt through. Pools of wax on the floor and furniture. Very strange.'

Livia rushed up to see for herself, as did others.

'Must have left in the night.'

'But why didn't they take the cart and horse we had ready?'

As the mystery grew a dark, sombre mood descended onto the household. Livia went into an erratic spin, like one of those waterspouts occasionally seen on the lake. She accepted the kind offer of the horse and cart, as everyone apart from her seemed to be convinced that they would have left for Perugia, Massimo desperate for news of Giovanni and his family. She meanwhile thought they had gone up the mountain, to reunite with her son who had died there. So a search party was organised, and up they went high onto its slopes shouting for 'Maria Celeste' and 'Massimo' among the trees.

Vittoria refused to stay at the castle and joined them.

'What's this *mamma*,' she said, pointing at a thin green shoot that rose through the undergrowth.

'Looks like an asparagus,' Livia said.

'Can we pick some to take with us to Perugia?'

Stopping to gather her breath, Livia noticed they were surrounded by green shoots of wild asparagus with purple knobbly tips.

****

Giovanni saw the last patient for the day out of the practice and into the street.

'Can I come in?' asked Livia, who was standing in the room next door.

'I'm free, yes come in,' he said. 'Are you ready?'

Livia entered the room to see Giovanni cleaning some medical instruments, before placing them in a drawer.

'Ready as I'll ever be.'

'I have a carpenter and his assistant standing by to take down the hoarding. You do want to see the house first, don't you?'

Her house was still boarded-up, left untouched for about a year.

'I don't know if I will have the strength.'

'Of course you will. I'll be by your side. We'll be together.'

She looked at him gratefully.

'You have been so kind to me and Vittoria. We weren't even supposed to be here Gio.'

'Livia, you have transformed our lives here since your arrival. The boys are so happy.'

'Vittoria too. But we will leave you in peace when Massimo eventually turns up,' Livia said. 'He will return won't he?'

'I believe he will. I think Maria Celeste just wanted to whisk him away, to have him all to herself for a while.'

'You think they are still alive? That makes me feel better. Stronger too. I've decided.'

'Decided what?'

'Let's visit Alessandro's grave first. Where you had him buried.'

'Shouldn't we take Vittoria too?'

In the end both the whole household, including the boys, walked hand-in-hand to the spot where Alessandro was buried.

****

The angel did return. This time it was Vittoria who answered the door, as everyone was home and it was safe to do so.

'And who might this little cherub be?'

'My name is Vittoria,' the cherub replied.

'She is Alessandro and Livia's daughter,' said Stefano, first of the boys on the scene.

'I thought as much. You my darling, are more beautiful than those boys are handsome.'

'Thank you,' she said.

'And her *mamma* is staying with us too,' said Paolo, butting-in.

'Aren't you lucky boys. Now, tell me, is your father in?'

'Yes, he is in his practice. Do you have an appointment?' asked Stefano.

'Are you his assistant?' the angel asked, light heartedly.

'We both are,' Paolo answered.

'Well then, yes I do. But not a medical one. The other day, when I bumped into your *papà* outside the *Palazzo*, he said he would take me to see where your *mamma* and sister are buried.'

'We can take you,' offered Paolo.

'I'd love that. But I do not want to be in your father's bad books would I?'

'No, that would be terrible,' lamented the boys.

'Why don't we all go together?' said Vittoria, breaking the impasse.

'What a clever girl you are,' said the angel.

They could not help but notice that Giovanni blushed when he came out of his practice to greet Lucrezia. Or that he held his arm around her while she cried standing over her best friend Ornella's grave. Or that afterwards, on the walk back home, their angel reached out to hold his hand.

'I didn't know angels could cry,' Stefano said afterwards.

Chapter 13. The Goddess of Dawn
127 A.D.

Maria Celeste led Massimo by the hand up the tight round stone staircase of the turret to her bed chamber.

'You must be exhausted.'

'Not a bit. I am so excited to see you.'

They kissed and fell into each other's arms onto her four-poster bed. At first they just held each other, looking deep into each other eyes smiling, tears streaming onto linen pillows. Selfishly, for a few precious moments they thought only about themselves. They made love almost fully clothed, hurriedly, as if the plague might return and envelope them at any moment. They climaxed together, so loudly they could be heard far into the still night.

They were alive once more.

'What's this?' Massimo asked as they lay pressed against each other afterwards. He reached into one of her pockets to find a miniature metal sculpture. He sat up and rested the object on the palm of his hand. In the candle-light, he could see that it was a young girl cast in bronze.

'That's our good luck charm,' his wife replied.

'You and your pagan worship!'

'Well it worked, for us at least.'

Now was the time to give him the news that had never reached him in Florence. Of all the lives shattered in their small circle of closest friends. She was dreading it. It took Massimo several hours to fall asleep, his head a revolving maze of disturbing images. The worst was seeing Livia becoming a recluse in a convent. The fate of so many widows.

****

Massimo awoke early. A cockerel was crowing in the yard, announcing another dawn.

'We forgot to blow out the candles again,' he said, while wiping the sleep from his eyes. 'What a waste.'

Molten beeswax had solidified in pools around their votive offerings next to their straw mattress. The bronze figurine he had found the previous night, alongside small clay idols of Jupiter and Mars.

'Never mind that,' replied Maria Celeste as she stirred into wakefulness, stretching her arms in a deep yawn. 'Let's get going. We have a busy day ahead.'

'It is the same every day, with you in charge of the kitchens,' said Massimo. 'What are my instructions today?' He knew perfectly well what his orders were, but enjoyed creating the impression of his forgetfulness.

'Ice from the top of the mountain. Then tomorrow, fish from *lacus trasimeno*.'

'Are all Britons as demanding as you?'

'Some are, yes. Are all Dacians as lazy as you, Maximus?'

'You deserve punishing for that,' he responded, reaching out an arm to drag her onto the mattress. But she was quick and evaded his grasp. Even though she was heavily pregnant.

'It took two long wars to subjugate us. Your tribe of Britons were a walk-over.'

He instantly regretted his comment.

'Sorry! Please ignore what I said,' he pleaded, as she marched across the tiled courtyard to the kitchens, scattering chickens and ducks before her.

While Massimo was a second-generation slave, Maria Celeste was the first of her people to be enslaved. Brought back by her master, who helped quell a rebellion in *Britannia* on behalf of Emperor Hadrian. The welt on her forehead was still so fresh by comparison to his, it almost glowed red. 'Tax Paid' was the inscription. Most of the slaves on the estate tried to hide their welts with head-scarves, although it was forbidden to do so by law. Unless they were freed.

Massimo walked across to the kitchen for some bread. He tried to speak to his wife, but she was busy.

'Why don't you accompany me up the mountain?' he asked hopefully, knowing she planned a foraging expedition. 'I know where the best wild asparagus are.'

She had started talking about the dishes she would prepare for the weekend's visitor. Massimo guessed patina of asparagus, a sort of egg custard, was likely to be on the menu.

'See you tomorrow,' she said firmly.

'As you wish,' said Massimo, resigning himself to a short period of purgatory.

Perversely, he was pleased about this reaction he had provoked. But he wished she spoke more about her past, rather than keep it deeply hidden. His parents had always spoken about their home village in Dacia, to keep memories alive, their customs and rituals. By contrast, his wife's past remained a mystery to him. She had adapted to her new life remarkably quickly.

A couple of hours later, Maximus was leading his mules along a path that wound between small beach trees. His three companions were some way behind him. He could see that spring had arrived several days later at this altitude. Infant leaves were just starting to protrude from the buds which protected them from winter's cold. To the left he saw the cliff faces of white jagged rock, the same stone they quarried and chiselled into blocks used to build the walls of the huts that now came into view. Stone buildings with thatched roofs that sheltered him, fellow slaves and other visitors periodically through the year.

They were used as temporary homes during the summer logging season. In the autumn they might be occupied by hunters, including overnight visits by his master, his guests and friends. They also offered a welcome sanctuary during the coldest weeks in winter, when they stayed on the mountain to replenish the ice house a few hundred metres away.

He thought about his wife and the child she was carrying.

'Now, do you believe in my lucky charm, Massimo?' Maria Celeste had said, a few months earlier when her bump first became noticeable.

'I am beginning to,' he had replied. Both had been so elated.

Then he thought about his doubts and the fights he caused.

'How can you believe you are not the father?' she had implored him.

'I know the master covets you. You are his most precious possession. Why did he make you head of the kitchen, before you could even speak Latin?'

'How many times do I have to tell you before it sinks into that stubborn head of yours? The villa's head chef died suddenly. He recognised my talents,' Maria Celeste replied. 'There is nothing more to it. Come on Maximus, why are you trying to kill our relationship like this?'

'Well, why is the master involving himself in the kitchens? It is not a man's place, certainly not an army commander's,' Massimo had persisted. He could not help himself.

Just then Massimo drew up alongside the ice house. As he was waiting for his colleagues, he remembered taking part in the construction; laying the stone floor, building the walls shaped into a dome as they rose, leaving a large hole in the roof for access. The site was a large natural hollow just above the treeline, located at the foot of a bowl in which large drifts of snow accumulated. Driven by north-easterly winds. After heavy snowfalls he and his team would shovel the purest snow into large baskets, which they would carry on their backs with padded handles resting on their foreheads. Once tipped onto the ice below, the men would stamp on the snow, as they would grapes in a later season, compacting it into ice before covering the area with straw. It was cold work and their feet froze.

The rest of his team arrived. Without delay, they began carving large blocks of ice. These they loaded onto the mules, packed in canvas bags stuffed with straw. They hardly spoke at all. Apart from Massimo, they had mastered only rudimentary Latin. One was from Anatolia and the other from the lands that were once home to the Carthaginians. Three hundred years earlier, Massimo was told.

'Time for *prandium*,' said Massimo, after an hour of hard work. No need to translate those welcome words. The kitchens had packed roasted chick-peas, white bread, cheese and olive relish. Massimo's bundle included sliced *lucanicae*, which he shared with his fellow muleteers.

She still cares for me, thought Massimo, as he savoured the sausage meat. This was food fit only for the *Dominus* and his family. Certainly not slaves.

'No time to waste. Can't have the master's ice melting can we?' Massimo said while rising to his feet.

The men led the mules and their heavy cargoes downhill. Massimo took short detours along the way to check the animal traps. They were empty but that did not worry him. The larder was filled with fawns and hares he had caught earlier. As they neared the bottom of the mountain, one muleteer turned towards the villa. The other three, including Massimo, headed for the lake.

****

'Maximus, is that you?' she said, in a startled voice. 'Maximus?'

Maria Celeste had lost track of time, and was now quite high up the mountain. She imagined it could be close to the ice house.

There was no reply. But the voices continued, one moment present and close, their echoes bouncing off the bark of the trees; the next muffled by the rustling undergrowth. They appeared to be calling a couple of different names, repeatedly.

'I'm here! I'm here, don't worry. Just got a little carried away foraging,' she shouted. As the voices began to fade into the distance, she looked down and spotted her first asparagus. A green shoot rising a few centimetres from the dark fertile earth. She saw another spear that had risen from the same underground root system, or crown. Then a third. She was in luck. There were still wild asparagus in season. Those forest spirits had come to her rescue.

It was not every day that she was asked to feed an Emperor.

But now that she had found more than enough asparagus, she was beginning to feel more at ease. Earlier, she and her two kitchen boys had collected a basket full of wild strawberries she spotted hiding in the thick undergrowth of the lower slopes. She had sent the boys back with these and baskets filled with cherries from the trees behind the villa.

Clutching her full baskets as she headed downhill, she began rehearsing what she would prepare with her foraged delicacies.

The asparagus would be ground in a mortar with onions, coriander, lovage and pepper. She would add olive oil and white wine, breaking eggs over the top before baking the mixture in the dome-shaped oven.

She planned to scatter the strawberries on *sprias*, slices of thin pastry containing crushed nuts and sweetened with honey. She would also try something new, making full use of Massimo's ice. It involved making a strawberry puree sweetened with honey. Once cooled in a bath of ice she would add iced milk, blending the mixture into a pink creamy paste.

As for the cherries...

'The *prunus avium*. Do you know, we should thank the general Lucius Lucullus for this delicacy. Brought them back from his conquest of *Anatolia*,' her master had told her, on one of his frequent visits to the kitchen.

'I did not know this *Dominus*,' she replied meekly, avoiding eye contact.

'This fruit,' he added, reaching for a peach from within a bowl she carried, 'follows our conquests in *Parthia*.'

'Now, that I had been told,' she answered, as he moved uncomfortably close to her. She could understand why Massimo had grown so jealous. Especially as he was away so much with his mule train.

****

'What have you got for me today then?' asked Massimo, as he tied up his mules outside the fisherman's home. There were a collection of nets hanging from tall wooden poles, drying in the sun. Behind them some willow trees, then a band of reeds which hid the lake from view.

'Depends, how much ice have you brought me?' said the fisherman, sitting hunched over a net he was mending. He hardly looked up, but he knew who it was and welcomed the idea of a short break from the monotony of this daily task. One that gave him lower back pain and a stooped posture of one much older than this 32 year-old father of seven.

'Enough for you to fill a whole wagon of frozen fish.'

'Ah, we are in business then,' he said as a smile returned to his face after a leave of absence. 'Let me show you what fish I have.'

While Massimo's colleagues unloaded the heavy blocks of ice, they walked across to some basins in the shade of a shelter made of dried reed poles.

'Well, here are the perch. Caught this morning. And over there the sand smelt, just as requested.'

The fisherman's wife appeared from inside their home, surrounded by a shoal of children of all ages with hardly a stitch of clothing between them, one refusing to detach from a mountainous breast as Massimo was caught in a suffocating embrace.

'How's that beautiful wife of yours? Not long to go now is there? How many months- two, three?'

'About that,' he said, recovering. 'By the way, she wanted me to give you her special greetings and thanks you again for the cooking lessons you gave her.'

'It was our pleasure,' said the fisherman's wife, beaming. 'Is she going to try my recipes on Emperor Hadrian, then?

'You heard?' said Massimo, taken by surprise.

'Of course!' she replied. 'Everyone knows Hadrian is taking a slight detour from his trip north to meet your master. Maria Caelestis told us how close they were in *Britannia*.'

'Now back to business. I have masses of *garum* for Maria Caelestis. It's just come in, the finest fish paste from *Hispania*. As well as fish roe. Very lucky to get that, you are.'

'Can you throw in some carp. For us slaves?'

'Just this once,' she winked. 'Especially as I hear you have lots of ice for us.'

'Thank you. Yes, we brought half the ice house.'

'While they are packing your fish, let's go in and settle up. I've got some fish soup for you and your friend.'

'Thank you! You always spoil us. Let me take a quick dip in the lake first.'

Massimo took off his sandals and shirt waded into tepid green water among the reeds. He felt the mud ooze between his toes. A snake swam idly by, which rather alarmed him. Once he passed the reeds he was chest deep in water that stretched almost to the horizon. He immersed himself fully and exhaled slowly, watching a stream of bubbles breaking the surface above him.

As he returned to the shore, he saw a group of boys splashing through the water. They were driving frightened fish into concentrated groups. Fishermen waited nearby for their arrival, some standing in the water, others in small wooden boats, all eager to cast their weighted nets to envelope their catch.

****

Hadrian was enjoying riding alone. Actually, he was never really on his own. Some of his personal praetorian guard rode a discrete distance behind him, while others rode ahead to clear the way. But at least they were out of earshot, far enough away to let him indulge in thought. To reflect on the important affairs of Rome.

He was grateful to have left his mobile government, that noisy and very needy retinue of administrators and advisers that accompanied him throughout the empire, behind in Perugia.

Hadrian was at his creative best when on horseback. He remembered the long hours riding behind Trajan during his military campaigns in *Dacia* and elsewhere on the eastern fringes of the Empire. When he began harbouring doubts about the sustainability of some of the recent conquests. Secretly, he had vowed if he were to succeed Trajan he would order the withdrawal from *Parthia*, marking a period of consolidation of the Empire along more defendable frontiers. The idea of building a wall across northern *Britannia* to mark the edge of the Roman Empire also came to him while he rode. The message to the barbarians to the north would be clear: keep out. Furthermore, it would be cheaper to patrol the border with a manned wall, than to maintain a large army in the north.

Now here he was riding to share his latest plans for government with one of his closest confidants on the *Britannia* campaign. Who had helped the governor of *Britannia* Quintus Falco quell the rebellion.

The Emperor wanted to divide Italy into four regions, each with its own governor. He would ask his opinion on his choice of governors from among a list of former consuls, the first of which he was on his way to appoint in the north of Italy. Clearly, this devolution of power would not sit well with the Senate back in Rome. But it was in line with the belief that the best way to maintain this great empire, was to bind the mass of peoples with a sense of belonging and common culture and to give them, under the watchful eye of Rome, a degree of self-autonomy.

Hadrian combined his idealism with a strong dose of pragmatism. He would purchase his people's loyalty. This required heavy investment in new buildings that propagated Roman culture, with the construction of lavish temples, theatres, sporting coliseums and public baths. He invested heavily in infrastructure, in the roads that tied his peoples together, the aqueducts that would water their crops and perimeter garrisons that would protect them from Rome's enemies. He had made it his ambition to travel ceaselessly throughout his empire to implement this plan.

Lulled by the motion of his horse, he began feeling drowsy. His thoughts turned to his Hellenic lover, Antinous.

How he wished he could join him in Italy. He would make sure Antinous would accompany him on the trip he planned to Egypt, when he would begin by paying homage to Pompey by restoring his tomb. In truth, Antinous had given him a renewed energy and sense of purpose, as being constantly on the road was beginning to tire him. He thought he might be falling ill, but kept this very quiet.

Hadrian continued to fantasize about his lover in short interludes between thoughts of matters of empire, when he came into sight of the villa.

****

Maria Celeste walked along the peristyle, the covered porch that surrounded the villa's central courtyard. She could hear the gentle sound of the fountains fed by a spring on the mountain behind. She smelt the sweet fragrance of the jasmine plants that wound their way around columns supporting the tiled roof. Statues of various gods adorned the yard, scattered between rows of lavender that had yet to flower.

In her hand she held a scroll with the menus for Emperor Hadrian's visit. She was grateful her master's wife agreed to her idea of focusing on recipes drawn from local produce and inspired by regional cuisine. She was therefore spared the trouble of preparing stuffed dormice, always a favourite among the ruling class, or serving roast peacock.

As she stepped into the *tablinum* opposite the entrance to the villa, she walked across a mosaic of black and white tiles. It depicted dolphins, tuna and other exotic sea life that surrounded the god Neptune bearing his trident at its centre. The walls were covered with frescoes, mainly of rural scenes with animals and birds that lived in the surrounding countryside. On the eastern wall, there was a very prominent portrait of Aurora, the goddess of dawn. It had only recently been commissioned and most embarrassingly, it bore a striking resemblance to her.

'*Servus*, is everything in order?' asked the mistress of the villa. 'We are expecting the Emperor to arrive any moment.'

Maria Celeste suspected, as did all the slaves, that her mistress was as nervous and excited about this momentous occasion as they were. That her imperious nonchalant air was but an act. They had all seen how she had changed since the announcement of the visit, proudly doting over a husband whom she had treated as a meddlesome pain since his return from Britannia, even forgiving him it seemed for bringing Maria Celeste into their lives and for promptly elevating her role to chef of the household.

'Yes *Domina*. The gods have been kind to us. I have brought you the list of dishes for the main feast, the *cena*,' she said, handing her a scroll.

Her mistress began reading. 'Let's see. The *Gustatio*. All based on local produce, as we agreed. Accompanied by *conditum paradoxum*. Good.' The mistress was very partial to spiced wine. 'Can you add some *lucanicae*?

'Yes certainly, *Domina*.' Luckily, Maria Celeste had not given all the sliced sausage to Massimo and his ice collectors. She was relieved, the fish soup, deep-fried sand smelt and patina of asparagus were all approved. Now for the main course.

'*Mensae Primae*. Perch roasted on reed embers. Fine. Saddle of hare with wine sauce. One of the *Dominus's* favourites. Roast duck with hazelnut crumb coating. Yes. Can you add another legume dish?'

They agreed on lentils, prepared with coriander seed, mint, rue and honey.

'And don't forget the cabbage.'

'Of course not, *Domina*.' Maria Celeste knew the Romans believed cabbage was the ultimate cure for hangovers.

'Finally, the *Mensae Secundae*. *Libum* and *spria* served with *passum*.'

Maria Celeste planned to serve the cheesecake with cherry sauce. If it worked on the day, the wild strawberry and honey iced cream would be served as a surprise.

'That will be all, thank you,' the mistress said, dismissing Maria Celeste.

****

'This is our chef,' said her master, proudly presenting Maria Celeste to Emperor Hadrian.

She stood fearfully in front of a middle-aged man of around 50. Here she was, a former enemy, a mere slave standing in front of a demi-god. Leader of the greatest empire of all time. One reputed to have a temper fiercer than that of Jupiter.

'Maria Caelestis. That is a heavenly name. What a talent you possess too,' the Emperor said, congratulating her warmly.

'*Imperator*,' she answered, while bowing deeply. 'Thank you.'

'I hear you are from *Britannia*. That you have adapted very quickly to life here. I commend you,' the Emperor said.

'*Imperator*,' she repeated, at a loss for words.

'With child I see,' he added, noticing her bulging tunic.

Maria Celeste's face reddened.

'Who is the lucky husband?'

She was taken totally off-guard. An Emperor taking a personal interest in a slave?

'His name is Maximus. His family were originally from *Dacia*, brought across at the time of Trajan,' she replied, this time finding the courage to respond.

She rose and found herself looking at him inadvertently in the eye. There was no sign of an irascible nature. The burdens of state seemed to have aged him, leaving his forehead scarred with furrows. He had a full head of grey curly hair, while his closely shaved beard still retained darker hair of youth. His skin looked faintly yellow, perhaps the cumulative effect of being on the road. She had heard he was seldom in Rome or resting at his villa in Tivoli. If he was indeed ill, he hid it well.

'What music you bring to my ears. It is what I strive for,' Hadrian pronounced, while addressing all those present in the room. 'To create a single family of people, all living peacefully under my benign rule.'

'I propose a toast to our *Imperator*. To *Imperator Caesar Traianus Hadrianus Augustus*!' said the host, sensing the moment was right.

'And to *Senatus Populousque Romanus*,' added Hadrian.

All the guests sat up from their reclining positions to toast to Hadrian and to *SPQR*, while kitchen slaves topped-up their goblets with sweet raisin wine using silver ladles.

'You may not know,' said Hadrian, after thanking his host. 'But I was brought up by a nanny from *Germania*. She had the purest soul. I freed her when I became *Imperator*. I believe all slaves should be able to earn their freedom through devotion to their *Domini* and to *Roma*.'

'My wife Vibia and I were not able to conceive children. So treasure yours,' Hadrian continued, looking once more at Maria Celeste. She thanked him, curtsied and withdrew from the room.

As she left, she passed by a line of musicians with flutes and lyres, as well as dancing girls and young male acrobats, all slaves like herself.

'Bring them in,' called the host. The entertainment was about to start.

****

Maria Celeste knew the day was near when the night sky turned green. Curtains of green hung from the heavens in between patches of pink.

Many thought that it was a poisonous rain falling from invisible clouds and ran indoors for shelter. But not a single drop of water fell to earth, green or otherwise. Domesticated animals shuffled nervously in their pens and sheep gave birth early. Premature lambs unable to stand up to suckle their mothers would die in their hundreds in the coming days.

The gods had not behaved in this manner in recorded history. Priests struggled to attribute the phenomena. It was unlikely to be Jupiter, god of the sky, as he kept watch during the day. But perhaps he had an axe to grind with Nox, the goddess of the night, wanting to claim the night his own? After all, he was the god of all gods. He might have fed Nox something that violently disagreed with her and made her ill. Then it might have been Erebos, the god of darkness, striking green with envy at the thought of Jupiter making advances on his Nox?

Fearful she would lose the precious bundle inside her, Maria Celeste retreated to her room in the slave quarters and told Massimo she refused to work again in the kitchen until her baby arrived.

'Giovanni would have been able to explain all of this. Where is he?' she asked her perplexed husband.

'Who is Giovanni? What a strange name,' he replied. 'Anyway, how would he know any better than us?'

'Your best friend we left behind. With Livia and Ornella and all the others. How could I do that, bring just the two of us here?'

She began to swear and shout at the bronze figurine for the first time.

'I told you that figurine was cursed. We should have traded it long ago,' he said, sympathetically. 'Or just thrown it away.'

'Never!' she replied, throwing him a piercing glance. He had never seen daggers in her blue eyes before.

Maria Celeste became overloaded with emotion and began crying, which Massimo had never witnessed before either. She never cried about anything, not even separation from her whole family and homeland in *Britannia*.

'Where is Sandra when I need her? I haven't seen her for so long,' she said, in between sobs.

Another strange name he had never heard of. He became convinced it was something to do with the green sky. Her mind had been poisoned.

'Look, sweat-heart, I will go and find the mistress tomorrow to tell her you are unwell. I will make sure your assistants prepare breakfast.'

'Thank you,' she said, while squeezing his hand.

The tears kept flowing, as multiple losses from another age overwhelmed her incomprehensibly. She did not know where the names Giovanni, Livia or Ornella came from, or why she had said he could understand what was happening in the night sky, or what she meant about leaving them behind. It just sprung from her subconscious. From an inner self cocooned deep inside her, one that knew exactly why the sky had glowed green. That it was a global aurora resulting from a massive solar flare.

But she did now firmly believe in the magic of her little figurine.

Massimo sat up almost all night holding her in his arms, until she eventually fell asleep. It was only when he saw the first hints of daylight in the east, that he in turn drifted off, comforted by the knowledge the goddess of dawn would ensure a return to normality.

The following morning Maria Celeste rose, splashed some cold water onto her face and left for the kitchen, as if nothing had happened.

When the day actually arrived, the baby was late. So late in fact, that when Maria Celeste's waters broke, Massimo was high up Monte Tezio laying traps.

'You will send a boy running up to tell me, won't you?' he had said, worry written in his face, etched in lines across his forehead.

'Of course I will. Where will you be- by the limestone cliffs?'

'Yes, beneath the ice house. Are you sure, sure, sure?'

'Maximus, we need more game. The larder is almost empty.'

'But I can send one of the muleteers.'

'You could, but remember what happened the last three times you did so?'

'They returned empty-handed.'

'Yes, so off you go,' she said, dispatching him with a brief kiss on his lips, and a purposeful pat on the bottom.

Later that morning her baby started to move.

'Now, don't you play any tricks on me. You kept us on tenderhooks so long. It is your turn to see what it's like. Wait until your father is back. It's an order!' she instructed, while preparing the ingredients for a hare stew.

'But slaves can't issue orders,' reminded her kitchen boy, who had been listening to her talk out aloud to her baby since the morning after the green night. At times, he even answered on the baby's behalf, trying to project his voice onto her stomach like a ventriloquist.

'Oh yes I can- go and fetch the last two hares from the storeroom. Now, before I get angry.'

Her baby must have thought anger most unbecoming of mother, for that instant there was an ominous splash on the orange tiled floor, following which Maria Celeste doubled-over in pain. The sharpest pain she had ever felt. She curled up in a ball and lay paralysed on the floor.

'On second thoughts, go and fetch Maximus. You know where to find him,' she groaned. He was a fit lad who had often accompanied Massimo on his hunts. He knew the mountain well.

'Yes *archimagirus*,' he said, suddenly looking very timorous. He ran from the kitchens and went straight to the slaves' quarters to raise the alarm.

'Help, help!' the boy shouted. 'The baby's arriving. Maria Caelestis needs you. She's in the kitchen.'

'About time,' said the household midwife, as she reached for the bedding and cloths that lay in wait for this moment. 'Here, take this pail and fill it with clean water from the spring. Then warm some on the fire.'

'But I am supposed to warn Maximus.'

'He can wait,' she said dismissively. 'His fault for not being here.'

About half-an-hour later Maria Celeste she was squatting on a pile of sheets with a woman slave holding each arm. The midwife stopped issuing orders to all and sundry, and started to focus on the birth.

'It's in a hurry. Look, I can see the little head already,' said the midwife.

'Is my baby green?' Maria Celeste managed to ask, in between pangs of pain.

'Looks normal to me. Dark hair.'

'What a relief!' Maria Celeste said, managing to smile.

There had been rumours among the slaves, that Maria Celeste had something to do with the green night. Some were even convinced she was deity, or at least the progeny of one of the gods. They were so busy procreating with humanity it was hard to tell who might a demi-god or demi-goddess. How else could you explain the sudden arrival of this majestic woman slave from a foreign land, her lightning-quick promotion to head chef and her audience with the mighty Emperor of Rome?

But others subscribed to less fanciful reasoning. That she was simply the apple of the master's eye.

'Come on darling, time to push,' urged the midwife. 'Extra hard. In case the child has second thoughts.'

The baby did seem to be slowing its entry into the world, and Maria Celeste was by now gasping for breath in between loud shouts of pain. A fourth woman in attendance began mopping her brow with a cloth she dipped into the bowl filled by the kitchen boy. He had been finally dismissed and was running as fast as he could to reach Massimo.

The shouts began to crescendo and now everyone in the room was providing encouragement. They couldn't wait to see if it was a boy or a girl.

Maria Celeste dug deep inside and found the energy for one last big push, accompanied by the loudest noise anyone had ever heard. Louder than the blast of a Jovian lightning bolt. Shock waves bounced around the room, then emerged through the stone walls and thundered up the mountain behind, followed by an almighty gust of wind that almost blew Massimo off his feet. As well as the kitchen boy, who had yet to reach him.

'That can only be my wife,' Massimo said, grinning broadly to himself. Now empty-handed, as he had just laid the last trap, he charged headlong down the mountainside, oblivious to the slippery pine needles and jagged stones that conspired to send him flying with every step.

'Now, tell me she's not normal,' challenged one of the women in attendance below, breaking the silence that followed.

This prompted a protest from the baby, who began to cry. The midwife began issuing orders again and they set about cleaning mother and child.

First to arrive on the scene, standing in the open doorway, was the master himself. All inside bowed to him and in further show of obeisance, he was handed the baby, freshly wrapped in swaddling clothes.

'What do we have here? A beautiful baby girl!' he said.

****

'What name will you give her?' said the Roman mistress, paying a rare visit with her husband to Maria Celeste's new home on the periphery of the estate. Massimo was away once again on the mountain behind.

'Good morning, *Domina*. We cannot decide,' she replied, bowing instinctively as if she were still a slave. Even though she and Massimo had been granted their freedom two months earlier.

'How about Aurora,' suggested her master. 'After all, she arrived at the dawn of your new lives.'

Maria Celeste blushed at the thought of her portrait in the villa's most important room. It would upset Massimo too.

'She is not deity,' the mistress declared dismissively, still suspicious of her husband's possible infidelity. In fact, she wished she had come alone.

'Well, what about Aurelia?' her master persevered.

'After Julius Caesar's wife? How could you suggest that hallowed name?'

As their disagreement escalated, as they often did now that the excitement of Hadrian's visit had subsided, Maria Celeste retreated into her own world of thought.

She quite liked the name Aurelia. It meant golden. Her golden daughter. A much more suitable colour than green.

Chapter 14. The Bureaucrat
Near Future

It was market day and Umbertide was very busy. Even though it was early December and there was a distinct chill in the air. Locals were out shopping, winding their way around large groups of migrants that milled about dejectedly. Their numbers seemed to grow exponentially every week.

'Forget Climate Change, it's a bloody Climate Calamity,' Sandra mumbled to herself, remembering the days she was a pink-haired protestor halting traffic. At least she stopped short of allying with those frightening political ideologues that helped pave the way for the new world order. One led by dirigiste regimes set on controlling the globe.

She took out her key chain and opened the announcements cabinet. Removing an advertisement for an old musical event in the main *piazza* to make room for hers, Sandra pinned a colourful promotional poster for the museum in its place. It had taken hours of committee meetings to approve her design for the poster, which all had agreed was necessary. Footfall numbers were still well below those visiting the *Museo di Santa Croce* before the Covid epidemic.

As she discarded the old poster in a nearby recycling bin, a short barrel of a woman barged past imperiously. It was Vincenzia. The living embodiment of that scourge afflicting everyone's life called bureaucracy. What an apt name Sandra thought, for a caste that issued diktats on the smallest aspects of daily life from behind barriers of desks.

'Be more careful!' Sandra remonstrated, as she watched an unmoved Vincenzia enter the newly restored local government headquarters in the 17th Century *Palazzo Comunale*.

'I saw that. *Che stronza!*'

Sandra turned around to see her friend Giulia, who she greeted enthusiastically with a hug and a kiss on both cheeks. Almost as if she had been expecting her to be someone else. But Maria Celeste was not around. She had vanished mysteriously. As she did, periodically.

'That promotion has gone to her head,' Giulia continued. Vincenzia had indeed recently been appointed head of department within *il comune*, where she had a seat in the executive body that advised Umbertide's town council and elected mayor. 'Just you wait, that dreadful brother of hers Cesare is going to take full advantage.'

No sooner had her friend spoken than they both saw Cesare entering the building. He was the local agricultural holdings representative of a conglomerate that owned and managed vast acreages of forest and agricultural land in the area governed by the *comune*. She heard he ran it as if it were his personal fiefdom, as if he were a medieval *signoria*.

'Not at all discreet is he? So much for all those criminal safeguards from Brussels,' said Sandra, before changing the subject. 'I'm freezing. Fancy a coffee?'

A few minutes later they were each sipping a frothy *cappuccino*.

Giulia was very fond of Sandra. In a different way from university days, when they studied archaeology together. She supposed it was a sort of girl crush then. But it never came to anything, as Sandra was fixated on that English woman. Still was, so far as she could gather, even though she was married to the concert pianist, Massimo. She too had married. Happily so, for the most part.

'How's that charming husband of yours, Roberto?' Sandra asked.

Quite short in stature and thin as a rake, her friend's husband exuded a southern charisma, always greeting one with engaging eyes that held contact for almost as long as his outstretched hand. He was proud of his dark complexion and pencil-thin moustache that he felt made him unmistakably Sicilian.

'*Bene grazie*,' Giulia replied. 'Been a saint helping get our holiday rental business back on its feet after the earthquake damage. Having to deal with unsavoury characters in the construction trade. The worst is a menacing contractor called Cafaro, who tried to intimidate him into giving him the business. We think he's tied to the mafia.'

'The mafia, in Umbertide? I suppose, nothing surprises me these days.'

'Yes, the other day my husband spotted Cafaro with a childhood neighbour from Sicily rumoured back at home to have joined the mafia. But enough of my news. What about you?'

'Me, oh, fine enough. I can't complain. The museums are keeping me busy. You should come to visit me. We have some new exhibits I think you'd like.'

'Any more additions to the Umbri collection?'

'Unfortunately, not. No, these are a few Renaissance works we were donated recently.'

'I would like to see those idols again. Still the most exciting event in my life, that find on Acuto,' Giulia reminisced, before correcting herself. 'Apart from my marriage and daughter, of course.'

'And your new passion, the painted Madonnas, surely?'

'My wooden icons? If only they would sell. I want to drop the price but Roberto refuses to let me. 'They are exquisite,' he says, 'don't undersell yourself.' So there they sit, collecting dust on the shelves of my studio.'

'I'll buy one,' Sandra said, enthusiastically. 'How about spending a morning together, starting at the museum and ending-up at your house?'

'Next Friday,' Giulia repeated, while consulting her phone. 'Yes, I'd love to.'

'*Ci vediamo venerdì,*' Sandra said as they parted ways a little later, both very pleased with their impromptu plan.

It started to rain, only a light shower but enough to wet Sandra quite thoroughly before she made it back to her car. Her damp clothes made the windscreen fog-up immediately, so she turned on the car's ventilator at maximum. While she waited for the glass to clear, she took out her phone and tried to call Maria Celeste once again. There was no answer, so she added another to the long list of unanswered text messages:

'Mari where are you? Please reply. I am so worried about you. Sandra.'

Sandra made a plan. That afternoon, after she had checked-in at the provincial museums' headquarters in Perugia, she would go to the university where Maria Celeste taught and inquire of her whereabouts. Failing that, she would ask for Massimo at the Conservatoire.

With the mist lifted and vision of the road ahead restored, Sandra set off for the picturesque hilltop village of Montone, just outside Umbertide. She managed another museum there, another poster to pin.

Fifteen minutes later she was driving beneath the sweet-chestnut trees that lined the road, about to arrive at her destination. The trees had lost their leaves. The chestnuts too were gone. Most would have been collected for Montone's famous chestnut festival earlier in the autumn, to be prepared as savoury condiments or sweet pastes encased in chocolate or simply roasted over the burning embers of outdoor braziers.

****

Cesare was pacing the reception area on the first floor. He was not used to being kept waiting.

'Can you remind Vincenzia that I arrived ten minutes ago,' he told the receptionist irately.

'Certainly, *signore*. She must still be in a meeting.'

'Meeting, my foot. She is probably gossiping by the coffee machines,' he muttered, walking back to take a seat.

'Between you and me, I think she has spent her whole career making people wait,' said a disgruntled woman sitting nearby.

'Mind what you say about my sister,' he snapped back at her, suddenly finding himself being protective.

'Oh my, she even keeps family waiting!' she replied, without a hint of apology.

Che stronza, Cesare mumbled to himself. *E anche una straniera,* he added, looking at her thick blond hair. Speaks good Italian however. He stood up and continued walking up and down the hallway. His phone buzzed loudly in his jacket pocket.

'Cafaro, you've called too soon. The meeting hasn't even started. I'll get back to you when I'm out.'

Vincenzia meanwhile was desperately trying to catch-up with her preparations for the day. She was lazy and some of the additional responsibilities that came with her promotion were tiresome. Top of her in-tray was a depressingly thick document with the words Strictly Confidential stamped in red ink over the title,

'*Climate Change- Contingency Preparations for Mass Migration.*'

She glanced at the preamble and saw references to past failures to take action. All very negative. There followed procedures recommended for local government services. Housing needs, employment, urban transport, rubbish removal. All very routine. Absolute silence on the real crisis measures she thought would be needed. How to maintain law and order, keep open supply chains, ration goods and services. Etc.

In any event, Vincenzia was not overly alarmed. She saw it as an opportunity for the *comune* to wield more power. She would delegate the work to her junior colleagues.

****

Vincenzia took two coffees from the vendor machine and walked past her colleagues sitting at their desks in the open area to her office, with its large wooden desk and high ceiling. She purposely left the door ajar.

'*Mi dispiace*, Cesare. I had a lot of catching-up to do at my desk.'

'That's alright. I used the time productively, speaking to potential contractors.'

'*Scemo*! This is highly confidential.' said Vincenzia, getting back up to close the door. 'What's more, it is all still at a conceptual stage.'

'I am not a fool! I was only joking. Vincenzia you are the last person I'd come to for inside information,' Cesare said, winking at her. 'But it doesn't take a genius to realise the *comune* may want my help to alleviate the pressure on public housing around Umbertide. The big rural repopulation.'

'Do you like my new office,' she asked, changing the subject.

'I was going to say, Vincenzia, this is impressive. Your very own office. How many years did it take?' said Cesare, as he sipped his cold coffee.

'Too many, I know. At least I didn't sleep my way to the top,' she replied, knowing this would irritate him. 'Would have been much faster.'

'What was the secret then? The right politics?' Cesare continued pulling her leg.

'I won't rise to the bait. My report said I was a meticulous worker, with good attention to detail. That I always met my targets, filled the quotas set by the *comune*.'

'So, it was all about being a *rompicoglioni* then. Making it excruciatingly difficult for people applying for citizenship; or residency status; or birth or death or marriage or divorce certificates.'

'*Basta* Cesare! You've made your point. Look, sorry I kept you waiting. Ok?'

'Fine, Vincenzia,' he replied. 'I went too far.'

'As always.'

'What about this meeting you arranged?'

At that moment there was a knock on the door.

'Come in,' said Vincenzia motioning a woman in her forties with short dark hair to take a seat. 'Sorry we are running a bit late. Cesare let me introduce you to the head of the housing department.'

After a short briefing, the three of them made their way to a large room next to the mayor's office. As the meeting dragged on and the tedium mounted, Vincenzia began to feel hungry. She had skipped breakfast, and worse still it seemed she might have to forfeit her mid-morning *panino di porchetta*.

****

Cafaro parked his car next to a red Porsche Cayenne connected to a charger and rang the doorbell.

'Cesare, it is great to see you,' he said, after shaking an outstretched hand. '*Che bella macchina.*'

'Cafaro *benvenuto.* Yes I am pleased. Is yours electric too?'

'I am waiting for hydrogen.'

'Could be a year or two. I was too impatient. Can I offer you something to drink?'

'A whisky. Single malt if you have one. To celebrate the good news you are about to give me.'

'Not so hasty. I have a twelve-year Oban. Sound good to you? Please make yourself at home,' said Cesare, pointing at the sitting room.

'Is your girlfriend in?'

'No. She is in Salerno with a few friends.'

'Good. We can talk frankly then.'

Cesare sat down in an armchair opposite, also armed with a malt even though it was only four in the afternoon.

'Nice place you've got here. Infinity pool. Look at that view across the valley to Monte Acuto. I wish I had a job like yours.'

'You are not doing badly yourself,' Cesare said, wishing now he had not invited Cafaro to his home. 'Now, let's talk about my meeting at the *comune* yesterday,' he added, pre-empting his visitor's next question.

'You don't need to tell me about the climate migrant tsunami report. It's already out of date. When are the bids due?'

'Not so fast, Cafaro. Bureaucracy here moves at its own pace, you know that. But I do have good news for you. The countryside protection legislation is going to be lifted in certain pockets.'

'You don't tell me! So what about the estate you manage? All those derelict farm buildings deserted in the 1960s?'

This man is a piece of *merda*, Cesare thought to himself, even by my standards. But I need to be close to this devil in the turbulent era that lies ahead.

'Well, the news gets better. They are thinking of building a whole new settlement on the estate.'

'Now we're talking!' said Cafaro smiling. '*Un brindisi.*'

They clinked glasses and Cafaro sank into the sofa with its garish yellow upholstery. The formal agenda was over quickly.

'Top-up?' Cesare asked, noticing the glass opposite emptied in a single gulp. This was going to be a heavy session. He would need to keep his wits about him.

His glass re-charged, Cafaro moved off-piste.

'Cesare, I've been meaning to ask you, how does one go about joining the shooting syndicate on the estate?'

'Simple, let me introduce you to the syndicate manager. There is an office in town. Near the museum. You are a club fisherman aren't you? That should shorten the waiting list for you.'

'I am an impatient man, Cesare, you know that.'

'I know. Let's see what we can do.'

'It's the off-season hunting at night that really interests me. When the wild boar are less wary,' Cafaro added. 'Does your office in town handle that as well?'

After a few awkward moments, Cafaro spoke again 'You know, I really envy you and the corporate flak jacket you wear.'

'How flattering. I wish it were true.'

'*Dimmi*, that outdoor prostitution racket that uses your estate. What's your personal take? Ten percent? Maybe more: fifteen, twenty? After all, there's others to pay-off to turn a blind eye. I bet you this isn't discussed at your board meetings up north.'

'Word has it you are an occasional customer, Cafaro,' said Cesare, grinning.

'*Parliamo di donne allora.* Much more interesting,' said Cafaro, enjoying the warm feeling of three glasses of good malt.

'Women, yes indeed. Are you married, Cafaro?' Cesare asked.

'No. Settling-down was never for me. Neither for you it seems?'

'I was briefly, but it didn't last long.'

'Now you have a much younger girlfriend, Cesare. I am told she is *una bellezza.*'

'She is rather. Always off doing her own thing. Like now for instance. A holiday along the Amalfi coast,' said Cesare, being uncharacteristically open. 'Cafaro I've been meaning to ask, whatever happened to Lucrezia?

'Good riddance to her.'

'Rumour has it she was gang raped and fled the country.'

'Nasty rumour. So untrue. It was an orgy, no rape. I tell you, she will regret ever setting foot back in Italy. Especially if she links up with that group.'

'You mean Giovanni and that lot?'

'Enough about women,' Cafaro snapped suddenly. 'It's time to leave. Thank you for the whisky.'

****

The meeting with Cafaro made Cesare feel deeply uneasy. He could not help thinking that he was sounding him out on behalf of a criminal organisation. Perhaps even the mafia.

Climate change, protracted regional wars, mass migration. All would lead to an explosion of criminal activity. Human trafficking was big business. The mafia needed to be in on the act.

One dark evening, two men appeared at his front door.

'*Buona sera, signori. Benvenuti,*' Cesare said.

It was a few weeks after Cafaro came to his home. Once again his girlfriend was away, this time in Milan. He had wondered how and when it would happen, and whether the men that approached him would look like characters from a film.

'*Per favore, entrate,*' he continued, motioning them with his arm into the hallway. 'Can I offer you a drink?'

They both asked for a whisky with single cubes of ice. Unexpectedly they were well-dressed and only mildly menacing. One was olive-skinned.

'*Vi abbiamo portato un regalo,*' said one of them, once they were seated in the living room. The man pulled out a dossier and laid it on the glass coffee table in front of Cesare.

Cesare took out his glasses and looked at the open page. There was a copy of a contract, the income from which he had never declared. He did not need to look any further. Although in closing the document he noticed some compromising photos of himself taken with long lenses.

'Well gentlemen, thanks for the gift. *Un brindisi?*' he said, offering his glass to be clinked in a toast.

They declined to participate.

'*Va bene*, let's talk business,' Cesare continued, while trying to regain his composure.

Half-an-hour later they left and disappeared into the night.

As he closed the door, Cesare mopped his brow. Never before had he been betrayed by nerves, by the large beads of sweat that glistened on his forehead.

Chapter 15. Santa Chiara
1230 A.D.

Massimo spotted the small wooden box on Maria Celeste's desk. He had always admired the inlaid icon of the Madonna, her vivid blue and red robes and the gold surround. For the first time, he saw a key with a blue ribbon in the lock. He could not resist taking a look.

Inside there was a bundle of documents held together with a maroon velvet ribbon, tied in a bow. He recognised them immediately. They were the letters from Livia that Maria Celeste would read out aloud to the family. Untying the bow, Massimo leafed through them gently, looking for the dates of each. They appeared to be in chronological order. He took out the first letter and began reading:

'My most beloved family,

Finally, I have found time to write to you. It is so difficult to find time to ourselves. But our Badessa has allowed us to write to our families once a week after Vespers and before our light supper.

I was so happy to receive your letters. So relieved and happy to hear you continue to live as I dreamed you would, full and healthy lives without me.'

He looked up, as the memories began to trickle back.

****

The founder of the Order of Friars Minor had just finished giving a sermon outside the Duomo of Perugia. The crowd was silent for a moment. Wishing him to continue.

'*Mamma*, that man looks like *papà*,' said Vittoria, holding the toddler Aurelia in her arms. Maria Celeste stood next to her, keeping a close eye on the two of them. Massimo was also nearby.

'You are right, darling,' replied Livia. There was vague resemblance. Except her husband had no beard or drooping moustache. They were lucky to have got so close to the podium to see him in detail. To feel his personal magnetism and his sense his aura of serene calm.

'Can we say hello to him,' the little girl asked. 'What is his name?'

'Yes, let's try,' Livia said. 'Can you let Massimo carry Aurelia in the meantime,' she suggested, increasingly worried the whole crowd had the same intention.

'His name is Francesco,' said Massimo as he swept his smiling daughter into his warm grasp. 'He has come all the way from Assisi to speak to us. He is the priest God spoke to about rebuilding the church, remember?'

'Good, I am going to tell him to ask *Dio* to bring back my father, brother and baby sister.'

'Excellent idea,' said Massimo, as they started to move forward to join a mushrooming queue.

Massimo's admiration for Francis had grown when he realised his capacity for forgiveness. Here he was preaching to Perugians, when only a few years earlier he had been their prisoner of war. What impressed him even more, was his ability to renounce his wealthy background; spend years restoring small churches by hand; and founding, with papal permission, a mendicant order seeking to emulate the life and ministry of Jesus.

'What a pleasure to meet you, my dear. And who is this smiling angel you are holding in your arms?' asked Francis, a while later. Safe at the front of the queue, Vittoria made sure Aurelia was back in her arms.

'That is my cousin Aurelia. Well, she is not really, but I call her my cousin as my *mamma* and I live with her and her parents since my father, brother and sister died. Massimo says you can bring them back.'

'Well, I am not sure where he gets that idea from,' Francis said, looking up at Massimo. 'But we can try to get closer to them. When you are a little older, you and your *mamm*a would be most welcome to come and pray with me and *Suor* Chiara.'

'Only if Aurelia can come too.'

'Of course she can. But you would have to wait a little longer, until she is older.'

****

Massimo continued reading. He noticed the twilight outside had succumbed to night.

'There is so much to tell you about my first month. I have to start with my new sisters. Our Badessa Chiara is such a saint. She is our inspiration, our guiding light on Earth.'

'Imagine my surprise to discover three of the sisters are members of Suor Chiara's family. Her mother Suor Ortolana joined the order, together with her sisters Catarina, now known as Suor Agnes, and Béatrice. They were most welcoming. There is also a group of noble ladies from Firenze and Assisi. We are small in number, but then so too are our dwellings at San Damiano.'

Such was the fate of so many noble women, thought Massimo. They either married or became nuns. Convents were full of highly-educated people. He skimmed through the remainder of the letter. Livia wrote briefly about the vows she had had to take and touched on their daily routine. She must have run out of time as she was clearly hurried and her fine writing became rushed.

'I must leave you for now my amore miei, or I shall miss supper. I will write soon. May our Lord keep you safe.

From San Damiano, this day the 6th March, 1217

Your loving

Suor Livia'

As he returned the first letter to the box, Massimo drifted back in time once more.

Vittoria had finally fallen asleep in the bed next to Aurelia's. She had not stopped talking about her meeting with Francis for over a week. How she couldn't wait to meet his sister Clare.

'She is not a real sister, darling, just as Aurelia is not really your cousin. She is a nun, a sister in the service of God,' said Livia.

'But she can help us get closer to *papà*.'

'Yes, I believe she might. Now, time for some sleep.'

Livia joined Massimo and Maria Celeste downstairs a little later. They were waiting to have dinner with her.

'That took a while,' said Massimo.

'I have been enquiring into the new religious order for nuns set up by Francesco,' Livia said, sipping a goblet of wine.

Massimo was not surprised. Neither was Maria Celeste. Livia had not been herself for a very long time.

'Tell us, what have you learnt?' Maria Celeste asked.

'Well, it seems that *Suor* Chiara and I have something in common. Chiara was equally moved by Francesco when she first heard him give a sermon. Apparently while still a teenager, she ran away from her wealthy family home above Assisi to take her vows at a small church rebuilt by Francesco, at Porziuncola.'

'Chiara must have made quite an impact on Francesco as well,' Livia continued. 'It was a Palm Sunday and Francesco ceremoniously cut Chiara's hair, gave her a simple robe and veil and placed her in charge of a new order.'

'Just like that? What is it called?' Maria Celeste asked.

'The Order of Poor Ladies. The Benedictine nuns have given them temporary shelter while their own lodgings are being built. Next to the church where the miracle took place. Where Francesco at prayer heard a voice from the wooden crucifix above him say, three times: 'go Francesco and rebuild my house which, as you can see, is falling into ruin."

It was a long time since they had heard Livia speak in such an animated tone.

'There's only one catch,' Livia added.

'Vittoria. We've told you many times we would be her guardian until she was old enough to decide her own future.'

'I know. You are like family to her and those two girls are inseparable.'

'No need to feel in a hurry, Livia,' said Maria Celeste. 'Take your time. We will support you whatever your decision.'

'Thank you for being so understanding,' she replied.

Livia did not tell them she would never be able to leave the convent. Joining the Order of Poor Ladies would be a sentence to serve God for life, from within one small self-contained world. Nor did she disclose that the community was supposed to live in seclusion, reluctant to accept visitors.

Afterwards, when Maria Celeste had retired to her bed chamber, Massimo and Livia remained together at the dining table. Both looked sad, Massimo acutely so.

'Maria Celeste was speaking for the two of us, when she said we would look after Vittoria,' Massimo said.

'I know what you are going to say, Mas. That I should wait longer. At least, until Vittoria is old enough to join me.'

'Exactly, Livia. Nor can you base your decision on what she says now. Naturally, she is totally captivated by the dream of joining you. We were all entranced by meeting Francis. Vittoria by the idea of joining Chiara's new order. But what if she changes her mind?'

'Massimo, I can't tell you how much I have agonized over this. Turning it over in my mind, while lying in bed at night next to her. During the day, while washing clothes or preparing meals.'

'So, why not stay longer? Wait until she is old enough to join you.'

'But I am hopeless as a mother. An empty vessel. I am a nervous wreck.'

'It must be all in your head. It doesn't come across like that to us. Most of the time, at least,' Massimo said, thinking about all the times she broke down in tears, or started shouting and swearing at nothing in particular. The worst was when she cursed herself and her Vittoria for still being alive. For they were no more worthy than the husband and two children she had lost. And Vittoria would come crying to Maria Celeste or if she was out, to him. Massimo. Her adopted father.

'The devil has moved in. I need someone like *Suor* Chiara to exorcise the evil.'

'Livia, you should not be running away from your demons. You need to confront them, face on.'

'And how do I do that, Mas? I am too weak.'

'Well, you do two things. First you stay with us. Continue being Vittoria's mother. She is the only family you have left,' he said, thinking about the news they heard of her uncle Giuseppe's passing. 'At least, stay until she can decide for herself, whether to follow you.'

'Mas, you are so kind to Vittoria and me,' she said, looking at him tenderly. The way she often looked at him in the past.

Massimo felt a torrent of emotion resurface and, struggling to maintain his composure, was lost for words.

'And second?' she prompted. She too was holding back. She wanted to say sorry for abandoning him, but then remembered it was he who abandoned her. It was a conversation that they had never held.

'Second,' he repeated, searching for his train of thought. 'Second, you need to give it more time.'

'That's exactly what Gio said. 'Livia, you need time for the wounds to heal."

'Which they will,' Massimo heard himself saying. 'The hurt will shrink in time. It always does.'

Livia continued looking at him soulfully. He wished she wouldn't.

'What I was going to say, was that you need more time to question that calling.'

'My calling? Yes, I realise it has turned into a bit of an obsession,' she acknowledged. 'Is it God that speaks to me? Or *Sour* Chiara? I don't know. Maybe I do need more time.'

For Massimo, it was not a calling so much as an escape. A refuge from her reality.

In the end, Livia did remain at Massimo and Maria Celeste's home in Perugia. Until one day, when Vittoria had turned 15 and a letter arrived from San Damiano. It was written in Chiara's hand and signed Abbess Chaira. She had been made an abbess already! She was reminding Livia they were still waiting for her, that room had been reserved for both her and her daughter, but that they needed to decide as others were waiting to join the order. At this point, everyone in the household agreed Livia should go and that Vittoria could follow after her sixteenth birthday.

****

'*Papà*, you are not going to stop us,' said Paolo, the older twin by about half-an-hour.

'We've packed already. Livia says she needs us as her bodyguard,' added Stefano, the younger brother.

'*Mamma* would have let us, if she was here,' said Paolo.

'I am sure she would be delighted to have your company. But no, we will not be needing any young warriors on this short journey,' said Giovanni. 'That is my final decision. *Mamma* would have agreed with me.'

The two boys looked angrily at him. Ornella would have let them go, they were sure.

'Anyway, I've arranged for someone to look after you,' he said, hoping to deflate the situation.

'I bet it's Lucrezia,' they said together.

'Yes, you are right. But if you'd rather, you can move in with Vittoria and Aurelia.'

They looked at each other, considering their options.

'Lucrezia!' they both said.

'Good. I will confirm with her. It's only one night, after all.'

Two days later, Giovanni and his twin sons walked across to the eastern side of Perugia, where Massimo and his extended family lived. Lucrezia accompanied them.

'It's time. A very sad time for everyone. Time to say goodbye,' Giovanni announced as they shuffled into Massimo's hallway.

There was a moment of jubilation, as everyone welcomed Lucrezia safely back. This was replaced by the acute sadness of imminent loss.

Massimo tried to lift everyone's spirits.

'Look, come across here,' he said, inviting the four youngsters to a room at the back of the house. 'What do you see through the window?'

'A mountain,' said Vittoria.

'Monte Subasio,' said Stefano.

Yes, and beneath it?

'Assisi. That's where my *mamma* will be.'

'Exactly, but to be more precise, do you see that little white building to the right of the walls? That is where she will be waving to you whenever you are missing her,' said Massimo, struggling to sound credible.

'That's impossible. She'll be too tiny to see. I can't even see the building. You are imagining things again Massimo,' said Vittoria.

'Well, she could light a fire in the garden and we'd see the smoke. You'll be gardening, growing your own food and burning the rubbish, won't you Livia?' said Stefano, as Livia approached.

'Yes, I will light a candle for each of you in turn,' she said. 'Every night in my heart, as I pray for you. And Vittoria- I will see you my darling, when you are sixteen.

****

They walked side by side down towards the south eastern gate. Giovanni had offered to organise horses for them to ride for the trip, but Livia felt uncomfortable doing so. She had no luggage anyway. There would be no more belongings in her life. She preferred to walk. It would only be a short journey, for the most part on the flat valley floors of the river Tiber and its tributaries to the east.

'That ale has really calmed me down. Such a good idea Gio to stop at the tavern, thank you,' Livia said.

'I think I needed it more than you,' he replied, putting his arm around her to draw her closer to him. 'You are like a sister to me, the sister I never had.'

'And you are my only brother,' she replied.

'Only brother?'

'Massimo's different,' she replied, gazing up at him. 'You know, I wanted to marry him so badly when I was younger.'

'I know,' he said, solemnly.

'Now, let's talk about the diversion I want to take you on!'

'Really! Not too far out of our way I hope, Livia.'

'Not at all, you'll see,' she replied. 'It's called St. Mary of the Angels.'

'Oh Francesco's chapel, where it all began. I'd love to see it. Didn't you tell me Francesco had helped with its restoration, hoisting large stones from the mountain to repair the apse, the single nave and vaulted roof.'

'I did.'

They approached the church in the early afternoon. They had been walking through a thick oak wood, which thinned out to give way to a small settlement, with the chapel to one side.

'This is where the Franciscan friars live, in these huts made of wattle, straw and mud. They hold their services and plan meetings within the church.'

'Will Francesco be here?'

'I think he is travelling. You know, he wants to replicate this model community throughout Italy and even abroad.'

Entering the small stone building both Giovanni and Livia felt compelled to fall to their knees in prayer. It was so simple and so humble. No famous artists had yet been commissioned to decorate the nave, there were no frescoes above the altar depicting the life of Francis. It was still too early in that story.

'Did you feel his presence,' Livia asked afterwards.

'I don't know, but I felt something very spiritual.'

'This is what makes me think I am doing the right thing. That I have a new sense of purpose. It helps me deal with my guilt.'

'Livia, you do not need to justify what you are doing. Definitely not feel any guilt. Everyone is behind you, even Vittoria. She cannot wait to join the order in a year's time.'

She was still crying softly an hour later, as they emerged from the wood into golden fields that fed the town above with corn, wheat and pulses. A large herd of sheep crossed in front, their shepherds returning them to their winter enclosures in the valley. Looking to the right, she could clearly see the town of Spello, its rooftops cascading down the right flank of the mountain.

'Look Giovanni, you can just make out the bell tower and buildings of San Damiano,' Livia said, pointing beneath the walls of Assisi. 'And that castle above the town, that's Abbess Chaira's family seat.'

'I can just imagine her father, the Count, sitting all by himself at dinner, saying, 'Where did it all go so wrong?"' Giovanni quipped, to lighten the mood.

It brought a smile to Livia's face.

As they walked through the fields and up into the olive groves behind them, Livia took Giovanni's hand.

'Ornella once confided in me,' she said. 'That if something were to happen to her, I was to tell you to go and find Lucrezia.'

'Really?' he replied, after a long pause. The pain of his loss returned, mingling with the sense of guilt that had tormented him every time he thought of their visit to Ornella's grave.

When they briefly held hands. Guilt which grew in progressive layers of grey cloud every time they met surreptitiously outside the *Palazzo dei Priori*.

'The boys adore her. You owe it to them too, to rebuild your family,' Livia said, as she wrestled with the painful irony of her words. Once again, she reminded herself that Vittoria would be joining her in the convent. Unless of course, she changed her mind.

'Thank you, Livia. So much. I was going to ask for your blessing. But you beat me to it!'

'You care for Lucrezia too, which is important.'

'In a different way, yes. You know, after our first encounter we met again one evening. A date. But somehow the spark had evaporated. The conversation stalled and the blossom of what might have been wilted like a stem cut,' Giovanni said.

'So much has changed since then. She too is a very different person.'

'I enjoy her companionship. She listens and cares and is so supportive. It pains me to say it, but I have come to depend on Lucrezia.'

Livia then hugged Giovanni. She squeezed him so hard he felt breathless for a while afterwards.

'I just wanted to say goodbye to you here, out of sight of my future sisters,' she said, drying her eyes on his shirt-sleeves.

After a short climb they arrived at Livia's new home. There was a stone courtyard in front of a portico with round arches. Behind it stood the church with a simple rose window. To the left were the outer stone buildings of the monastery. Giovanni tried to picture the cloister around which the key buildings, the refectory, dormitories and prayer rooms would have been built.

A Franciscan friar came to greet them and to lead Livia into the monastery. He was one of the friars assigned to help the nuns behind the scenes. He wore a brown robe of coarse material, with a white rope tied around his waist and had sandals on his feet.

Giovanni turned around and began his walk home. He did not look back, to see Livia waving at him.

****

Massimo took out a second letter, addressed to Livia's daughter.

My dearly beloved Vittoria,

How are you my most beautiful and precious one? I think of you so much, when I can. I bet Aurelia's parents are looking after you so well, and you in turn your little 'sister'.

Let me tell you about my day. It starts far too early, with our first prayers, the Matins Laud. For this we assemble in the Oratory, a room close to our dormitory which Badessa Chiara had built for personal prayer and dedicated to la Madonna. It is so dark and cold outside, after prayers we all retreat to the dormitory and in no time, are back asleep. I always think of you as I drift to sleep. It took me a while to get used to sleeping on the floor, with a thin covering of straw as a mattress. But do not let this put you off joining the Order, my darling.

The dormitory is among my favourite rooms and my preferred seat is a stone ledge by the window from which I can see the cloisters and Monte Subasio behind as I do my needlework.

At first light we assemble downstairs and across the courtyard of the cloister to the refectory. We break the night's fast with fresh bread and beer, or water if supplies are fresh which thankfully, is very seldom. This is followed by two sessions of prayer (the Prime and Tierce) held in the community prayer room. It is also known as the choir room as it is in this room, which is open to the church, where we sing acapella while services are held next door.

I was very pleased to be selected to sing in the choir as all my life I have been teased for being tone-deaf. Suor Agnes tells me it is a ruse to keep an eye on me and stop me causing any mischief during all that free time I would otherwise have. Suor Agnes is my moral guardian whose enviable role includes enforcing my vows of silence.

Two hours are then set aside for communal chores, gardening, cleaning the rooms, the washroom and kitchen before the Sext None. This is the fourth session of prayer. We then eat our main meal of the day in silence while being read to by one of the sisters.

In the afternoons we are free to pursue activities such as needlework and embroidery, reading, writing and illustrating of manuscripts and choir practice. The fifth prayer session, or Vespers is followed by a light supper and yet more prayers, the Compline at seven in the evening, before we retire to bed.

We also attend various services held in the church, with the Eucharist administered by the priests of San Damiano as nuns are not allowed to do so. Most unfair.

Tesoro I must end now. I love you more than you can imagine. I cannot wait for you to join me.

Your loving mother, this the 15th March, 1217

Suor Livia'

Massimo suspected her letters were monitored and was pleased to see the real Livia he once knew slip through occasionally. He set the letter aside and continued to glance through others. He spotted the girls' favourite. It told the story of how Francis tamed a large lone wolf that had started preying on the inhabitants of Gubbio and their livestock. For weeks afterwards both girls drew pictures of Francis and a wolf, along with drawings of Francis talking to birds and small mammals. Some still adorned the Oddi family home.

Then he came across his own favourite. It recounted how Francis joined the fifth crusade to meet with Sultan al-Kamil.

To broker peace between Christianity and Islam. Francis managed to have a lengthy audience with the Sultan, during which hostilities were suspended and concessions made. That the Sultan secretly converted to Christianity on his deathbed, a few years later, was a story more for the realm of folklore, thought Massimo.

Glancing through some of her later correspondence, it became clear Livia had never really settled into her new life; never really reconciled herself to having left Vittoria and her old life behind. For it soon transpired, that Vittoria did change her mind. After she met a very persuasive young man in Perugia called Claudio.

****

Sandra was standing by her mistress in the fading light of the window. It was filled with small panes of glass, held together with lead. Outside was a view of a distant Monte Subasio, the last rays of the sun bathing its western summit in gold.

As she finalised her mistress's hair, which was curled meticulously into balls on either side of her neck, Maria Celeste was rereading a letter from Livia. She could see it was dated 1228 A.D. The words she read seemed to calm her. They brought a smile to her face.

Downstairs servants were applying the finishing touches in the dining hall. A large fire had been lit and flowers filled the central hallway and drawing room. They could hear the occasional clash of pots and the reprimands that followed in the kitchen and scullery, as the cooks finalised their preparations. They were uncertain whether their guest would stay for dinner, and if so whether he would dine alone, as apparently was his custom. To play it safe, the dining table was laid for one.

As Sandra reached for the gold earrings with their inlaid emeralds, Vittoria walked into the room.

'Maria Celeste, your hair looks stunning.'

'It's thanks to Sandra,' she replied.

'She is the best lady-in-waiting you've ever had. I just wanted to say, I am off to join Claudio and other friends by the *Fontana Maggiore*.'

'That is a good idea. You can follow the papal retinue from the *Duomo* back here.'

'Exactly. And by the way, Giovanni and Lucrezia have arrived.' Vittoria said.

'Tell them I will be down shortly,' said Maria Celeste. 'Is Aurelia going with you?'

'She wants to stay in the kitchen watching the preparations,' Vittoria answered as she closed the door.

For her part, Sandra found it hard to contain her excitement. To see the Pope in person, to perhaps receive his blessing too along with the other household servants. What unimaginable good fortune. It meant better prospects for an afterlife that was as important to her as the present one.

Maria Celeste was looking at her most beautiful. Even though she must have been in her early forties. Her skin remained white and soft with hardly any blemish or wrinkle betraying her age. Sandra could see her long neck and back and in the reflection of the mirror ahead, her face and velvet robe. As she had done before, Sandra allowed fingers that had fixed her earrings to brush down her neck, to rest gently on Maria Celeste's shoulders. To massage them gently. Sandra had been very nervous the first time she did this, but as there was no resistance, she saw it as an invitation to explore their boundaries further. Both their heart rates rose in unison, every time. On this occasion, Maria Celeste's arm crossed her chest and she rested her hand on Sandra's for quite a few seconds, before withdrawing. She smiled while looking deep into

Sandra's eyes in the reflection in the mirror, to acknowledge their secret connection.

****

Maria Celeste could still not believe their good fortune. A papal visit to her own home. All due her dear friend Livia.

As Sandra applied the finishing touches to her hair, she read the passages in Livia's letter that touched her soul so deeply every time.

'Can you imagine the excitement among the sisterhood, when Badessa Chiara announces, before Vespers one afternoon, that il Papa would be visiting San Damiano. Suor Ortolana, the most devout of our sisters, promptly fainted.

The next two weeks were spent in preparation for this momentous occasion. It was just the tonic we needed, after Francesco's death two years ago.

We worked on adding texture to the standard Gregorian chants of the Kyrie eleison, Gloria in excelsis, Agnus Dei and the rest of the sung Eucharist. This involved some of the choir singing harmonies alongside the main melody, which we practised well into the night.

On the day itself, after the service, we all assembled in the refectory for a meal. Then a miracle happens. We all witness it, even il Papa. Il Papa asks Badessa Chiara to bless the loafs of bread. As she does so, before our very eyes, a cross was formed on every loaf. Suor Ortolana fainted a second time and had to be caught before her head hit a refectory table.

Suor Béatrice our baker swore it had nothing to do with the beaten egg she had applied to the loaves as they came out of the oven in the shapes of crosses and we all believed her.

Il Papa takes this moment to announce that he was on his way to canonise Francesco. That they would start construction of a Basilica bearing Francesco's name that would almost rival his own in Roma. That future pilgrims would be able to visit San Francesco's remains in a tomb deep in the heart of the church.

This could mean only one thing, to me and all present. That Badessa Chiara herself would one day be canonised. Santa Chiara too would have a vast and beautiful church of pink and white stone built in her name. Her Rules would also, one day, be sanctioned by il Papa.

Il Papa then asked to speak to one of her sisters. Would you believe it, Badessa Chiara asked me to step forward. She must have told him of my role in nursing Francesco, as he asked me about his final days. He must have been touched by my personal story too, as he said would come to bless you all during his stay in Perugia.'

Just as she finished reading these words she was drawn back to a pleasant reality. It was the soft touch of Sandra's fingers on their short journey down her neck to her shoulders, sending shivers down her spine and making her heart thump. Some time ago she had surrendered her resolve to fight the illicit emotions generated by Sandra's touch. Maria Celeste did not know where this might lead, nor cared of the consequences. She just did not want it to stop.

****

Abbess Clare had a problem to solve. That problem was called Sister Livia.

'*Badessa*, we no longer recognise her,' said the prioress.

'She used to be so withdrawn and vulnerable,' sister Agnes agreed. 'And now she is irrepressibly busy and very noisy.'

'Yes. She breaks the vows of silence almost every day, she's always making the novices giggle,' said another senior sister.

Indeed, the abbess thought, she was charismatic and loved to make the sisters laugh. But laughter was not appropriate in an order that required total silence for much of the day, apart from prayer. Livia had always struggled with silence. It was not in her character to remain silent for long.

'I know. I've been wondering what to do for some time,' said the abbess. 'Livia is a white dove couped in a cage. She needs to be freed.'

'But you can't let her go, *Badessa*. She is loved by all the sisters,' said the fourth nun in the closed room. 'They would be heartbroken. Moreover, if you break that sacred rule, what's to say most of the junior sisters wouldn't leave after her?'

She was right, thought the abbess. The problem was not just Livia, it was that dreaded precedent. Joining the order required seclusion for life. It was one of their core vows.

How ironic also, that her problem was the very same person who would present the best face of her order to the outside world. Who she did not hesitate to choose of all the sisters, to speak to Pope Gregory.

'Sisters, this quandary is of my own making,' said the abbess. 'It was my own misjudgement.'

'With all due respect, *Badessa*, I do disagree,' continued sister Agnes. 'How were you to know her daughter would not join the Order; that she would never be at peace without being reunited with her daughter?'

'I see now, she only joined us to escape the tragedies of her life. To start a new one. I was too young and inexperienced then,' lamented the abbess.

Abbess Clare would offer Livia the opportunity to leave. She just needed to find the right moment.

Chapter 16. The Boar Hunt
Future

The doorbell rang at the worst possible moment. Cesare's team Roma had just been awarded a penalty kick against their arch-rivals, Lazio.

Who the hell would be calling at this hour? The Serie A semis. Let them wait.

The bell rang again.

'Goallllll!!!' shouted the commentator.

'*Va bene, arrivo. Che stronzi però.*'

'*Sig-nori*,' he stuttered, struggling to regain his composure. He recognised the darker man, even though he had aged, just as Cesare had done. He could not recall the crooked jaw or broken nose, however. The younger man was new. 'Do come in. What's kept you so long?'

'Look, we'll be quick. We know you are watching the match,' said the darker man.

Like almost everyone else in the country, thought Cesare. Unless you are a Napoli fan, perhaps. As he imagined these visitors to be.

'How can I be of assistance? What is it, ten years since you were last here?'

'And you don't look a year older Cesare,' remarked the darker man with a tinge of sarcasm.

Although Cesare kept fit in his home gym, gravity had started to work on his expanding belly, the chins continued to multiply in the mirror and he had lost the struggle against a balding head. Those scientists had finally found a cure for cancer and were close to being able to regrow human limbs. But what about a cure for ageing, for people like him that were too vain to opt for plastic surgery?

All things considered, he was not doing badly for someone in his late 50s. As for his career, he was surrounded by the material trappings of success. Especially his precious Porsche, now hydrogen-powered (he dreaded the thought of having to trade it in soon for an autonomous vehicle). But he took the greatest pride in the exalted status in which he thought he was held. His popularity, whether in the boardroom in Turin, among his hunter friends or working the police. Now he was being courted by the Mafia. He resigned himself to considering it the ultimate compliment.

The younger man waved a manila envelope in front of Cesare's face.

'More snaps of me I imagine- can't wait to see them,' said Cesare. 'I hope you've improved on the resolution.'

He was finding it hard to disguise his annoyance.

'And copies of more contracts we got hold off. You have been a busy boy Cesare, haven't you?' remarked the dark man, in a casual tone. 'Look, let's get straight to the point, your friend Cafaro says you do the coolest night hunting.'

'Well as you probably know, I'm no longer President of the syndicate,' he said, before realising they would not take no for an answer. 'But I'm sure something can be arranged.'

'*Va bene*, we'll be in touch. *Buona notte* Cesare.'

Cesare walked across to his entertainment room, but found it hard to get back into the match.

The mafia had returned. They had obviously been told to stand down after the big police break-through in the 2020s. Hundreds of suspected mobsters had been imprisoned. As it happened, the countryside development plans had also been put on hold. A combination of a successfully coordinated campaign from various conservation groups. As well a lack of money during the prolonged recession. The migrant housing shortage, meanwhile, was worsening by the day.

****

Cesare reserved both the hides in the middle section of the Nese Valley for a week night in early October. One was near a remotely-controlled feeding station under an old oak tree that bordered a field. The other overlooked a shallow ravine that served as a passageway for families of boar setting out as darkness fell into the fields in search of food.

He had monitored the remote camera footage and had a good idea of when the boar would emerge at the feeding station. Acorns had not started falling yet and the boar could not resist a feast, especially after the lean dry weeks of late summer. They were clever and were less likely to visit the station with its risk of death, once food was plentiful elsewhere.

Cesare borrowed a friend's open top Jeep and set about assembling the equipment and provisions. Two hunting rifles with telescopic infrared night sights, ammunition, ear-muffs, high intensity torches, blankets, a pre-packed dinner, water and flasks of both whisky and his finest *grappa*. There were also tarpaulins with ropes attached to drag their quarry to the Jeep.

They began the hunt after parking the Jeep a few hundred metres away from the feeding station. They had moved into the first hide overlooking this station by sunset, while the boar were still asleep in their dens.

'How long before the boar show-up?' asked the younger man, impatiently. This was evidently all very new to him.

'*Direi una ora o due*,' Cesare replied, before anticipating the obvious question from the younger man to follow. 'But you need to be well settled-in before they arrive. They get very nervous with the approach of the hunting season.'

'It also gives us a chance to talk. Very quietly of course. *Dimmi*, why are you still interested in me? I am about to retire from the company you know.'

'Let me turn that one around. Why wouldn't you be interested in us?' said the older of the two.

'I would be if I knew how I could help.'

'Property. We want that tower and *chiesa* you can see on the way here. And the *borgo* behind. The whole *borgo*.'

They fell silent, while Cesare took stock of the news.

'Shhh, here they come,' Cesare whispered. 'They must be hungrier than usual.'

Two young boar appeared and began feeding greedily.

'Wait,' Cesare said, tugging the younger man by the arm.

Within five minutes, the whole family were on the scene, including a large male. Moments later, two shots rang out in unison, their echoes bouncing off the hills to warn all sentient creatures in the valley. The wild boar scattered, leaving two inert shapes on the fallow ground.

'You've done this before,' Cesare said, feeling rather exposed.

'I'm hungry,' announced the younger man after a few moments, just as silence returned to the valley.

'Let's eat. Where's that dinner you packed?' agreed his companion.

Ignoring the two of them, Cesare reached for three glasses he had bought for the occasion, filling them with *grappa*.

'First things first. Here's a toast to your marksmanship, gentlemen,' he said, raising his glass.

'And to lots more hunting together,' replied the older man, before adding, 'We've been meaning to ask. What's happened to the wolves in the valley?'

'They've moved on. I think we scared them off. The weekend hunts during the season. All the shouting and barking of dogs flushing out the boar.'

'What a pity. I'd like to add one to my trophy cabinet.'

Cesare was not going to tell them that he had ordered for the wolves to be poisoned. Rather like the dogs belonging to the last remaining farmer in the valley. As a warning to him, to ignore the illegal night-time activity in the valley.

'Let's head back to the jeep, where some food awaits,' he said. 'The pigs will be too skittish to return tonight.'

They descended the ladder of the hide and walked up to admire their kills.

'Can you help me drag them off the field?' Cesare asked. 'We'll cover them with the tarpaulin to hide them from prying eyes, until they are collected tomorrow early.'

After a quick snack, Cesare drove them back to their car parked just off the *strada bianca*. One of the mafia men amused himself as they drove to their car, shining the high-powered LED beam of one of the torches haphazardly across the valley, as if he were looking for escapees from a concentration camp. They declined the gifts of wild boar *salame*, but accepted the bottles of Inama *grappa* and Oban malt whisky.

'You will hear from us soon,' said the elder of the two, as they departed.

****

Sandra heard the tell-tale 'ping' of a new message and immediately reached for her phone in her handbag. No matter that she was in the middle of printing tickets for a family of four. Her publicity campaign, that began the day she pinned a poster near the main piazza all those years ago, had clearly had an effect in raising awareness. She hardly had an idle moment.

'Yes!' she exclaimed aloud, before looking up at the mother and apologising.

It was a reply from Maria Celeste. 'Sandra, so sorry. We have been so busy on the road but are finally back. I promise we will meet soon. xx MC.'

Sandra was so excited she forgot to open-up the Etruscan exhibit room across the courtyard.

****

A few weeks after the night hunt, Cesare was contacted as he approached his parked car one evening. He was told to pack a small case for a three-day trip, to include outdoor clothing. He thought this was good news, as he guessed he might be taking part in some mafia initiation ceremony.

He was right about the initiation ritual. What he had not imagined, was that he would be gagged and blindfolded and bundled into the back of a van for several hours. He felt they headed south, although they were not driving for long enough to reach the mainland mafia strongholds of Calabria and Puglia. Along the way, they came off the main road to collect two other passengers.

He was also right to be very apprehensive. Both about the tests he would be set, the psychological and the physical, and the 'family' celebration that would cap the event.

If anything, he found the physical test was the easiest. He was dropped-off in a secluded valley surrounded by large, jagged mountains- not the rounded hills around Umbertide- which he guessed to be the Abruzzi Mountains east of Rome.

Here he was told he would take part in a boar hunt, armed only with a hunter's knife.

'What sort of joke is this?' he asked with a sneer.

'Just keep quiet and follow me,' said one of the mafia team, restraining two large mastiffs pulling on leashes.

The dogs looked a bit like pit-bull terriers. Cesare knew enough about hunting to realise that these dogs were trained to catch and hold the boar by their hind quarters or rear legs. He meanwhile was expected to administer a killing blow with his knife.

There was a group of men with skinny bay dogs, who set off ahead into the forest. After an hour of waiting, listening to the bay dogs bark and huntsmen shout, a family of boar rushed past them. The catch dogs were released and Cesare ran after them. One dog managed to lock its jaws onto the rear right leg of a young male boar. It was large enough to pull the dog along, as it swiped its tusks from side to side, desperately trying to gore it and shake it off. The second dog returned to bite into the boar's left hind-quarters.

Cesare caught up with this frantic melee. He knew what to do. Catching his breath, he stood behind and to one side of the first dog. Picking his moment, he lunged towards the base of the boar's neck. It took him several attempts before his knife plunged between the boar's shoulder blades. In the process, the boar's tusk managed to leave a large gash in Cesare's left leg, which began to bleed profusely.

Somehow all this seemed relatively painless compared to what followed. Another long drive in the van, his wound bandaged by one of the mafia men, into the depths of Calabria. The ritual of blood- letting onto a card, that was then set alight and passing around all those attending while it still burned. The recitals of mafia vows, the *omertà* or code of silence and the code of honour. Then there was the terrible food, the endless plates of stuffed dormice and the heavy drinking. All in the company of unsavoury, violent men who would not hesitate to kill him on the slightest suspicion.

Worst of all, was the humiliation that he, Cesare, was no longer the man in charge. As he had been for so many years back in Umbria. He was to start as a humble soldier, at the base of the pyramid. He was told to expect a fast-track promotion to *capodecina*, or head of ten who would report to the elected boss of a local *familia*. They said what they had in mind for him was eventually to be nominated as a *consigliere*, or adviser of a local family. He learnt there were other chains of command further up, such as the *mandamento* or district head, but that he would never attain them as he was not from the south.

The following morning Cesare was dropped-off near the train station in Cosenza. He would have to make his own way back home. He had an almighty headache and judging from the moisture in his left trouser leg, his wound was still open.

****

'*Sono preoccupato*,' she said.

'*Amore*, who are you worried about now?' Giovanni replied, looking over his half-moon glasses at Lucrezia.

He had been ploughing through reams of research papers which he needed to distil into a keynote speech on radiology he was to give at a medical conference, and was a little testy. To add to his growing state of nerves, the conference organiser was pestering him with update messages every hour. Charming and rather pushy, she reminded him of Ornella.

'Not that skinny little Samburu orphan girl we met on our African safari again?'

'No darling, not that cute button. We've been through that endlessly.'

'Nor the bouncy Bajuni boy on the coast?'

'Not him either. It doesn't work that way, remember. The adoption agencies decide for you.'

'I know. It makes no sense that here we are inundated with migrants. And the bloody bureaucrats still make adoption almost impossible,' he said. 'I digress, *amore*. Who, what are you worried about?'

'Aurelia.'

That stopped him in his tracks.

'Aurelia. She's fine isn't she? A lot better since we helped advise on the right medication for her.'

'She has not been herself recently, have you not noticed?'

'*Francamente*, I haven't.'

'I thought as much. Which brings me to the root of my concern. Has Massimo opened-up to you recently?'

'About what? His frequent visits to Livia since her nervous breakdown. They are just friends, *amore*. I go to see her almost as often. I even took her to the home. Are you worried about me too?'

'Of course not! But there's more. Have you seen the change in Maria Celeste, since she reconnected with her long-lost friend?'

'Sandra? Never thought anything of it. Except.'

'*Che*?'

'That I have wondered from time to time what the two friends shared in common, apart from the love of antiquities at the museum.'

'And art and music and travel and,' Lucrezia hesitated, before committing herself. 'Each other.'

'No!'

It took him a moment to absorb the news. He had always regarded Maria Celeste as impeccably faithful. But another woman?

'It can't be true,' he said, still shaking his head from side to side.

'You never noticed their physicality? Sandra had always been very demonstrative and tactile. But for a while now, Maria Celeste has also been holding Sandra's arm, or knee or shoulder at any opportunity. And the way she greets her!'

'I can't say I have. Am I the only one? What about the boys? What do they say?'

'They say not we should not be concerned. That these things happen in families. That Aurelia is tough and says she can cope. What's more, she likes Sandra. She is worried for Massimo, however.'

There was a time the boys would confide in him on matters like this. But that was before the angel alighted on their lives.

'Not many families have had to cope with tragedies on the scale we've had to face,' he said ruefully. 'You are right. I must go and see Massimo. After the conference.'

'Long overdue, Gio.'

'*Allora*, don't make me feel bad,' he said. 'What about Vittoria?'

'Well, as you know she is moving out into an apartment. She is older. She'll be fine.'

Lucrezia adored Vittoria. Had done from the moment she returned to live in Umbria. Secretly, her biggest regret was that she arrived too late on the scene for her and Giovanni to be Vittoria's guardians. But then, who was to know they would end up together? This thought revived a sense of guilt that lay simmering under the surface of her daily existence. The sense that she had no right to have taken the place of her best friend. Although, that was nothing like the torment of her persistent nightmares.

****

Giovanni did call Massimo immediately afterwards, but it was a while before their diaries coincided. The conference had gone well, prompting Giovanni to consider a change in direction, away from his clinic and onto the stage. It was time to share his knowledge and experience and young medics lapped-up his quirky performances, filled with anecdotes from outer space and earning him a second sobriquet among his friends, *il astrodottore*.

He had tried to organise an activity, such as going to watch an AC Perugia Calcio match, or a long walk or even a weekend camping trip, but in the end they just settled for a drink in a central bar near the *Palazzo dei Priori*.

Massimo was also busy, balancing teaching music with low key performances in small town halls and private events. After a foray into painting, he returned to the keyboard, which was his real love.

'You think it goes back to the museum visit, all those years ago?' said Giovanni.

'It was something about her reaction. Sandra was so startled, to have her long-lost friend suddenly appear before her. The chemistry. You could feel the crystals forming an arch between them.'

'*Stai esagerando*, Massimo,' Giovanni said. 'Well maybe Sandra's infatuation was evident. But Maria Celeste. I don't believe so for a moment. You had only been married what, two or three years? Impossible.'

Now it was Massimo's turn to be lost, deep in troubled thought.

'And Mas, think of all those loopholes she went through to get her family's approval. Her father in particular. Organising the surprise ceremony. Come on, Mas. She was in love with you.'

'What really gets me,' mired in his own train of thought. 'Was that Maria Celeste was already attracted to Sandra back then. That really hurts.'

'Nonsense. I don't think she was at all. I think it was very recent. In fact, I think you can salvage your marriage. Lucrezia does too, by the way.'

'I am not so sure. You see, our marriage is missing an essential ingredient.'

'Oh come on, most marriages run on the skimpiest fumes of passion after a few years. You must be good friends, surely. That's the real glue.'

'No Gio, I disagree. One's children are the strongest binding force. Anyway, she has fallen out of love with me, most emphatically.'

'If she fell out of love with you rather than in love with Sandra, then there is hope, surely?'

'I've dug too deep a pit for myself for too long. It's my insecurity, my lack of self-worth she can't handle. From very early on, I doubted her fidelity, Aurelia's parentage. The thought of a woman as well. That's hard to cope with. Maria Celeste is just too big for me.'

Giovanni could see his friend had dug himself deep into a pit. Although to be fair, it was not entirely of his own making. Maria Celeste always carried an air of mystery about her. Sandra too, was a riddle. It had initially escaped his notice. But now that he saw them basking in the glare of the headlights, he realised that mystery and riddle belonged together.

'You were never able to solve that mystery, were you?' Giovanni said, sensing where his friend had wandered.

'You mean my sponsor? Never,' Massimo replied. 'If it was her, why withhold it from me. Worse still, why deny it? What could she possibly gain from not telling me?'

'Perhaps. Maybe she was embarrassed about her secret. How she used her family wealth so surreptitiously?' Giovanni posited, enjoying his own meanderings. 'Then, maybe she was afraid it would change the dynamics of your relationship?'

'Possibly. But it could only improve it, at least from my perspective. You know, all the flirtation, the fun of the early days. They had long gone. Why not try to revive it? Show how she cared deeply for me. How she believed in me.'

'MC, the eternal mystery,' Giovanni concluded.

'Instead, we became lonely. Each of us confined to the silos of our own making.'

It was time to move on.

'Another round?' Giovanni said, noticing two empty glasses. 'Where's our waitress?' He cast an eye around the high vaulted room that may once have been a medieval hall. It was filling quickly as a gig was about to start, featuring a home-grown Perugian artist with a burgeoning following on social media.

'I'll join you with another beer,' said Massimo, before sitting forward, as if he wanted no one else to eavesdrop. 'You know Gio. It took me a long time to realise this. But I don't think she was ever in love with me.'

Giovanni stretched his long figure as he leaned back in his chair and sighed loudly. He remembered the time, in a similar bar but much smokier, when he had been quite dismissive about Massimo's chances. 'Not a hope that she'll accept.' Or something along those lines. Giovanni had been wrapped-up in his own dreams then, about proposing to Ornella.

A waitress appeared and took the order. She reminded him of Laura, and of his impulsive plan to serenade Ornella. A masterstroke of genius, even by his own standards. It worked so well, they were married within weeks. He often thought of Ornella. How she and his daughter had been snatched away from him. But then she sent down an angel to look after him and the twin boys.

For a while neither friend said a word to each other. They sat absorbing the scene while the bustle and excitement grew around them. The atmosphere was so out of tune with their serious conversation it seemed an anachronism.

'Well, if that's really the case,' Giovanni said. 'This is my advice to you. Go, drive out to that hospital and bring Livia back into your life.'

'Gio!' Massimo said loudly, as if alarmed.

'What? Have I got it wrong?'

'No. You never get anything wrong,' Massimo said, smiling now. 'How did you know?'

'That you might be thinking the same? Dreaming of collecting Livia from the home one day? I hoped you might. But you are loyal and stubborn. Just the sort that would have stayed on the Titanic. Playing your piano until it slid into the frigid ocean.'

'Gio, how melodramatic of you. Is that a metaphor for my marriage?'

'You tell me.'

'Well, I suppose I should have seen that iceberg coming,' Massimo said. The joyful expression that lit his face seconds earlier began to disappear into a cloud of thought. 'You are right, though. I don't feel right about taking to the lifeboats.'

'Livia is no lifeboat Mas. It was meant to be. Written in the stars. Just like Lucrezia was for me.'

'You and your stars, Gio. Anyway, what makes you think Livia would welcome me?'

'I can tell.'

'How?'

'From her letters.'

****

Vincenzia was rather surprised to find two rather handsome *carabinieri* waiting for her one day in her office. They wore immaculate blue uniforms with red stripes down their trouser legs, red bands on their epaulets, pressed white shirts and dark blue ties. She was annoyed she had been caught with two *cornetti alla crema* in a paper bag she had bought as a mid-morning snack. She offered the officers a coffee and even signalled she would relinquish her precious croissants, but they declined both offers.

'*Signori, buongiorno.* How can I help you?' she asked, lightheartedly.

'*Buongiorno, signora.* Sorry to disturb you, but we would like you to identify someone for us. *È solo una formalità.* Please can you follow us.'

Vincenzia collected her coat from the stand and followed the policemen through the building. She knew all eyes would be on her and that unwarranted suspicions and rumours would play havoc with her office life for a while to come. Once outside, she was asked to step into a Fiat police car.

'*Dove stiamo andando?*' she asked, nervously this time.

'To the mortuary.'

Twenty minutes later Vincenzia was looking at her dead brother Cesare, lying under a sheet on a metal trolley with wheels. He had one bullet hole in the centre of his forehead. He also had a nasty gash in his left thigh which had not healed properly. Vincenzia remembered he had told her he had suffered a small hunting accident. Strangely, there was a piece of cardboard in a transparent plastic bag next to him, on which was written a word in red ink she did not recognise.

'That is Albanian for traitor,' said one of the policemen, anticipating her next question. 'His body was found on a stretch of country road worked by one of the prostitutes owned by the pimps.'

The policemen and mortician left her alone in the room. Vincenzia stood next to her dead brother, holding his hand while she cried.

The following day, Vincenzia resigned her position at the *comune*, collected her belongings and walked back to her empty home. If there was any consolation, this was in any event the year she was due to retire.

Chapter 17. A Late Renaissance
Future

Cafaro sat in his sitting room with his two minders. They were the same two men Cesare had taken hunting.

'I was at his funeral. It was big. Half of Umbertide were there to pay their final respects,' he said, exaggerating the facts as he usually did. 'He was unlucky.'

'No, it was our mistake. We should have seen it coming,' said the man with the darker complexion and beaten face.

'It falls to me to take them out, I suppose.'

'Eventually. We need to be patient, to pick the right moment. That will be your job, to choose the location and time. You've had no dealings with them, right, the pimps?'

'No,' he replied. 'They may know me as an occasional customer, but that is all. But tell me, why Cesare? Wasn't he getting a bit old?'

'His contacts were useful to us. Also, he had a more subtle way of doing business.'

'I can be subtle too,' lifting one lapel of his jacket discreetly with his right hand. 'Seriously now, what did you want him to do that I couldn't help you with?'

His two visitors looked at each other.

'Well, let this be your first test. We want to sweep up all the properties on the estate he managed.'

'A bit of money-laundering? You can count on me. What's my budget?'

****

Aurelia had come by her parent's home to collect some of her belongings. Vittoria had asked her to move in with her in her new apartment in Perugia. As usual, the rummaging extended to her mother's room, as they both seemed to share each other's clothes and jewellery.

'Look what I came across!' exclaimed Aurelia, walking into the sitting room with the bronze figurine in her hand.

Sandra was sitting next to Maria Celeste on the sofa. They were watching a holographic tourist guide to Mexico playing on the table in front.

'Aurelia, shame on you! I was keeping that to give to you on your 21st birthday,' said Maria Celeste.

'I remember you telling me about your lucky charm when I was small. I absolutely love it. Alright, I'll wait and pretend I never saw it,' Aurelia said. 'Where does it come from?'

'We believe it was cast by the *Umbri* tribe around the sixth century B.C. They used these figurines as votive offerings, to pray for better harvests, or healthier livestock,' said Sandra.

'Or in this case, a young girl,' said Aurelia, completing Sandra's sentence. 'You still haven't told me where it comes from.'

Aurelia saw the two women looking at each other, before her mother replied.

'The truth is Aurelia, we just don't know. It just appeared in my pocket one day, on a walk to the *Umbri* religious site on Monte Acuto.'

'Hmm. Does Massimo know this?'

'He thinks Sandra pinched it on an archaeological dig and gave it to me,' said Maria Celeste.

'Does he really? That is quite a special present.' Aurelia was still trying to come to terms with the tectonic changes taking place in her small family. 'Where is *papà*, by the way?'

'He has gone to visit Livia at the home.'

'Of course, Vittoria mentioned he would give her a lift. But she was busy,' Aurelia replied. 'When I last spoke to Livia, she said she was ready to come out. Do you think he might be collecting her?'

It had been several years since her nervous breakdown, after multiple deaths in the family. Alessandro, her son and youngest daughter in the same car pile-up that killed Ornella and her daughter.

'No, it is just a visit,' Maria Celeste replied.

'*Mamma*, you know what we need to do, to help you remember how that little sculpture came into your life?'

'Yes, I know. I've researched it and even have a number to call, somewhere. But I could never face it on my own. Maybe if you come with me?'

****

You could not help but like Aurelia. Kooky, nutty, clumsy, inadvertently funny. Some would say, just plain mad. *Pazza*.

Calling her clumsy is a bit unfair, as she was very co-ordinated and had a black belt in karate to prove it. She was socially clumsy.

'There's a cure for ADHD on the market,' Vittoria once said.

'But I don't need it. There's no cure for me,' she replied, quoting one of her favourite artists from way back, Aurora with whom she shared a love of nature.

'I like me,' she declared.

Her mother had told her it was a toss-up between the two names.

'And you chose to name me after a car. Thanks. Anyway, I am far from golden.'

Aurelia was tall and had dark hair like mother, except she kept hers short and curled forward to accentuate her jaw-line. The one good thing she inherited from her father as the others, the music and art, were not encoded in that lucky strand of DNA that reached home base. She had been told everyone in the neighbourhood heard her parents that night when they made love as they had been apart a long time and were not at all surprised at her late arrival some nine months later. But she was not so sure.

For much of her life Aurelia had watched and heard and lived the strains of the relationship between her parents. She found herself naturally siding with her mother and over time became increasingly estranged from her *papà*. In her imagination, she liked to toy with the idea of different possible fathers in history as she was convinced Maria Celeste was a time portal, although her mother denied it vigorously. The fact she carried around a bronze figurine from around 550 B.C. only confirmed it. But her mother was in denial. Which is why they needed to see that psychiatrist and get her under hypnosis.

Like her mother, Aurelia was sexually ambivalent, although unlike her mother it did not take her almost half a century to realise it. On balance, she probably liked girls more. At least then there was no chance of getting pregnant.

'*Chi sano di mente* would want to bring a child into this planet, collapsing under the weight of 10 or 12 or whatever the number, billion homo-sapiens all intent on killing each other? Where's the wisdom in that?'

'Well I want two,' announced Vittoria and Aurelia conceded that her gene pool was superior and that she deserved them. Calm, sturdy and stable as a rock, as Livia once described Vittoria's father Alessandro, whom Aurelia never met. Vittoria was that and much more. Determined to have a short but successful career in finance before settling down to raise a family and live happily ever-after.

'You'll need to find a man for that,' Aurelia teased but Vittoria was a bit of a bombshell and a queue of candidates had formed soon after she reached puberty.

Aurelia was almost 21 and had not a clue what she wanted to do in life. Maybe just skip the first two stages and go straight into the 'live happily ever-after' bit.

When she heard Maria Celeste and Sandra were planning a holiday to Mexico she pestered them night and day to let her join them, but they steadfastly refused saying she needed to focus on her combined archaeology and anthropology degree.

She decided to major in these subjects as it was not enough to read about the past like her mother, she wanted to feel it, to absorb the human energy in the stones and artefacts she found on digs.

'But I can tell you all about the Mexican Nahua Indians and their contract with nature,' she said, only to realise Sandra had rented a similar plug-in circuit on the Aztecs, the best known of the Nahuatl-speaking peoples. Which was not too surprising as she was still an antiquities specialist and museum curator and was not going to Mexico just for the sunshine and tequila.

Aurelia liked so much about Sandra. Her passions for archaeology, for the preservation of the past and for saving the planet. She had done her bit for the planet as a young radical, dying her hair pink so that the truck-drivers could spot her lying prostrate on the road trying to block their way. Above all, she could see happiness for her mother in their relationship.

'Well, I can be your bodyguard then,' she offered, but did not pursue this line of reasoning as she knew Mexico had more guns per head of population than any of those failed states that dotted the globe. She was a pacifist anyway and would not hurt the tiniest insect if she could help it outside her martial arts gymnasium, where she now taught children self-defence.

After the Mexican holiday rebuttal, Aurelia announced in a huff one day that she was planning to emigrate to Australia, to live among the few remaining aborigines that remembered something of their ancestry. She rented a plug-in circuit on aboriginal culture and made the most startling discovery.

'Did you know that the aborigines had a very sophisticated explanation for time? That the future, present and past all happen in parallel?'

Her mother and Sandra looked at one another in dismay before Maria Celeste replied she was welcome to pay her way there, once she had graduated.

****

It was an exciting day for Lucrezia's new family. Not only had the boys, who no longer lived at home agreed to come for the weekend, without their partners, but Giovanni had two days free from work. Lucrezia immediately made an appointment with an English real estate agent, whose office was across the bridge in Umbertide. He specialised in selling country houses in the region, mainly to foreigners.

She had always dreamt of having a weekend and holiday retreat in the hills nearby and in no time convinced the family. They needed a large space for their two golden retrievers to roam, a night sky free of light pollution for Giovanni's telescope, and above all, a reconnection with the beauty of nature.

They had a quick drive up from Perugia and were sitting having breakfast at the ex-pats bar, while the agent was busy on the phone next door. A large, very old-fashioned flat TV screen shone vigilantly down on them from above a mirror that covered the length of the room, reflecting the bar and its customers.

'*Sono un po' in ritardo. Perdonami*, Lucrezia,' said the Englishman in his best Italian, kissing her on both cheeks as he arrived. 'Giovanni, so good to meet you finally. And the two young men, welcome. You look the same age as mine. A bit younger perhaps. Did you know that Lucrezia was once a top property agent in Northern Umbria?'

'Yes, father told us. She even said she might start-up again, isn't that right?'

'*Chi lo sa*,' Lucrezia replied obtusely. 'Got to keep *l'inglese* on his toes.'

'Well if she does, she is welcome to join forces with me. Wouldn't want you as a competitor, *amore!*' he winked harmlessly.

'Are we all set? Do you mind following me in your car?'

Half-an-hour later the five of them stood on a spacious balcony above the gate house of the B*orgo di Santa Giuliana*. There were panoramic views over the valley and hills beyond. Olives were being harvested in the groves behind. Above them, near the top of Monte Corona, they could see the edge of one of the hermitage buildings. The monastery bells were tolling, as if on cue, to add to the idyllic atmosphere.

'Well, as you can see, there is no disguising that we all love it,' admitted Lucrezia, against her professional judgement.

'Everyone seems to fall in love with this view. In fact, everyone is enchanted with this whole medieval fantasy, which comes complete with the latest utilities and communications,' the agent said.

'What about water?' asked Giovanni.

'They pumped water from a nearby spring for the longest time, but are now on the mains.'

'Any offers out?' asked Lucrezia.

'None so far. But as I said to you over the phone, there is one very wealthy buyer who wants to snap up the whole valley, including all the apartments in the *borgo*. They are trying to convince the owners of the *la Torre di Santa Giuliana* below to sell, I'm told.'

Lucrezia could see the church far below them, next to a tall defensive tower.

'Any idea who?'

'No, they are with another agent. But their front-man is a guy called Cafaro.'

'Cafaro?' Lucrezia repeated, startled.

'Are you alright,' asked the agent. 'You look a little faint. Let me get you a glass of water.'

****

Giovanni reached a hand across the bed to wake her gently. Lucrezia had been trembling and moaning aloud, muttering unintelligible words.

'*Scusa* Gio. Did I wake you up again with my nightmares.'

'I am so worried for you. I think you should see someone. It's finally time for some professional help Lucrezia. You've kept this bottled-up for so long.'

'Oh, it's nothing Gio. Let's speak about it in the morning.'

She turned around and he shuffled over the sheets to lie pressed against her as she lay curled in a ball, his body following the contours of hers. He stroked her forehead softly a few times, then found her hand and held it tightly in his.

'Goodnight again, Gio. *Ti amo così tanto.*'

Lucrezia was going to see someone, definitely. It was getting worse. She was terrified that psychopath Cafaro would be after her, now that she was married. Hearing he would be competing with them for the *borgo* came close to sending her back over the edge.

'*Buonanotte*, my guardian angel.'

The following morning, they both sipped coffee while scrolling through messages and emails on their phones. Gio was up first as usual. He had already taken the dogs for their first walk of the day.

'Gio, what time are you going in?'

'Mid-morning. Which is good. Gives me time to prepare some lectures I will be giving to my medical students.'

'What are your plans for today, *amore*?'

'The agent wants to know whether we'd like to make an offer,' said Lucrezia.

'We should drop it. It makes no sense competing with big money, especially criminal money. Having that man snooping around us. No. Tell *l'inglese* we want to try somewhere else. What about the Niccone valley?

'I am not going to give this up. We all loved the *borgo*.'

'If that's the case, we need to come up with a strategy. I have a friend who works for Interpol. I could ask him to dig around. See if there is any dirt to discredit Cafaro. Better still, find out who is behind him.'

'Gio, you know that would be playing with fire.'

'Well, then, we need to go all the way. Take him to court. Although we'd need to trace that witness first.'

'No way Gio. Now you are being horribly insensitive.'

'Sorry. Sorry my love.'

'While you mention that subject,' Lucrezia said. 'I got an appointment with the best psychiatrist in Perugia. Tomorrow at six.'

'Fantastic news. I'll be there, if you need me.'

'Yes, I would love you to be there by my side. But maybe it would be best for you to stay in the waiting room Gio.'

'You decide *amore*,' he answered.

Lucrezia looked away for a moment. 'Now, back to the *borgo* strategy,' she said, after taking a deep breath to recover her demeanour.

'Tell me. You are the professional.'

'By all means get your friend to do some checks,' Lucrezia agreed. 'It will be useful. What I suggest I do, is call our agent and start with our reservations. There is a lot I could mention. Cesare's assassination by that gang. The Sicilian's mysterious disappearance. Our concerns about the other potential buyer. Smells of money-laundering to me. I remember it well from my days working in Spoleto.'

'My word, you have done your research. Impressive my darling.'

'There's more. Then there is the lifting of the countryside development freeze by the *comune*, the plans to build a settlement in the valley below the *borgo*. They were put on hold many years ago, but could be reactivated at the flick of a switch.'

'None of this sounds good to me. Are you building up to a hefty discount?'

'Wait for it. No. Then I say that in spite of all these reservations, we would like to make an offer for all three apartments at the asking price. On the condition that, we get to meet the sellers.'

'You've lost me.'

'Giovanni, we need to convince the sellers not to touch Cafaro's money. In fact, we need to meet the owners of the other apartments in the *borgo* to make sure Cafaro never gets anywhere near them.'

Giovanni stood up and put both their cups in the dish-washer. He agreed Lucrezia should make that call. She was most impressive most of the time, but especially when she had the bit in-between her teeth.

The following evening, the two of them sat at the psychiatrist's waiting room, looking distinctly apprehensive. She was running late. Half-an-hour late.

Suddenly, the door to the practice opened. Out walked Maria Celeste and her daughter, Aurelia.

****

After the surprise of bumping into their friends at the psychiatrist's, Maria Celeste walked home feeling quite drained. Aurelia apologised and ran off to join her friends for drinks followed by pizza next to the *Duomo*.

Maria Celeste had no idea what had emerged from her subconscious. She'd have to wait to hear from Aurelia, or until the next session. Judging by the psychiatrist's expression when she returned from her trance, she must have said some bewildering things. Aurelia meanwhile just smiled mystically, as her mother came to.

Looking at her phone, Maria Celeste saw two messages from Sandra.

'I've booked a table at Il Caldaro, near Umbertide. 2morrow @ 20:00. S'

The second just read 'xxx'.

Perfect. Massimo had planned to take the two girls to visit Livia, adding that they were going to spend the night and following day in Rome.

Returning home, Maria Celeste went straight to the kitchen to pour herself a restorative glass of wine, before googling the restaurant. It would be a half-hour drive from home. When she received a further message, saying simply '+ room booked next door xx', the dinner beforehand was the last thing on her mind.

****

'Change of plan,' read the message. 'Meet me at the museum in Umbertide at 19:00 first. I hope you can make it. Sandra xxx.'

Maria Celeste replied she would and could not wait to see her. What did Sandra have in mind, she wondered? A private viewing? Perhaps she had a new collection to show her?

In any event, Maria Celeste arrived so early she had time to have a coffee at the bar across from the school where she once taught. Her first job on arrival from England.

After her brief reminiscence, she walked across the railway track to the museum to find Sandra waiting for her.

'So happy you could make the diversion,' Sandra said, after giving her friend an almighty bearhug for a greeting. 'I have something that I have been meaning to show you for a very long time.'

She took out a key and opened the main entrance to the museum. Then she turned sharp right and took out another key to open the door leading up to the Etruscan and Umbri rooms. Once upstairs, she turned on various light switches and walked into the figurine room, with Maria Celeste following close behind.

'Now, which one is it?' she said, fumbling through another set of keys until she saw one with a patch of red tape.

'You are going to show me your find? From all those years ago.'

'Exactly. Long overdue,' Sandra said, finding it hard to contain her excitement.

She opened the cabinet and gently withdrew three figurines to hand to Maria Celeste, whose heart was by now thumping loudly. That hypnosis session had opened a window to another past and she knew what was coming.

'This one is supposed to represent Mars. Then that slender one, is a boy. The third, a petite girl,' Sandra said.

'I know,' replied Maria Celeste. 'They were mine once.'

****

'Livia, are you aware that Massimo is your most frequent visitor,' said the nurse, looking at the clipboard in her hand.

'Don't tell me you keep records of individual visitors?' answered Livia.

'We don't. But I just know. A four-hour return journey, he told me. That's some commitment.'

'I suppose so, come to think about it.'

Livia had known this nurse for some time, but never spoke to her from the heart. She felt her diffidence evaporating, like a morning mist beneath a strong sun.

'And may I say, you are always so joyful, exuberant and funny in anticipation of his visits; so downcast and quiet after he's left. We all notice it,' added the nurse.

'It's true. You know, Massimo always used to be my pillar of strength, my unfailing support. But now......' Livia faltered.

'Now?'

'Now, I think he needs me.'

'We think he does too,' replied the nurse, hoping her encouragement might sever the final chord that kept her at the home.

'I think it is time for me to leave.'

The nurse smiled with approval and gave Livia a long hug.

Massimo collected Livia one week later, along with the few belongings she had taken to the psychiatric home. There were some tearful farewells among fellow patients she had got to know well. The doctors and nurses that looked after her, stood in a line applauding her as she walked by at the entrance.

On the way home she noticed they had taken an unfamiliar route, the eastern arm of the Via Flaminia, with signposts to Spoleto.

'Massimo, where are you taking me?'

'Ah, now that is a surprise.'

As pre-arranged with the Spoleto music festival organisers, he had been given the key to Sala Pegasus. A tuned Steinway was awaiting him, along with a faded copy of the programme he had played so many years earlier, in July 2020. The concert which was meant for Livia.

*****

'Vittoria has just messaged me,' Livia said. Her private recital had ended, and she was walking next to Massimo towards Spoleto's main *piazza*. Their hands were tantalisingly close, occasionally touching with the finest of brushes. 'Aurelia is moving out of her apartment so that I can have her room. She can't wait to welcome me back. Did you plan this?'

'It was her idea. You know me, I don't really think things through,' he replied.

'Massimo, you mean to say you were just going to leave me on a bench somewhere in Perugia with my suitcase?'

'Exactly. With the homeless, by the bus station,' he smiled. 'Vittoria and I have agreed to take turns bringing you food parcels.'

'How considerate of you both,' she said playfully.

Massimo stopped in front of the *Caffè degli Artisti*. 'Fancy a drink?'

'Do we have time? Isn't Vittoria expecting us?'

'Yes. But she agreed to wait a bit longer.'

They both ordered negronis, which were served along with a bowl of olives and crinkly homemade potato chips.

Livia had not had an alcoholic drink for a very long time and after just two sips she felt very giddy.

'Massimo, you are going to have to finish this for me. On second thoughts, no. You're driving.'

'We'll see,' he said enigmatically.

They sat in silence for a long while. Revelling in each other's presence. Livia began to enjoy glimpses of what her life would have been like if she had been at that concert, all those years back. But then she thought there would be no Vittoria. No Aurelia. It was meant to be. The temperature started dropping and Livia began to shiver.

'Mas, shall we go? My sweater is in the car.'

'It's getting chilly isn't it. Let me settle-up.'

As they walked away from the bar, Livia dropped any pretence that they were just friends. All inhibitions deserted her, like grains of sand lost in the Saharan wind. She grasped his hand and Massimo seemed quite content to let her swing their arms back and forth in long arcs, keeping time with the pendulum in the clock tower above them. For a brief moment time came to a halt, as clocks around Umbria synchronised in approval. She felt the child in her returning. In her state of euphoria, she did not notice that they were not heading towards the escalator and car park. Instead, they ambled down an alley and past the Sala Pegasus.

'*Signora e signore*, your keys,' said the hotel receptionist looking at Livia then Massimo, some ten minutes later. '*Avete bisogno di aiuto con i bagagli?*'

'We don't have any luggage,' a still bewildered Livia replied. 'Do we?'

'Livia, you go and settle into your room, and I will go down to the car to fetch your case.'

'What about yours?'

'I forgot to pack one,' he said.

Later that night, after a light dinner in the hotel restaurant, Massimo heard a light knock on his door.

'I thought you might like to borrow my tooth-brush,' Livia said. 'Can I come in?'

****

They were in no hurry to leave the following morning. A sun shone through the open shutters onto their bed, warming their bodies. Through the window they had a view of the fortress that overlooked the town, and of dark cypress trees that dotted the landscape randomly beneath it.

'You spoil me, Massimo.'

'Livia, you need spoiling. Lots and lots of pampering.'

She reached her arms around his neck and they spoilt each other once more.

Later, she stood up and nibbled at a cherry in a bowl on the trolley, draped in white linen.

'The coffee's cold,' she said, feeling the silver pot.

'I'll ask room service for another,' Massimo replied.

'No Massimo, let's get dressed. It's time to go and see Vittoria,' Livia said. 'I can't wait to see her apartment.'

They drank their cold coffees and showered and after Massimo had paid the bill, they walked down to the car park in the sunshine.

'Massimo, why did you book two rooms?'

'I was not going to presume otherwise. Anyway, it was the same price. For two people.'

'What if I hadn't offered you my toothbrush? Would you have come to visit me?'

'Possibly,' he said, ducking slightly in anticipation of her reaction.

'No, definitely,' he added, too late to avoid a gentle remonstrative blow to his back.

'Now Massimo. I hope you haven't got any more tricks up your sleeve,' she said, climbing into the car. 'No more diversions.'

'*Nessuno.*'

'*Mi prometti?*'

'Promise. Well, there may be one,' he was not going to lie. 'A little detour.'

'Honestly! Are we ever going to get back to Perugia?'

'Vittoria is expecting us for dinner.'

'That's hours away.'

She had an inkling. She imagined going to the Sibillini mountains. To see one of the best spectacles of nature that Umbria had to offer, the vast expanses of wild flowers in the national park there. Incredibly, she had never been. But they turned left onto the highway to Perugia, not right. Perhaps he would take her to the Temple of Clitumnus, another site she had never visited, which was quite shameful given its proximity to her childhood home. Her childhood home! That was Massimo's plan, surely?

'Spello,' she said excitedly, as Massimo exited the main highway.

'*Hai indovinato!*'

They drove past the Roman arch, with its cordon dutifully in place, and up the winding alleys, snaking their way up to the small house that once belonged to Livia's parents.

He parked the car just outside the garage.

'Massimo, you are making me very tearful,' she said, flooding with memories of Donatella and of her father Mauro, who died so soon after her mother's early passing, heart-broken.

'Can we drop by the shop?'

'All in good time,' he said. He had been in touch with Livia's floral team- or rather, those that were still alive- and arranged for them to meet in the stock-room later that afternoon, with the permission of the current owners of the shop. To top the surprise, he had hoped Giovanni would be there as well. Along with Lucrezia, Vittoria, who had the afternoon off work at the bank, and Aurelia, who always welcomed a break from uni. Although they quite liked the idea, it was agreed they would prepare a welcome dinner back in Perugia.

'In the meantime, I want you to try this for size,' he said, walking across to a rented Vespa and extracting two helmets from a black compartment at the back. A shopping bag, containing their lunch, was hanging from one of the handles.

At this point, Livia burst into tears.

By the time they arrived near their favourite picnic spot on Monte Subasio, Livia's cheeks were caked in hardened brown crusts.

There were no sheep dogs to greet them and their secret site was hard to find, as the vegetation had grown and changed almost beyond recognition. But the lunch was the same. The cheese, the fennel, the bread, although he added some salami to the takeaway order. And two beers.

'No cherries,' he said, searching the lunch bag.

'Massimo, so forgetful of you,' she joked. She lay with her head on this stomach, watching harmless white clouds drift by. 'Mas, I never thanked you for my concert,' she added, after a while. 'You are very good you know.'

'Some people tell me that.'

'But not Maria Celeste?'

He didn't answer. Instead, he looked at his watch. 'Livia, you are going to be late for your meeting.'

'What meeting? You mean dinner with Vittoria?'

'No, your team meeting. But before then, I am allowing myself one further indulgence. Come, follow me.'

They quickly packed away the remnants of their lunch, then walked along the contours hewn by countless animals over time. They reached the rim of the sinkhole. There beneath them, was the same name written in blocks of limestone. Only this time, he had added his.

'Massimo, how old are you?' she asked.

'Twenty-one,' he answered.

'Are you sure you're not twelve?'

Chapter 18. Stella di Natale
Future

Maria Celeste and Sandra's Mexican adventure had exceeded all expectations. Worries about the travel risks soon melted under the hot sun, while the vibrant colours, soft tropical air, exotic smells and the slow tempo of daily life lulled them into a sense of security. Which for the most part, was justified. Drug lords and cartels may have ruled over much of the country, but foreign tourists were still welcomed and protected. So long as they did not venture too far from the paths beaten by many generations of visitors.

They had face to face encounters with the stone heads of large serpents at the base of tall pyramids; stood outside temples at their summits where priests once held up the beating hearts of luckless enemies; and battled acrophobia as the descended their perilously steep faces into the lush green embrace of the rainforest below. This was in the Yucatan Peninsula, where they managed to stay clear of the hordes of tourists by avoiding the beaches and limiting sightseeing to the very early mornings or late afternoons. In the heat of the day, they lay in the shade beside the pools of hotels that were once grand *haciendas*, reading books about Pre-Columbian art and the remarkable Mayan civilisation, with its three calendars and use of the numeral zero.

Maria Celeste and Sandra were among a growing number of traditionalists that clung to old habits, such as reading books. Who liked the tactile sensation of turning pages. The illicit touch of skin on paper, now quite rare, as pulp forests were replanted with indigenous trees to help re-introduce diversity back into nature.

Behind closed doors at night, they cuddled and kissed and made love under whirring ceiling fans. They had a very physical relationship and Sandra was quite insatiable, as if she was still a young woman in her twenties or thirties.

'Sandra, not again *amore*. I am getting too old,' Maria Celeste would say, before succumbing to the soft warmth of her lover's touch.

In central Mexico they toured towns whose Spanish colonial heritage had been surprisingly well-preserved. The air was cooler and more invigorating here than on the coast as they were at altitude, and they were grateful to have packed sweaters and jackets that they shed only when the sun stood high above them. It was early December after all. They walked on high grey stone pavements alongside cobbled streets, bordered by painted walls of vivid blues, ochre, red and umber. Every so often twin towers of churches reached high above tiled rooftops, preceding the pregnant domes that covered the apses to the east. Their favourite memories were pushing swing-doors with peeling paint as they entered tequila and mezcal bars; and befriending local *charros*, who taught them how to ride *ranchera*-style, after they had admired women in long purple dresses in the style of revolutionary Mexico cantering in formation around the ring at an equestrian event.

Now suddenly, the holiday was coming to an end. It was their last morning before the night flight back from Mexico City. They had just been to the Frida Kahlo museum and it was Maria Celeste's turn to select an activity. They always took turns to maintain equality in the relationship, although it was hardly necessary, as they had so many interests in common.

Maria Celeste had read about a popular district filled with artisan boutiques, art galleries and trendy bars called the Zona

Rosa. 'We still need to buy a few Christmas presents, remember,' she told Sandra. One hour of heavy traffic later, the taxi had left them outside one of the galleries, that also coupled as a café and book store. It was called Galeria Zarita.

'Two coffees and a *nopal* and orange juice,' said the waitress in Spanish, as she set the cups and glass on the table.

'*Grazie*,' replied Sandra, still relying on a combination of Italian and her rudimentary English to get around.

'Are you Italian?' the waitress asked. Both women nodded in response. 'Well, isn't that just typical,' she continued. She spoke perfect English, with an American accent. 'We've had a young woman pass by every day this week asking whether we've seen two Italian women. Except today. She said her father might come instead.'

As she spoke, Maria Celeste was looking at a dark-haired lean man sitting alone at a nearby table. He was handsome mixture of European and indigenous Mexican ancestry. A *mestizo*, as those of mixed race were once known, in the distant past. He was on his phone and looked troubled.

'Is there anything else I can get you?' the waitress asked, having not drawn a reaction from either woman.

'Yes,' replied Maria Celeste. 'Those paintings on display. They are for sale, aren't they? I particularly like that charcoal of the Nahua Indian.'

'Yes, all the pieces are for sale. As for the head profile, that's a Diego Rivera. You won't be able to take it out of the country I'm afraid. A national treasure. Plenty of tourists have asked about it.'

'Pity,' she said, realizing it was hopelessly beyond their reach anyway.

'What about the painting of the tree in purple flower? I love that one,' said Sandra. 'In fact, I'd like to go there,' she added, while admiring the scene of a seated man with a tall sombrero dwarfed by the tall tropical tree above him. Behind him was a light blue lake and dark green hills thick with Mexican pine.

'The jacaranda painting? You'll have to move quickly. There is another customer sitting in the corner over there considering it.'

'Where do you think that scene is?' Sandra asked.

'Zarita told me it is by an artist based in Santa Maria Ahuacatlán, in the State of Mexico. You see the street in front is unpaved, and there is an open drain running down the centre. She says it must have been painted in the 1970s. When the village was still unknown and very poor.'

Just the handsome *mestizo* man stood up from his stool, turned around and walked straight past them out of the gallery.

Maria Celeste had a strong premonition. Her face turned ashen.

'Sandra, I'll be back soon,' she said, before turning to the waitress. 'We'll take it! The jacaranda.'

Maria Celeste wanted to give the painting to Giovanni and Lucrezia, as she pictured it hung above the fireplace in the sitting room in their *borgo* back in Umbria. She had another present in mind for Sandra.

She rose abruptly and ran outside into the street to intercept the Mexican man. For some reason she felt she needed to meet him. Unfortunately, he disappeared into a taxi before she could reach him.

****

Giovanni had suggested they buy space tickets. But they were hugely overpriced and anyway, they were in no hurry. So they flew sub-stratospheric.

The loudspeaker burst into life again. The announcements never seem to stop, thought Sandra. Always in duplicate. First in English, then in Spanish, for the benefit of the small percentage of passengers that did not understand any English.

'Ladies and gentlemen, this is your first officer speaking. My apologies to those of you who have already settled down for the night. We have something exciting to report. One of the best-known stars in the night sky has just exploded into a supernova. Some of you may have already noticed the bright beacon on the right-hand side of the aircraft.'

There was a short break in the announcement to allow passengers to absorb the news, before it continued.

'The star is Betelgeuse and it is in the constellation of Orion. There is nothing any of us need worry about, it is so far away. The captain tells me the last supernova to be visible to the eye on Earth was several hundred years ago. Enjoy this very rare spectacle while you can.'

In the excitement of the moment, the Mexican crew did not offer a translation, which Sandra imagined was a relief to all on board.

Maria Celeste sat up suddenly, whipped off her eye shades and opened the electronic blind.

'Look, there it is,' she said from the vantage point of her window seat. 'Giovanni will be excited,' she added.

'You almost need dark glasses, the light is so intense. Look at the reflection it casts on the sea!' exclaimed Sandra.

'Not sure whether this is a good or a bad omen,' said Maria Celeste. 'Either way, I feel it will affect us somehow.'

'I think it can only be a good sign. Our very own *stella di natale*. No need to worry, the pilot said.'

After a while normality resumed aboard their flight home, with a quick change in London. Sandra dozed while day-dreaming about her holiday, comforted by the constant hum of the jet engines and the soft vibrations she felt through her premium economy seat. Maria Celeste slept fitfully, worried what the omen had in store for them. But she was much more concerned about her hunch in the gallery. That it was not pure coincidence, she was certain. It made her so worried, she thought about getting in touch with her psychiatrist again. This time, on her own.

****

'*Va bene*, Aurelia, time to tell us what you've learnt,' said Stefano. 'We've got the *borgo* to ourselves.'

Their parents had left for Umbertide a little earlier, just as the sun rose above the ridge, only to hide behind an obstinate layer of cloud. They were off on the last food shop at the Co-op before Christmas.

'Come on, Oracle, out with it,' said Paolo, joining the chorus. 'Where did our golden girl come from?'

The four youngsters sat huddled at the large kitchen table in the *borgo*. The central heating was struggling to keep the large stone room warm. Two coffee pots on the stove began to bubble and hiss, drawing smiles from all of them.

'And what about that latest tattoo of yours. The huddled rabbit. What's that all about?' Stefano mocked.

'That's Metztli, the Aztec goddess of the moon, isn't it Aurelia?' said Vittoria, filling four empty cups. 'Anyway, leave her be.'

'Exactly. My tattoos are none of your business. As for what we've learnt, my mother does not know,' Aurelia declared.

'What an anti-climax. Come on, you must have learnt something from all those sessions,' said Paolo, not letting go. He was the older of the two twins, by a few minutes. He was a neurologist, specialising in mental illness. His younger twin Stefano was in AI, working on the regulatory side. Without people like him, many believed AI would have destroyed humanity by now.

'*Basta, ragazzi*. It's a very private matter. Just like Lucrezia's,' said Vittoria.

That shut them up.

'Actually, I did learn a few things,' Aurelia said unexpectedly.

'We are all ears,' said Stefano.

'You remember my papa's musical studies at the Royal Academy? *Mamma* disclosed under hypnosis who sponsored him.'

'Who?' they asked in unison.

'She did!'

Their jaws all dropped. They were dumbfounded. Noone knew that she had also taught him as a young teenager.

'She's kept it a secret all this time,' Aurelia continued, before dropping another bombshell. 'I also now know why my parents' marriage broke-down.'

'A little something to do with Sandra, perhaps?' Paolo ventured.

'That is so insensitive of you, Paolo,' said Vittoria, continuing to defend her. 'Honestly, you two are monsters when you are together.'

'No, it wasn't her,' said Aurelia impassively. When she was in an introspective or meditative mood she was quite mellow, not easy to rouse. 'Well, maybe in part. It was also *papà*. He steadfastly refused to believe he was my biological father. He still does, to this day.'

They sat in silence for a while.

'And,' said Stefano, mustering the courage, 'Is Massimo your *papà*?'

Just then they heard a buzzing sound outside.

'That drone is back again.'

The young men rushed onto the terrace to see a small mechanical robot hovering menacingly above them. Drones had been banned from public use for many years in Europe- since being weaponised in Putin's war.

'*Va fa'n culo*,' shouted Paolo, gesticulating angrily at the black lens that glared at them.

'Where are those stones I collected to throw at it?' asked Stefano, as he searched the terrace.

'Giovanni must have cleared them away,' said Vittoria, while filming the drone from the kitchen door on her phone.

'Good thinking, Vittoria,' said Paolo. 'Send that footage to Giovanni now. Weren't he and Massimo going to the police station to report the harassment?'

As they settled back in the kitchen to finish their coffees, Aurelia spoke again. She had not moved during the whole commotion.

'My *mamma*,' she started.

'Yes, what does she say?' Stefano asked, quick as a flash.

'She is not entirely sure who my *papà* is either.'

'What?' they all exclaimed at once.

'That is horrid. You should have your DNA-tested, all three of you,' said Stefano.

They looked at her for a response, but Aurelia was in her own world.

'It seems time-travellers do get to enjoy some frequent-flyer benefits,' she Aurelia, enigmatically. 'A few romances across history.'

'A few! *Quanti esattamente?*' asked Paolo.

'*Tre Amori.*'

'She told you that? Seriously now. Who is your *papà*, really?' asked Vittoria, joining the inquisition at last.

'You must first swear to keep all that I tell you a secret.'

They all nodded in acknowledgement. She knew they could be trusted.

'Well, I am not quite sure,' Aurelia continued. 'It's either Raffaello. Or Michelangelo. Or'

'Michelangelo?' interrupted Stefano. 'Can't have been. Wasn't he gay?'

'Or?' prompted Vittoria, enjoying the fantasy.

'Or, he might be a Roman tribune.'

****

Giovanni had offered to drive in his new hover car. The word drive was actually a misnomer as AI did all the work.

'Doctor's privilege!' he always replied, when asked how he was allowed to own one. Like drones, they had been largely banned since being weaponised and driven off-road by criminals able to reprogramme their navigators. It was highly illegal to take the hovers outside prescribed air corridors, which for convenience and safety generally followed above the road networks, especially in urban areas.

As the four adults hovered comfortably above tree height over a tarmac road towards Umbertide, they passed fields Giovanni remembered were once planted with tobacco and sunflowers.

'It's as if we are living in Florida. Look at these rows of avocado and mango trees. One farmer is even experimenting with papayas.'

'And lime trees too, I hope,' said Lucrezia. 'There have to be some benefits of climate change.'

As they crossed the Tiber, fields gave way to areas of new urbanisation, some still under construction but others already occupied by the thousands of migrants that had been allocated to the Umbertide region.

'How long before the developments move into conservation areas, such as your valley?' Massimo asked.

'Not long.' They had all seen illegal settlements in the woods consisting of tents and makeshift shelters with plastic sheets as roofs. Tented cities had started to overrun large areas of Italy. They must have passed over a hundred people walking along the road, trailing suitcases on small spinning wheels or carrying them strapped to their backs.

'Especially as the hunting syndicates have lost their political clout, with membership numbers plummeting,' Giovanni continued.

'*Veramente?*'

'There is so little wildlife left to shoot. Biodiversity has given way to rapidly growing carbon quota trees and solar panel farms.'

All four parents were quite downcast when Giovanni parked the car, just beside the Rocca di Umbertide.

****

Massimo sat with Giovanni in the office of the chief of the *carabinieri*.

'Here, officer, the drone is back as we speak,' said Giovanni, showing him his phone. 'Look at the footage I have just received from one of my sons.'

'Well it not one of ours,' the officer said. 'So it's probably illegal. However, it's more a matter for the *polizia*.'

'*Si, lo so*. We are very concerned this campaign of intimidation is the work of a criminal gang. Maybe the mafia itself. Especially as we are going into peak holiday period over Christmas, with fewer officers on duty. I have family and friends staying and we feel very exposed,' said Giovanni.

'Don't worry, we and our colleagues at the *Guardia di Finanza* are monitoring Cafaro. Have been ever since Cesare was killed. Thanks to a tip-off of yours to the Interpol, if I remember rightly. In fact, here is a member of my team to confirm his location,' he said, as a colleague dropped a black and white photocopy of a map on his desk. 'See that cross,' the officer said, turning the map towards Giovanni. 'That's where he parked his car earlier this morning.'

The officer would not normally disclose this type of information to members of the public. But wanted to put their minds at rest, to be left to get on with more pressing issues.

'Very close to the *borgo*. The drone must be his,' said Giovanni.

'I suspect so. Now if you do not mind, I have a busy day ahead before *Natale* is upon us.'

'Thank you, officer. Just one more thing, we noticed a lot of unusual activity in the base of our valley before we left.'

'The hunters preparing for the day's shoot, most likely.'

'No officer. We know many of the hunters by sight. It wasn't them.'

'Fine, I will alert my colleagues. *Buona giornata, signori.*'

Giovanni and Massimo walked to their hover car.

'Time for a coffee?'

'Not if we want to be in trouble with the girls; and I need to buy the wines first, remember?' said Giovanni, before reconsidering. '*Dai*, if you insist.'

When their men eventually made it to the Co-op, Livia and Lucrezia were waiting for them with two full shopping trolleys. As well as a half-empty box of takeaway pizza.

'How did it go with the police?' asked Lucrezia, as they drove off in a very loaded car.

'Usual nonchalance, wouldn't you say Massimo?'

'Maybe, but the good news is, they put a tracker on his car.'

'*Oddio*,' remarked Livia. 'Feels like we're in a cop series on TV.'

'Your Interpol friend said his phone is tapped as well, didn't he Gio?' added Lucrezia.

'Yes. It doesn't stop him borrowing other cars and phones when he needs to shake them off, unfortunately.'

'Just like TV,' said Livia, refusing to be drawn into the gravity of the conversation. '*Dai*, let's forget him for a while and enjoy Christmas together. When did you say Maria Celeste and Sandra were joining us?'

'Well, they only returned from their holiday yesterday. They wanted a couple of days to re-adjust. The 26th they said,' Lucrezia replied.

'Have you got room for all of us?'

'Yes, and more. We are about to close on the sixth and last apartment in the *borgo*!' said Lucrezia.

'Isn't Lucrezia amazing. Not only that, but she also stopped Cafaro from buying a single property in the valley,' said Giovanni.

Lucrezia's Revenge, thought Massimo, quietly to himself.

On arrival at the *borgo*, they were very surprised to see Sandra getting into her car under the hamlet's tall medieval walls.

'*Bentornata*, Sandra! Lovely to see you,' said Lucrezia, winding down her window. 'How was Mexico?'

'*Muy bien gracias*,' answered Sandra, before continuing in Italian. 'I've just dropped off some *Babbo Natale* presents on the way to the museum. Must rush as I am late for a meeting. Can't wait to see you all after Christmas.'

****

Cafaro bought the drone through his black-market contacts to monitor the movements of the Albanian gang, to corroborate the accuracy of the intelligence provided by his informants. He also took great pleasure in flying it around Lucrezia's *borgo*, both to intimidate Lucrezia and her family and to learn its every passageway and possible hiding place.

Lucrezia had almost cost him his life. She and her husband had outwitted him, launching a smear campaign which foiled all his attempts to build a property portfolio for the mafia. As soon as they realised this, they withdrew their plans and re-assigned him to other tasks, with a clear warning.

The sudden appearance of the supernova was very auspicious for Cafaro. He felt his fortunes were about to change. He was alerted by social media, while he was sipping a *cappuccino* at breakfast. He would need to wait until the constellation of Orion rose in the evening to see it for himself. But watching the coverage on social media he could see how anarchists, climate activists and doomsday sects the world over were trying to capitalise on this omen to build on people's fear. He would do the same.

There was plenty of opportunity. The demand for synthetic drugs such as fentanyl had rocketed. Gangs were also making a fortune people-smuggling. It was time take to control of all this illicit activity.

But first, he had to win back the confidence of his handlers by destroying that Albanian gang.

The day before Christmas Eve, he heard the news he had been preparing for. An informant had identified a safe-house at which Albanian gang-leaders were planning to assemble, on Christmas Eve itself. As luck would have it, it was a partially-developed site in the lower Nese valley. Just beneath Lucrezia's *borgo*. He had just the cover he needed- gang warfare- to pay a visit to Lucrezia's afterwards.

He sent a very simple encrypted message to his principal handler and within half-an-hour he received the go-ahead. His only problem was that at short notice, they were short of transport. He would have to use his own terrestrial car, which he never did on mafia business, in case it was tracked. But he would make sure he left his phone behind.

****

The clouds broke soon after sunset on Christmas Eve, revealing the beacon of intense light that had been playing a tantalising game of hide and seek with Giovanni since Betelgeuse exploded. The covers came off his telescope so quickly they were left in a crumpled pile on the tiled floor. The extended family took turns, while Giovanni launched into an astronomy lesson. He was in his element.

'Was the *Stella di Natale* that guided the three wise men to Bethlehem a supernova as well?' asked Vittoria.

'Good question! We don't know. It might also have been an occlusion of two or more of the brightest planets, or a bright comet. Equally, the story could have been a total fabrication, to boost gospel sales.'

Giovanni then got carried away and began talking about the Periodic Table and how these massive stellar explosions created and dispersed through space all the iron in their blood, the calcium in the bones, the gold in their rings and necklaces, the silver of the cutlery and the lithium and sodium in the batteries of their health monitors and phones.

Noone had the heart to remind him they all had copies of his book which dwelled on this topic.

'How long ago did this explosion take place?' asked Aurelia, who had been staring silently at the whole scene. She was sad that Betelgeuse had died but equally, liked the idea it was surrendering its life to new generations of stars and planets. Maybe one day there would be a new Earth on which intelligent life might evolve not so intent on self-destruction.

'Over 600 years ago. That's how long the light it created took to travel through our galaxy to get here,' answered Giovanni.

'Travelling at just under 300,000 kilometres a second,' Stefano added, looking at his father. 'See, I read your book!'

'So Betelgeuse exploded at around the time the altarpiece fresco was painted in the church below.' Aurelia was referring to the church next to *la Torre di Santa Giuliana*.

They looked around at the family mystic in unison.

'*A tavola*,' announced Livia, who had been darting back and forth from the terrace into the kitchen, helping Lucrezia at the kitchen stove.

Everyone, apart from Giovanni, was grateful for this summons. It was a cold night.

Lucrezia kissed Giovanni on the cheek as they re-entered the apartment.

'*Sono così felice*,' she whispered in his ear. 'This is going to be such a special family *Natale*.'

'The best,' he replied, presenting a second cheek for attention.

After dinner they all gathered around the fire in the sitting room, from where they could see the Christmas tree on the mezzanine floor just above them. Vittoria and Paolo picked up their guitars and the whole group sang carols and their favourite songs from Lucio Battisti and Lucio Dalla. Lucrezia lit a candle by the nativity scene, walking around the room lighting other candles to add to the atmosphere.

'Who's coming to evening mass at the monastery?' Lucrezia asked, after checking her watch.

'*Oh cavolo*, it's already 11:15,' observed Massimo. 'How the evening has flown by.'

'Do we have to?' said Stefano. 'We are so settled in here.'

'It's so frosty out too. Why don't we go to the service tomorrow?' added Vittoria.

'The monks are expecting us all. They have even prepared a special brew for us,' said Lucrezia, trying to nip the rebellion in the bud.

But then Paolo and Aurelia joined the ranks of the midnight mass rebels.

'We promise we will go to Massimo's concert at the *Badia di Monte Corona* tomorrow evening.'

'I wouldn't miss Beethoven's Tempest for anything,' agreed Paolo.

'Ok, it's your loss,' said Giovanni. 'Don't forget the dogs need to go out.' They all kissed and hugged each other before the parents walked out of the apartment into the night.

'Who's for some more *grappa*?' asked Stefano.

'Green tea anyone?' offered Vittoria.

The rebels got out the scrabble board, but soon ran out of energy.

'I'm going to bed,' announced Paolo.

Stefano and Vittoria followed his good example, leaving Aurelia behind on her own to re-stoke the fire. She stared for a while at the twinkling tree that rose from a mound of wrapped presents, then put her headphones on to listen to music. She made a mental note to let the dogs out briefly before going to bed.

Outside, darkness returned to the moonless sky as Orion dipped beneath the hills to the west, taking his burning prize with him. The line of cypress trees, the tall, pointed sentries outside the *borgo* resumed their vigil in the black night.

****

'*Cazzo, finalmente*,' muttered Cafaro in the valley below. This was the moment that he and his men in the valley below had been waiting for. For the hunter to strike.

He double-checked his machine gun was loaded; the grenades in his pouch; the pistol in his harness; the belt of ammunition. Before giving the signal.

****

'*Mamma*? Oh, thank God you answered your phone. You won't believe it, we are under attack.'

Maria Celeste had felt her phone vibrating, and seeing it was Aurelia, walked out of evening mass at the *Oratorio di San Bernardino* in Perugia. Sandra remained behind on the pew, looking concerned.

'What do you mean attack?'

'Automatic gun fire. I was about to take the dogs out when I heard a machine gun. We think Cafaro has broken into the *borgo*. Coming to get us any moment. We are trapped.'

'Have you called the police?'

'Yes, Vittoria is on the phone to them now.'

'Vittoria? Where are Giovanni and Massimo?'

'The grown-ups are at Mass. They didn't pick up my calls.'

'And the boys?'

'They locked the front door and blocked it with that hallway table. Now they are desperately trying to find the keys to Giovanni's gun cupboard. Oh *mamma*. *Cosa faciamo?*'

There was a moment's silence, as Maria Celeste gathered her thoughts.

'Now listen carefully. Have you got your figurine?'

'Of course. Aurora is always with me,' said Aurelia.

'Assemble the others, quickly. Gather by the Christmas tree.'

'We are all here. What do we do now?' Aurelia replied, after a few frantic moments.

Even Maria Celeste could hear the loud shouts of men trying to break through the front door of the apartment. She could also hear one of the boys remonstrating.

'What the hell are we doing here by the tree? Let's try and escape onto the roof.'

'Shut up Paolo,' said Vittoria. 'We can't hear her instructions.'

'Find the presents I bought from Mexico that Sandra dropped by,' Maria Celeste continued. 'Look for the framed painting.'

'Got it.' Aurelia said, as they ripped the wrapping off several gifts. 'It's of a large tree, with a man sitting in the shade wearing a Mexican hat.'

'That's it. Now, do you see the date on the back of the frame? Each of you must, you must learn that date. And the location...' she shouted, as the line went dead.

****

The monastery bells were tolling after the service as the four parents walked through the small cobbled *piazza* outside the chapel, through the wrought iron gates of the hermitage and out onto the short driveway. This beautiful sound would have been heard by countless generations living in this landscape.

Just then they heard machine-gun fire in the valley.

'Oh no. It's Cafaro,' said Lucrezia. She felt her heart being ripped from her chest.

They jumped into the terrestrial car and Giovanni drove as fast as was safe on the slippery *strada bianca*.

'They've got the bastard!' said Lucrezia, repeating what she was told while on the phone to the police. 'Two of his men were killed along with six Albanians in a shoot-out in the valley,' she continued, relaying more information.

Turning a corner, they could see a line of police hover cars by the *borgo*. Flashing blue lights were reflecting off the medieval walls. There was even one that had landed on the terrace, presumably a police hover bike.

'What about our children?' asked Livia, who was about to vomit with dread.

Epilogue
Future

Umbria had not received so much news coverage since the aftermath of the student murder near Perugia in 2007.

The police had not been able to solve the case and the 'Missing Person' file remained open. The officer in charge on the night was commended for his timely arrival and for arresting Cafaro before he could break into Lucrezia's apartment in the *borgo*. But the disappearance of Aurelia remained a mystery.

'Alien abduction!' had been the headlines among some of the online tabloids that regularly ran unidentified aerial phenomena stories to improve sales.

Later, when word got out from the exhaustive police interviews that Aurelia had an obsession with time travel, social media was inundated with time chatter. The public bought time travel T-shirts and other merchandise in record quantities, unscrupulous merchants sold fake bronze figurines in their thousands and some academic institutions ran courses on worm-holes and other conjectural time-altering phenomena. Mainstream astrophysicists fought back. They maintained it was impossible to travel backwards in time. As for travel into the future, they argued that while time could be stretched relative to other observers by, say, floating next to a heavy object such as a black hole, you were unlikely to survive the experience.

Public interest eventually began to wane and so too, the media hounding. The traffic caused by inquisitive day-trippers to and from the *borgo* also subsided.

One Saturday morning, Maria Celeste took a call between lectures. For a change she was the student. Learning to become a psychiatrist. In spite of all the talk of neuroscience cracking mental illness, there was still huge demand for personal advice and the industry was secure. Paolo confirmed it. It was this new academic challenge, and her relationship with Sandra that prevented her from falling into full depression.

'Lucrezia, how wonderful to hear from you. Where are you?'

'*Siamo a casa, al borgo.*'

'How's the agency doing?'

'*Bene, grazie.* Had our first completion this week. Have another two properties on the books too. So, it's looking positive. How are your classes?'

'Making progress. Luckily, I am not the only senior student.'

'We've got Livia and Massimo spending the night and it just occurred to me, do you and Sandra want to join us? I think Stefano, Paolo and Vittoria are planning to drop by as well.'

'Let me check with her and I'll get back to you. I'll have to bring my books. Final exams coming up soon.'

'Fantastic. Something odd has happened I want to show you,' said Lucrezia.

'*Veramente?* Anything to do with Aurelia? Can you tell me now?'

'I'd rather show you, but now that I've raised it. You know that oil painting you gave me of the purple jacaranda tree in flower? It featured one person didn't it? A man in a straw hat sitting in the shade?'

The painting had pride of place in their living room.

'That's right. Why do you ask?'

'Well, there is a second figure now, standing next to him. Looks like a young woman with short dark hair. She just appeared yesterday evening. The paint is dry, the pigments, just like the original.'

'Oh, that is the most incredible news,' said Maria Celeste, almost dropping her phone with the excitement. 'It seems she made it to Mexico after all.'

'What did you say?'

'Oh Lucrezia, I can't explain over the phone. Let's talk later.'

Acknowledgements

One of the first questions asked by friends has been, what is the genre of your book? A love story? An historical novel? Time travel? Is it a work of science fiction?

Eventually I came to consider the novel a sort of historical fantasy, a blend of the two. There are historical underpinnings to many chapters but as time lord, I have massaged some facts to fit the narrative.

For instance, the earliest reference to the ice-house on Monte Tezio is in the seventeenth century. However, ice was stored at altitude in Roman times, so perhaps it did have an earlier heritage? The Oddi family did own a castle in the area, although it was in the nearby Niccone valley and not on the lower western slopes of Monte Tezio. Nevertheless, count Oddi Baglioni is on record as mentioning the ice-house in 1864, establishing a link borrowed by this story. Equally, so far as I am aware, there was no Roman villa at the site of the castle. But that location, which basks in the warm afternoon sunlight near Lake Trasimeno is so bountiful, its olive trees so knarred and ancient, that it simply cries out for a wealthy Roman's home.

As for the title, *Tre Amori*, those of you with the character Giovanni's aptitude for maths may consider it misleading. All the main protagonists have their own love stories to tell. But so too does the backdrop to their lives. The nature that surrounds them. The rich cultural legacy that binds them. And a past that awaits them.

I would like to thank first and foremost my immediate family, for their support and patience during the lengthy writing process. My wife Francesca for her advice throughout and for her companionship during the many site visits; as well as for her magical map and mystical cover illustration.

Next on the list is my goddaughter and editor, Charlotte Whittle. A poet and playwright in her spare time, I was very fortunate she agreed to edit my manuscript before starting her master's degree in Creative Writing. The story features quite a large cast and my editor provided thought-provoking insights on character and relationship development. Especially on her favourites. Thank you Charlotte, for your help in taking this novel across the finishing line.

Four family friends to whom I owe debts of gratitude are Robert Pimm, Caroline Langan, Andy MacLachlan and David Ferrabee. Bob, who is in the publishing field, for his frank and invaluable guidance after reading the first manuscript. Caroline, for her feedback on the story as it evolved in the early stages, and for her linguistic touches. Andy for encouraging perseverance. David, a self-publishing guru with four titles to his name so far, for guiding me through the publication process.

My thanks also extend to local friends, notably Laura Brugnoni and Mauro Vitini, who have enriched our Umbrian experience over the years.

Finally, although they are no longer with us, I am deeply indebted to Francesca's parents Lisa and Alfredo Pelizzoli for setting-up a family home near Umbertide all those years ago.

Printed in Great Britain
by Amazon